ACROSS THE RUNNING TIDE

by

Michael J. Cohen

illustrations by
DAVID H. ELBERT

COBBLESMITH
PATTERSON'S WHEELTRACK
FREEPORT, MAINE 04032

The author is grateful for the contributions, editing, research assistance, advice and materials offered by the following individuals:

Gary Hirshberg, Diana Cohen, Frank Trocco, Cris Idzik, Beth Nagusky, Otis Sawyer, Kathleen Lignell, Ryerson Johnson, David Ebert, Sonya Cohen, Bethany Aronow, Tina Hubbard, Charles Lewis, Gene Boyington, Scott Meridith, Doc Hodgins, Jaqui Robb, John and Penny Cohen, Richard Diana, Robert Binnewies, and all fellow participants on expedition education programs, for this is their story.

© 1979 by Michael J. Cohen

All rights reserved. No part of this publication may be reproduced, in whole or in part, in any form or by any means, electronic or mechanical, including photocopying, recording, or by any information storage and retrieval system, without permission in writing from the publisher.
Inquiries should be addressed to:
COBBLESMITH, Box 191 RFD #1, Freeport, Maine 04032

ISBN #0-89166-010-0

NOTICE

Most of the incidents which appear in this work are drawn from actual occurrences. All names, dates and places have been changed to protect both the innocent and the guilty.

To the spirit of Dan Miller found in each of us

I

As the mighty Fundy tide began its two mile march back to the ocean, it appeared to be a curtain opening on a great stage. The words to part of a song suddenly came to mind:

I danced in the morning when the world had begun
And I danced with the moon and the stars and the sun.
I danced through the night and I danced so free
For I am the Lord of the Dance, said He.

Dance, then, wherever you may be,
I am the Lord of the Dance said He.
I'll lead you all, wherever you may be,
I'll lead you all in the dance said He.*

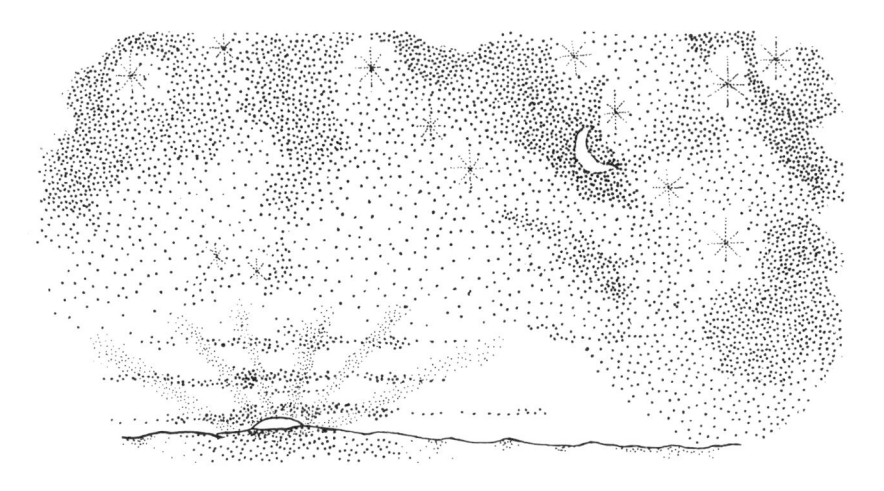

From a composition by Dan Miller, age 16.

Item from "Refinery News" a weekly column of *The Downeast Gazette,* January 8, 1977
Ory got his dory and he rowed out in the bay,
Ory got his dory, but the herring'd gone away.
There was oil upon the water and tankers at the docks,
And the herring and the white gull were dead upon the rocks.
This folk song, circa 1966, was popularly played on Maine Coast radio for eight days then suddenly, for unknown reasons, removed from the airwaves.

* Paraphrased from: LORD OF THE DANCE © 1963 by Galliard Ltd. All rights reserved. Used by permission of Galaxy Music Corp., N.Y., Sole U.S. Agent.

The March 25, 1977 Sunday edition of the New York Times contains an unusual feature article. It centers around a half page picture of several young men and women pack-hiking through spectacular wild canyons deep in the back country of Utah. They are described as being part of an accredited environmental education expedition which is traveling across the USA for a year. The expedition consists of ten college students, two graduate students and eight high school juniors and seniors along with four specially trained guides.

The academic goal of these young people is relatively simple. They want to learn first hand about their environment and its people. They are committed to letting themselves be caught in the web of life as it exists throughout America as well as within the social microcosm of the expedition. They want to discover the problems and effects of varying environments while seeking workable solutions or alternatives through real life encounters. The article mentions that perhaps the most important thing they learn about is themselves as individuals.

The provocative all season camping trip is described as "a pioneer and innovative concept in environmental education. It is perhaps the most valuable revolutionary school in the country today." It may also be the most controversial. It is based on the profound, but unpracticed, idea that the most productive way to help a student ask important real life questions is to have him choose to remove him/her self from the overprotective home or school environment which blockades thought-provoking experiences.

This book is a unique story about the expedition's twenty formative years and some of the people who lived through them. It contains many startling past occurrences which appear as narrative flashbacks or written journal entries. For clarity they are distinguished by a change of typeface, as follows:

Journal entry by Sarah Bryce: January 8, 1977, Everglades National Park. Clear, cold, windy. A.M.: Students canoed to Bird Rockery Key. Ecology seminar. P.M.: Food shopping.

Kathy discovered that one of the boxes of fudge she had bought for dessert had been opened and one piece was missing. Perplexed, she asked, "Who ate the fudge?" No one answered. She became quite upset about the incident. At our travelling school's evening meeting, she brought up the idea that people should not eat food bought for group meals because it meant that someone else wouldn't get their share. She thought whoever did eat it should say so. All the other students agreed but no one admitted to it.

Two days later a package of doughnuts was discovered open and one was missing. Matt was upset about it because he had bought the meal. He said it was a rotten thing to do — but again nobody would admit to it.

Silence. The subject changed to the flock of Roseate Spoonbills which flew overhead. Suddenly, Dan Miller exploded furiously. Nobody had ever seen him quite so angry. "This expedition is some kind of fraud," he shouted. He banged his fist, insisting that the school would only work if members were honest with each other. This expedition was based on trust so that everybody could live comfortably together for a year. Some people were breaking that trust by stealing. That was bad enough. But everybody else seemed to be accepting the stealing as inevitable. That was worse! Worst of all, some people were so mistrustful that even though they knew there would be no punishment they still wouldn't admit they took the food.

"This group is nowhere," he yelled. "This is the biggest idiot joke going! People are so blasted out of their skulls that they're willing to live in and continue to sustain an environment which is nothing short of stupid. Well, I'm not going to do it. I've had enough of that kind of horseshit at home! Screw it! I'm going on a sit-down strike until this crap is straightened out once and for all! I don't have to live in a mistrustful madhouse. I object to it — I won't do it!"

Up to that point Arty Miller's reaction and attitude had been just like everybody else's. "Oh, ain't it awful — well, boys will be boys. Isn't that just too bad. I guess that's life, that's people, what can you do." Arty and others had been conditioned into inaction.

Dan's explosion brought down the house. People really began letting out their hurt and angry feelings about the lack of trust they felt; guilt over the games they were playing; cliques they were forming or watching being formed; holding back their feelings; their distance from each other; other areas where trusts were being broken but not discussed. Tears, frustration, depression, understanding — all went into a meeting which lasted from sun-up to the wee hours of the morning for two solid days. During the process people became more open, and the atmosphere became more honest. I doubt there will be any more theft for the rest of the year.

The scene was not unusual for Wally and Sarah Bryce. The unique expedition school they had founded and directed had come to study the ecology of the Everglades. Now they were confronted by the area and each other, which was precisely their intent. While others had for years sat in classrooms and offices arguing the depressing pitfalls of the American school system, Wally and Sarah had built a school which did something about it. Shaken, but seldom stopped by the doubters addicted to their own ways of life, Wally and Sarah had experimented for a decade and discovered what worked. They then established a travel/study environmental expedition. Their school did what the dreamy words and promises of the ivory towers had failed to do. It dramatically eliminated the gnawing problems which often undermine and waste the individual in public school. Now their seemingly tireless energies were constantly engaged in sharing the problems of maintaining the expedition and its vital rewards.

Dan Miller was just one example. The same quality in Dan which caused him to trigger off the long meeting almost made him a jailbird the previous afternoon.

"Shoplifting!" That's what the store manager called it. "He took a chocolate bar from the shelf, he ate it, he put the wrapper in his pocket, and he walked out of the store without paying for it!" Wally had put in a long hour at the police station trying to explain that it was Dan's nature to act that way.

"He wasn't trying to steal, he was . . . uh . . . how could you say it . . . forgetful . . . absent-minded . . . yeah, that's it — he didn't intentionally steal the chocolate, he just forgot to pay for it."

Dan was most apologetic. He never denied the manager's accusation and could appreciate his irritation. This was not the first time this had happened, he explained, but try as he would it happened again and again.

"It's like an incurable disease," said Wally, trying to convince the store manager not to press charges. "Please try to understand."

"He ought to be put away," said the manager, "but OK, I won't do anything. You better keep him on a rope. I hope you can do something for him. You've got a problem on your hands. I wouldn't want it."

Dan was not the only responsibility facing Wally and Sarah. "Problems" was the name of the game. Yesterday morning the problem was how to get to study ancient Calusa Indian shell mounds deep in the

Everglade mangroves. The resolution was to cautiously swim across an alligator and snake inhabited channel. The hostile water did not dampen the students' spirits. To the contrary, the encountered insects, snakes, scorpions and poisonous plants just made their exploration of the Everglades' environment even more exciting. Each encounter was a problem. Each was carefully dealt with by painstakingly learning about it. It was more instructive, more fun and more lasting than learning the same thing from a book or classroom.

Cold and wet, but in high spirits they returned from the channel crossing to the school bus parked on the end of a remote dirt road. Waiting for them there was a very official looking sheriff from Miami. He had cleverly located the bus, and had patiently spent the morning waiting for the group's return.

With little formality he served Wally and Sarah a subpoena to appear before the Attorney General at a June 11th grand jury hearing in Augusta, Maine. In no uncertain terms the subpoena stated that the Attorney General was still actively investigating the school for the purpose of closing it down. It further stated the school was being charged with (1) aiding and abetting truant students, (2) operating without state approval, (3) practicing psychological counseling without a license, (4) illegally operating a motor vehicle, (5) conducting tours; acting as a travel agent without a permit, and (6) practicing medicine without a license.

"Run for the hills, the shovel just broke," murmured Wally after the sheriff had departed. His attempt at humor did not conceal the concern he and Sarah felt. Here was a continuing problem, one which could overwhelm them. Frustrating as it was, it could not be dealt with immediately. Time would have to run its bumpy course before the end of this problem would be in sight.

They returned to the campsite. Wally called Charlie French, a lawyer and longtime friend. Charlie was surprised and worried. He said he would look into the matter and would call back in a few days.

That night frost painted the palm trees and sleeping bags. The air temperature dropped to an alarming 28 degrees. Tropical fish were beginning to float to the surface of Florida Bay. A severe cold front had worked its way down the Florida peninsula from the north. The front had been preceded by the equally chilling effects of a lot of hot air emanating from a state capital in the same general direction.

II

To make the non-people world, only four ingredients are necessary: soil, water, sun and air. Mix them well, chill in the winter frost and serve yourself the greatest show on earth. With care, there should be enough to go around. I realize now that I've spent much more time savoring its delights than I have spent being with people. It's not been an escape. To the contrary, I've had nowhere else to go. Now, I'm not sure that I desire to go anywhere else, for all else seems to fall far short of its grandeur.

From a composition by Dan Miller, age 16.

Item from "Refinery News" a weekly column of *The Downeast Gazette*, June 12, 1975
The approved site for the refinery is land deeded to the city specifically for the purpose of creating a public park. The deed specifically stipulates that the land be returned to the donors' heirs if not used for its intended purpose. Nevertheless the land will go to the oil cartel; the heirs can go to hell.
Sandra Jones
City Council minority.

The January subpoena delivered by the sheriff was a rude but legal message, a continuation of unsettling events which had started back in September before school had begun. At that time Wally, Sarah and Charlie had originally been subpoenaed to appear at a Grand Jury hearing to answer the same six charges. On the phone back then, Charlie was somewhat discouraging. He said it was urgent that Wally bring down all the papers and materials in his possession concerning the school.

"How about my journal?" asked Wally.

Charlie's voice brightened. "That might be very helpful. I didn't know you kept one. Right, bring it! Listen, do you have any materials about your contacts with Ben and Carol Miller?"

"Dan's parents? What do they have to do with this?"

"Perhaps nothing, but I suspect much of what is going to take place here, in Augusta, centers around your relationship with them. I hope I'm wrong. I'll know more by the time you get here."

"I have close to twenty years worth of notes and essays in my journals. Much of it refers to the Millers. I have tape recordings of our meetings and discussions with their therapist. Do you know that both their kids, Dan and Arty, will be on the expedition this year?"

"Yes, and that may be precisely why these hearings are taking place. You'd better review that material and bring it all down with you. It may save your life but that depends upon what it says. It could just as easily hang you if it proves the Attorney General's point."

"Charlie, what the hell is this all about?" Wally was getting excited.

"I'll explain what I think is happening when you and Sarah get down here. Just be sure to bring the stuff and be familiar with it, OK? And don't worry, you won't get more than three years with good behavior — just kidding, just kidding, Wally. I'll see you Friday."

It was a very unhappy Wally and Sarah Bryce who drove down to Augusta that September evening. Wally described the trip in his journal. Five pages vividly convey his attitudes and outlooks, outlooks that had brought him into his present dilemma:

Journal entry. September 4, 1978, Augusta, Maine. Clear and warm.

To begin with I was in no pleasant mood. I was angry, that's what I was. Who could feel even mildly pleasant about being subpoenaed to appear at the state capital in order to be cross-examined by the Attorney General and some jerkwater commissioners. Conceivably I could end up in jail and/or out of business, such as it was. Who could be happy about that? Here I was driving down the highway to the statehouse when this dope in a car from New Hampshire just about tips the proverbial overloaded manure cart; getting me to think back to what had filled it in the first place.

'Live Free or Die' — New Hampshire License Plate Number CL73 — something or other — the numbers became fuzzy as the S.O.B. shot by me. Hell, I was doing 57 down Interstate 95 when this mother buzzed down the left lane like a rocket with an empty load. CL73. N.H.?!X-$ I hate your guts. You're a god-damned low life if I ever saw one and I don't even know you.

Now, that's me right there — in my car I'll curse that bastard but if I met him face to face at the next garage I'll bet I wouldn't say boo to him no less ask politely, 'weren't you going a bit fast back there on the highway?' I have every right to say something to him — That's my freedom — freedom of speech right? But I say nothing, tongue-tied Wally that's me. Somewhere deep inside me is the feeling that that ape might just deliver me a handsome knuckle sandwich followed by another blow which would kill me for sure. There's no honesty in government nowadays. They should take the license plate slogan and shove it . . . put the truth instead: 'Live free *and* die'.

CL73 N.H. Even though we're total strangers, I know you. With few exceptions, you're no different than NC17ON.Y. or L1875 Calif. You're a jackass puppet to your surroundings — your society or culture or whatever other high flouting word you want to use to label the environment which the children of Plymouth and Jamestown inflicted on this continent. You're the end product of humanity's hand upon land, iron ore, coal, fire, limestone, petroleum, oxygen, steam, Madison Ave. and the like. You're the monument we have built from nature's gifts to protect us from her temperment. You're a punk who couldn't explain your way of life if you spent the rest of your life trying (no fair using the cop-out that God made you what you are). If you were in the least bit interested in being honest you would get your butt over to the nearest home for the bewildered and wisely spend the rest of your days in the local nut house! You're crazier than hell, so friggin' crazy that you can't even see it. Don't look to me or anybody else in the area to tell you what makes me think you're nuts. God knows we should all be in there with you. Hey CL73, avoid the rush. Do the world and yourself a favor. Go now, get a room with a good view. The scenery will improve sharply as the rest of us finally do something right and move in with you.

At the moment you passed me, our respective headlights illuminated a small object — a moving object — an animal — a hopping ball of fur, with long ears. It was on the road ahead, flitting first slowly, then frantically, from one lane to the other. I jammed on my brakes wondering when it was going to find the grassy side of the road and a freedom which has long escaped either you or me. But the tell-tale brake light on your car never went on. Why not? What happened? Where the hell were you! Don't lie. Don't tell me you were in the car driving. I know you weren't there because you would have slowed down or made some attempt to save that rabbit which had begun its final dance.

Your rocket streamed onward but where were you? Drunk? Stoned? Tranquilized out of the brutal reality we have created? Where had you gone to escape it? Into the arms of your girlfriend at 65 M.P.H.? Daydreaming about some babe you'd like to screw? Maybe not. Maybe you had the radio on and were totally wrapped up in a murder mystery which was somehow more important than the road and the rabbit. Perhaps it was the news broadcast whose authoritative tones were distracting you with routine war, murder, rape, theft, competition, exploitation, violence and lies for your entertainment and information. Or was it the deceiving sound of a rock band paid to set all these other themes to beautifully weird screamy music for your listening pleasure?

None of these? Well then, I guess you were daydreaming. Which dream was it? Power? You were overpowering something in your personal life which was bothersome. Money! Maybe that was it! You were thinking about some new shrewd business deal, or what you would buy next to make you happy . . . depression . . . an escape dream. You would win two free weeks in Las Vegas.

Not a dream. No, Huh? Well, let's see: You were forming a meaningful relationship — you were shouting at the top of your lungs to your idiot wife. Or were you the shoutee? She was laying it into you. Maybe you were hitting a home run in Yankee Stadium.

None of these? My goodness, you must be unique. Our world is filled rotten with all these wonders with which to escape. Where were you? Reading the newspaper — reading a comic book while driving? You wouldn't be the first one. Watching TV? How about that — oh, wait — I've got it — talking on C.B. How about: you were putting mustard on a hot dog? How about: you were putting mustard on your hot dog? That might be a first, but I doubt it.

I still haven't guessed it? Well, it makes little difference. You were lost somewhere in the gross national product. I know you. You're the product of it.

Could it be — oh no — you're not one of the maniacs who have fun killing. You stupid son of a bitch! Did you purposely hope to kill that little rabbit? Is that why I can't guess where you were because you were there all the time — never left? Is that your escape? You kill for the kicks it gives you? Asshole!

I'm sorry. I didn't mean to call you an asshole. Killing for pleasure just hits me harder than do the other escapes. They're all just the same thing taking place in one way or another. The least I can contribute in this time of need is to be fair and not pick on any one booby in the hatch.

With relief, I watched the rabbit stay in my lane as Apollo 95 swiftly approached it. Then, as if purposefully, at the last possible second, it leaped into the left lane before the onrushing lights. Maybe he missed it, my innocent mind screamed. Split seconds later, headlights sorrowfully revealed the final steps to the dance. A pitiful bloody rabbit lying on its side jerking in spasms of pain and finality then disappearing suddenly in the cold darkness as I flashed by continuing southward.

I was shaken. Tears welled up distorting my vision. I asked Sarah to drive. We changed places and I tried the radio escape. WCBS N.Y. came on strong with the news that already the death toll was twenty-seven persons for the Labor Day weekend. They didn't say how many rabbits.

They couldn't care less, I thought. Why should I? I was bothered. Why did I let it bother me? Who is nuts anyhow, them or me? They're happier than I am right now. Friggin' queers. Killing off the world and saying nothing, feeling nothing, doing nothing and being nothing. The Boston Strangler took five lives and they've done nothing about the world that created him.

Will it ever come to . . . "This is the WCBS world roundup at 9:00 P.M., Jack Samuels reporting. The death toll this Labor Day weekend stands at 984,000. The breakdown by states shows N.Y. in the lead with 16,054 rabbits, 8,124 skunks, 1,631 frogs, 11,621 mice, 900 possum, 1,123 turtles, 1,463 birds, 94 snakes, 4 cows, 89 dogs, 4 persons and a General Sherman Tank. The tank was destroyed on Interstate 95 by an infuriated rabbit that cried, 'Live Free or Die' and then hurled itself before the brute after chug-a-lugging a fifth of nitro-glycerine during happy hour. The four persons were scared to death by ghosts of spring peepers and mosquitoes past."

Such a thought was unusual for me during waking hours and I became aware of being half asleep. I switched off the radio and sat quietly in the turmoil of my thoughts. As I dozed off my mind drifted to a phone call I received from Ben Miller many years ago. Wally Bryce, who thirty years ago shot innocent woodchucks and squirrels with a smile, uneasily fell asleep to escape pangs of unhappiness, anger, and memories of frustrating hassles with public officials.

III

Camping out and living on the bay island brought many delights. For five days I watched the seal colony move onto the striking rock formations as the tide came and went. They were completely aware of its motion, arriving an hour later each day, sunbathing, and then proceeding on to the higher rocks as the water flooded. I donned my wet-suit one day and covering myself with seaweed, lay on the rocks awaiting them. They crawled up real close until they finally discovered my presence. Then they flopped off the rocks, as if the world had come to an end.

From a composition by Dan Miller, age 16.

From "Refinery News" *The Downeast Gazette,* April 3, 1975
It is illegal to reduce the air quality in a national park. This park is located three miles from the proposed American refinery which will, by the refinery's own admission, lower air quality. It would endanger many local marine mammals which are now protected by law. Canada has refused permission for tankers to sail down the dangerous passage into the U.S. It would be illegal. Therefore it would seem impossible for the refinery to obtain a permit, but it has done just that.

Merril Crockett, Superintendent
Fundy Marine National Park

Sarah and Wally arrived at Charlie's house in Augusta around 8:15 P.M., September fourth. They were somewhat tired from their drive. Charlie, bearded, sprightly, and congenial, took their coats after a warm greeting. He led them into his office in the rear of the house explaining that there was a great deal to discuss and although they had a whole weekend, their conversation tonight would help plan an immediate course of action for tomorrow.

"For Chrissake, what is this all about?" demanded Wally, who was still in no joyful mood. "What's going on?"

Charlie lit his pipe while explaining the nature of the subpoena and the grand jury inquiry.

"There are laws on the books of this state which protect the public from being hurt by people supposedly unqualified to perform certain services. A doctor has to have a medical degree and a license from the state. A lawyer has to pass the bar exam. For some reason the Attorney General is under the impression that you two are performing services for which you are not legally qualified or licensed. The penalties can be pretty stiff."

"Do you think we are?" asked Sarah.

"That's what I'm going to try to determine tonight," he said relighting his pipe. "As you can see on the subpoena, there are quite a few different areas being questioned. Each one will be looked into."

"But we've been operating close to twenty years and we've never had any mishaps or any static from the state. Why now all of a sudden?" inquired Sarah, upset and flustered by the mystery.

"Good question," replied Charlie. "I've done some snooping around. The only thing I can come up with is that the Psychiatric Division of the Public Health Department has received a complaint about the school and yourselves. Specifically, the complaint is to the effect that you are practicing psychiatry or doing psychological counseling without a license or training."

"Who lodged the complaint?" asked Wally.

"I'm not sure," said Charlie. "I think it has something to do with a practicing psychiatrist, a Dr. Sullivan, Dr. Richard Sullivan. Have you ever heard of him?"

Wally looked shocked. "I'll be a son of a bitch. I can't believe it! Yeah, I know the guy; I met him once a long time ago. He's worked with the Miller family since Ben was a kid. Ben, Carol and Dan have seen him off and on for about twenty years. He threatened to file a complaint about twelve years ago when we had a consultation about what was happening to Dan. He and I did not see eye to eye. Why is this happening now though? Danny is sixteen years old. I don't understand. All I know is that Dan is coming on the school this year."

"I don't know either," said Charlie with frustration. "I can't find out any more than I've told you at this point. I think I know what's going on with regard to the subpoena though. I've found out that the Public Health Department has checked you out with every other department, and between all of them they've come up with the charges listed on this." He waved the subpoena in the air and slammed it down on the desk.

"We're going to get to the bottom of this; I'll find out if they can make these charges stick. I think the most damaging one is from Public Health . . . 'offering your services as a psychologist or psychiatrist when you are not licensed to do so.' If we can get rid of those allegations there may be less pressure on the other departments to prosecute. Then maybe they'll drop the whole thing. That's why I asked you to bring down all your material, especially about your relationship with the Miller family. If my hunch is right," he said, suddenly standing up, "most of the information they have about your activities is coming from Dr. Sullivan. If I can find out from you the exact extent and nature of your relationship with the Millers and Sullivan, it will give me a clue as to how to defend against their allegations. Steve Gitman is a psychiatrist, a respected one. If I think he can help us I've got to call him first thing in the morning. He says he'll spend the day with us tomorrow if need be." Charlie was pacing up and down the floor now. He stopped, went to his desk and took out a tape recorder. "Are you two ready to answer some questions?"

"I don't know how much help I'm going to be," said Sarah. "Ben Miller was a student of Wally's back in the mid-fifties. I've only known him casually since Wally and I were married."

"How did you meet him, Wally? How did you originally get involved with him?"

"Ben was a straight 'A' student of mine when I was teaching science at the local high school; highly inquisitive and always wanting to be sure he knew everything that could be known — especially in science. If I was explaining electrons he'd want to know where they came from, what they looked like, what made them move. I finally ended up holding an 'advanced question' class after school. Too much class time was being taken up by Ben and a few other students while everybody else sat around bored."

"What kind of a guy was he?" inquired Charlie.

"Strange! Ben only had one friend, Jim Garmish. When Ben wasn't doing imaginative science projects with Jim, or sitting in science class, he was a different person — morose, depressed — damned close to being some kind of monster out of a Boris Karloff movie. He was kind of ghoulish. I guess you'd say, pre-occupied, especially with death. Some kids were frightened of him, teachers, too. To the contrary, I really liked him — perhaps because I rarely saw his sadder side — it seldom appeared in science class. He was a Jeckyll-and-Hyde type and we hit it off real well. We enjoyed conversations about science, although he was at times a bit time-consuming and pressing.

"Jim Garmish was Ben's best friend in an important way. He was worried and genuinely concerned about Ben's depression and ghoulish ways. Evidently he and Ben had many lengthy heart-to-heart conversations about how Ben felt, until Ben began to realize that it wasn't normal or necessary to be so depressed. That didn't stop the depression by any means — it just gave Ben one more thing to be depressed about and more to discuss with Jim.

"Jim came to me one day after school, told me he was scared about Ben being depressed so much, that even Ben was becoming frightened of it. Jim felt that there was nothing he could do except make things worse and since I was one of the few people with whom Ben was comfortable, maybe I should talk with Ben about it. I was willing to do anything I could to help, and, before long, entered into several conversations with Ben.

After becoming aware of the extent of the daily depression, not to mention torturous, nightmarish sleeping hours, I decided that Ben needed psychiatric care. I had learned about this kind of depressed personality in many graduate level psychology and counseling courses which I had taken. The effective work of many latter day psychologists such as Ruth Axline, Rollo May, Alexander Wolf and Carl Rogers were convincing and, in retrospect, final, for I knew of no other answer or person to which to turn.

"At first Ben was quite resistant to the idea of psychiatric help. It was a statement, in his eyes, that he was crazy, a concept upon which his depression eagerly fed. I remember it took many months of discussion until Ben became strong enough to accept the reality that he needed help. His depression was indeed distressing, and since he could do nothing about it, perhaps a psychologist could help him. He'd just have to temporarily live with the depressing, frightening thought that he was crazy."

Wally stopped for a second, stared at the ceiling as if to try and remember something. He turned, bent over, and opened a box which contained about forty uniform notebooks. Glancing through them he removed the first one labeled '1956 January-June', leafed through it and read for a minute or two.

"I don't know how much detail you want, Charlie. I have notes on what happened because it was very disturbing to me. My relationship with Ben is what got me into the habit of keeping a journal. It would help me see things more clearly when I wrote them out, and I found it useful to refer to it to see how my feelings or perceptions might have changed over a period of time."

"Does any of what you have there refer to the subject of counseling, or something related to it?"

"Very much so," replied Wally. "That's how I became involved with Ben."

"In that case you'd better tell me whatever is applicable. It can't hurt and it might help. I'm not sure where this is all going, but if it's got something to do with you and practicing psychotherapy it's probably damned important at this stage of the game. I'll continue taping it so I can refer back if need be. You were saying that you were trying to get Ben to a psychiatrist. It might be helpful if you describe what you did and why. It may just be that we'll have to prove your competency at the hearings. I hope it doesn't come to that because that line of discussion would probably only be used to get you a reduced sentence."

"Jesus, this is scary," gasped Sarah.

"Better safe than sorry," said Charlie. "Go ahead, Wally."

"In looking back on the situation, it was not quite as simple a matter as I have described, Charlie. Lord, it was more like a battle, a game between forces which would appear and then retreat within each of us. The rule of the game was not to let Ben's depression get him so depressed about being depressed that it would overwhelm his better judgement. The object was to get him to seek help to relieve himself of this depressing depression.

My own fears began to be aroused as to whether I was doing the right thing playing the game at all, no less as to whether I was playing it correctly. My only salvation was that I had entered into a therapy group to help me with these same fears which I originally had to face while doing field service as a counselor in another school district. With Ben the lack of any other ethical choice in the matter helped me keep at it. What else could be done? Ben could not or would not talk about the situation with anyone else except me. I was the one chosen by fate, if you will. It was not easy, fair, or right to quit and say, 'goodbye Ben.' Frankly, I was under the distinct impression that if I did nothing, suicide (his, not mine) would result. How was this different than premeditated murder?"

"Did you ever get a Ph.D. counseling degree?" asked Charlie.

"Almost," replied Wally.

"Go ahead."

"You can well imagine my great relief when at the end of the school year, Ben finally decided to seek psychiatric help of some kind and then went to the guidance center to see what was available.

"It was with profuse tears and staggering sadness that Ben returned to inform me that in no way would his father let him see a psychologist.

"There's nothing wrong with Ben," said his dad, "why, he's an 'A' student."

"Depression? At that moment there was nobody who could have convinced me that depression was not a contagious disease like chicken pox, because now, through contact, I had it too. Ben convinced me that the only thing that could be done about *our* situation was that I speak with his father. I agreed, and made an appointment to visit the following evening . . . Hey, you want to hear something interesting. Let me read you the next couple of pages from the journal. I dramatized the meeting with Ben's father. I don't even remember doing it."

"Sure, go ahead," laughed Charlie. "It will be amusing to hear what you wrote twenty-one years ago."

Journal Entry: June 26, 1956, Whitehorse, Maine. Cloudy, humid, warm.

During the next twenty-four hours, as I was getting ready to visit Ben's father, the real me, Wally Bryce, Mr. Nice Guy, was joined by none other than Sherlock Holmes. I welcomed the company. The game was indeed afoot! I had to be prepared for anything and I figured the more I could deduce about what I was getting into the less of a shock it might be; the more I might be prepared to handle it.

The primary question which came to mind was, what made Ben so depressed? Was it going to get me, too, just by visiting his house? I was shaking in my shoes. What would happen if a situation came up at the house about which I could do nothing? Would I be overpowered by that environment? Would I ever be able to see it and thus have a chance to avoid it?

I'm so blind. I go about my daily business (what an interesting term to use to describe living — so revealing) thinking that I have some integrity, some will-power, some sense of direction or sense of right and wrong. Yet, if I walk down a dirty street full of paper and assorted garbage I often catch myself discarding my gum wrapper by throwing it in the messy gutter. However, if the same street is immaculately clean, I look for the nearest garbage pail or put the wrapper in my pocket for future disposal.

There's the problem, Sherlock! I'm a puppet to my environment. So is everybody else, the difference is that the rest of them out there don't realize it. But one must be aware of 'reality' if one is to cope with it. One can't expect to wrestle with an invisible giant and win. Good Lord, you wouldn't even be able to see the rascal. The environment is master — a powerful, invisible dictator which commands each of us to act in a certain way in a certain setting.

"I don't think this environmental entry has much to do with this," said Charlie.

"You're dead wrong there," exclaimed Sarah. "If you want to fully understand our qualifications and what we do you'll have to understand our environmental beliefs. It's part and parcel of our so called counseling procedures and why the Millers' kids are going on the school. People are so self-centered, so conditioned to perceiving the world from an egotistical point of view that we've blinded ourselves to the environment which surrounds and supports us."

"What do you mean?" said Charlie looking at Sarah as if she was some kind of kook.

"Well, have you ever thought what it really means when you say, 'I'm going swimming.' The subject of the sentence is 'I'. The verb 'to swim' refers to what the subject 'I' does. Where is the environment in the statement?"

Charlie thought for a while, then questioned, "I don't know — where is it?"

"It's hidden and invisible, yet it's there," replied Sarah. "Our "I"-ness won't let us see it. What the statement 'I'm going swimming' really means is 'I'm going to change environments.' I'm going to place myself in the water — a completely different environment than on land. The new environment, the water, immediately, authoritatively demands that I act in a certain way, and if I don't behave in the proper fashion, I will not survive in that environment. I will drown. In other words to contact reality demands we understand that what 'I' did was to choose to change environments. That *the environment* as an entity insisted that I behave in a certain manner. In reality any sentence or statement *always* has *two* subjects: the *written* subject and the *hidden* subject; *the hidden subject is the environment.* Every action has two participants, the *actor* and the *environment."*

"So what," said Charlie.

"Just take a close look at anybody or anything," persisted Sarah. "Look at yourself and you'll easily be able to figure out what the mold was that formed you, supports you and continues to keep you in your present form. The only way you'll ever change anything is by changing the environmental mold that keeps it what it is. For example: The escaped Nazi war criminals who slaughtered eleven million people aren't killing people now because they're in a different environmental setting."

Wally looked up. "It's like today," he said. "Patty Hearst wasn't a murderer or gun moll until the kidnapping environment molded her differently. I suspect if she was let free it wouldn't happen again unless she was again placed in an incredible stress situation such as being kidnapped. I wouldn't want to predict what I might end up doing in that predicament, would you? Perhaps in the right environment we'd be criminals too. Why don't they punish us now, just in case?"

"That's the main thrust of what we teach at our school," added Sarah.

"I see," mused Charlie, "go ahead with it then."

Wally continued reading from his journal:

Sherlock, the question at hand is what could the mold be which formed one Benjamin Wake Miller. Why is he so intelligent, yet so depressed? Why does his environment keep him in this state of mind when instead it could possibly get him some psychological help? What is Ben's real environment? What makes him morbid? What images and feelings does he live in? Why? Will it happen to Wally Bryce, too? Am I immune?

It was with some trepidation that I, both Wally and Sherlock, rang the bell of Mr. B. K. Miller on Hill Street in Whitehorse, Maine. "Sherlock" was excited and looking forward to getting a few first-hand impressions and maybe some evidence. Wally was scared.

Ben met me (us) at the door and with a pale, tense smile showed us into a dimly lit, walnut-panelled living room. A large, leather chair sat squarely against the middle of the far wall. Above it hung a bayonet. In the chair, sporting a blank gaze, sat B. K. Miller himself. To his left was a small darkly stained table upon which sat the lamp that lit the room. Good Lord! The lamp's base was made of a human skull with a hole in it. A brass tube jutted out, holding the bulb and shade. ("That's a bullet hole," said Sherlock, "But I'll hold judgement.")

"Hi, I'm Wally Bryce, Ben's science teacher. Nice to meet you." ("I'm not terribly delighted," muttered Sherlock.)

"Good evening, I'm B. K. Miller. I'm pleased you are so interested in Ben that you've come over this evening," he said insincerely.

"Well, Ben's one of our best science students — he did a wonderful job on that reactor project at the science fair — took second prize . . . that sure is an unusual lamp you have there."

"Yes, it is unusual. That's the skull of a Jap I killed during the war. Had a hell of a time sneaking it back into the States. I had his skin made into the lampshade as a memento of my soldiering days at Wake Island." ("I've seen and heard enough," said Sherlock, "I know why that kid is depressed. Wait till Watson hears about this . . . see you around Wally — Tally ho," and he vanished.)

"Uh, uh — yes, it certainly is unusual," I admitted. "Well, the reason I came was that I'm concerned about Ben's performance at school."

"He's a straight 'A' student — what's there to be concerned about?" B. K. asked, genuinely this time.

"Yes, he is a good student, but he's emotionally depressed a good deal of the time . . . feels badly inside . . . you know what I mean? Jim Garmish and I were worried by it. We thought Ben ought to get some help so he might feel better." (I brought Jim into the picture because with Sherlock gone I was alone and maybe B. K. might respond better to a crowd. Besides, I was damned lonely. If an evening with B. K. was first prize for being the most concerned teacher in town, then three evenings with him was second prize. As companionship, my mother he wasn't.)

"Oh," said B. K., "he's just going through some kind of teenage fad or stage. He'll be O.K. Besides, what have his feelings got to do with his grade in science?"

"Why, nothing — nothing at all. It's just that . . ."

"He'll be O.K., B. K. said, "but if his grades go down, let me know, will you? He's not crazy — he'll be O.K. . . . Was there something else?"

"No — oh — no," I said, and with the usual formalities, beat a hasty retreat.

Wally stopped reading, looked at Sarah, then Charlie. "It was that summer," he said, "that Ben attempted suicide by shooting himself through the head with his father's army pistol which fortunately contained blank cartridges. The doctor treating the powder burns on his head reported them as being due to the accidental discharge of a weapon. Three days later, Ben took an overdose of morphine, but not enough.

"At that time I didn't have the guts to sensitively ask Ben if he felt depressed because he tried to commit suicide twice and couldn't even do that 'right'. It seems like a crude question, but sometimes they're the ones which uncover the source of many evils or provide a smile. Ben and I would sometimes end up kidding each other in that harsh way. It was one step better than depression.

"Then what happened?" asked Charlie.

"Attempted suicide was able to provide what his depression and my visit could not bring about. Ben's doctor prescribed psychotherapy in which Ben occasionally indulges to this day. That's where Dr. Sullivan entered the picture. He provided the different environment which Ben so desperately needed. The changed mold has produced a changed person. Ben was seldom depressed. He became happier and more productive than he ever had been. A few hours a week for the past twenty years have been enough to offset many effects of an oppressive childhood and adolescence. It's been a long time coming and a rocky road to get where he is now. One of the rocks on the road was morphine, which has led to other drugs and other problems."

"Looks like they're our problems now," sighed Sarah.

IV

I would stand upon the highest boulder and stare for hours at the magnificent rocky habitat stretching before me. The tide went out, leaving the pools among the rocks painted with algae of all shades and descriptions. One could almost sense the bases of sea life now laid bare, exposed by the retreating waters. Here the rockweed washed about in the white foamy waves hissing as they threw themselves headlong onto the seaweed-coated rocks. One could smell the pungent salt air, barnacles, urchins; kelp, open sea and living things. As my eye would descend from the rock tops to the water, the color would change from olive green to the brown reds of the dulse and its relatives. The rich wild forest would be exposed for but a few short hours, as if to say, treasure us for we are your legacy. Then the sea would again reign, hiding its offspring, protecting them lest they be disturbed by my presence.

From a composition by Dan Miller, age 16.

From "Refinery News"; *The Downeast Gazette,* September 6, 1974
"Both ships were traveling through fog so dense the Master could not see the masts of his own ship. They could see each other only by radar. A third ship's radar saw the two dots come into one. Then he heard a terrific explosion. The dots separated and one disappeared. Sixty-three miles away buildings rocked. 40,000 tons of oil were released on the water.

Captain Harold Benson, Master
VLCC Spirit of America

The ordinarily quiet visitor center of Everglades National Park had suddenly become an old time New England town hall complete with instruments, musicians, callers and dancers. The impressionable might be led to believe last night's cold front had carried the dance down south, like a rock on a glacier, dumping it on the visitor's center museum for preservation. That was just a little less unheard of than the three inches of snow it had actually deposited in Miami and the Bahamas.

Quite suddenly screams of laughter resounded above the music and calls, followed by Wally shouting, "Reel Danny, reel! The call is reel — not kneel."

Crouched on the floor, Danny Miller appeared to be praying on both knees at the head of a contra dance set; surrounded by students and park visitors who were immobilized with laughter.

"What in God's name is going to be next with him," said Wally under his breath. "At least this is just a simple mistake. He probably didn't hear the call, or misunderstood it."

Danny got up, a foolish grin on his face. With bravado he waved hello to Wally, turned to the crowd of friends and strangers yelling, "Got it!" and proceeded to reel his partner down the astonished lines of dancers wildly but with impeccable accuracy.

"Now there's the screwball I know and love," said Wally to himself returning his hands to the buttons of the antique accordian. "Head couples reel down," he called briskly and started to pump out the rollicking dance music.

As Wally put it when he looked out of his sleeping bag that morning, "Somebody must have knocked the thermometer off the wall; the temperature has dropped." A voice returned from one of the twelve frost covered tents housing Wally's twenty college and high school students in the Everglades' campsite. "Maybe we should run off a contra dance to keep warm." After some discussion the heterogeneously-aged community members enthusiastically agreed. A few thought that other park visitors might want to warm themselves by joining in on the exhilarating fun. Hurriedly, they contacted park headquarters and within an hour arranged to have an old fashioned barn dance replace the regularly scheduled bird walk which would never have found any birds in such cold weather.

People were warm now; and so was the unheated visitors center. "Let's do another one," said Dan, completely undaunted by his hilarious mistake during the reel.

Sarah called out new dance instructions. Wally removed his gloves and began to play "Smash the Windows", a lively jig which caught the spirit of the dance. He carefully watched the lines of dancers who, in short time, had mastered the series of figures and were now joyfully "chaining ladies", "half promenading" or "swinging". "It's such an incredible source of fun," he thought as his fingers automatically played the old tune over and over. "It's like the school itself: a miniature community of people from all over America. Each dancer depends upon the other to carry out his part of the dance. Each is dependent yet independent. If people make a mistake others help them learn to correct it while the dance is going on; they teach each other. There is a group spirit here, close contact, physical contact, between people actively having fun by being together without the bug-a-boo of competition. Too bad this kind of dancing has all but disappeared."

Danny was outstanding in his own peculiar way. He was not the most graceful nor rhythmic dancer, but he did change from one repeated dance pattern to another without batting an eye. Whenever anyone else attempted it they would hesitate, become confused, or make mistakes. The essence of being Dan was to be unable to fall into habitual patterns of behavior. When people ordinarily made mistakes Dan wouldn't make any; when people would shy away from a touchy subject Dan would sail into it no holds barred. That's why the expedition spent that afternoon oblivious to the Everglades' enrapturing ecology. They sat at a meeting by the shore, a meeting which Dan had called.

"I'm really uncomfortable about a conversation I heard going on in the bus before lunch," Dan declared. "I think it affects a lot of people here and I know it's affecting me. I feel crummy about it; that's why I want to talk about it. In some ways it's even more bothersome than what happened with the doughnut being stolen except that this time a lot of people are aware of what's going on and nobody seems too concerned about it. I told the people involved that I thought they ought to discuss the incident with everybody. They don't feel concerned about it I guess, but I sure do."

There was dead silence. You could feel the tension rising. Even though Sarah had been through nine years of situations similar to this one she could feel its impact: her heart beating faster, harder; her face becoming flushed.

"I didn't hear any conversation," stated Ed. "Will somebody please say what's going on!"

"I don't mind telling you what I heard," replied Dan quite comfortably. "I just think that the people who were involved with the subject should talk about it. It's not like the doughnut which was stolen. They know who they are and what happened. I don't see why they want or expect me to take care of them, especially since I talked with them about this already. I also don't know if everybody wants to discuss this now. We had all planned to observe shore birds this afternoon."

"I think I'd rather get to the bottom of this," exclaimed Jill. "It looks like the openness we had at the doughnut meeting is gone. Things feel tight as a drum. I don't want to have them build up and undermine everything as they did last time." More silence. "This really stinks," she said with frustration, "we didn't learn anything from the other meetings. What a waste of time!"

"Jill, I'm not sure I agree with you," declared Wally. "I don't know what's going on but whatever the subject is, it seems to have a great deal of fear tied up with it. It seems to me that people are going to have to cope with that fear or discomfort before they can discuss the topic. Perhaps at home they can escape the subject or are not confronted by it. Maybe at home they hide from the feelings which are bottling them up right now. Maybe people tranquilize problems away so they don't have to face them. People here have already talked about how they have just about buried themselves alive getting wasted by drugs just so they can avoid feeling put down or uncool."

"That's not true at all," said Cindy, "I took drugs because they make me feel good. I feel better when I'm high. The problem was I was getting high all the time and being taken advantage of by other kids who were into getting wasted. I also was flunking school, but I felt good."

"I've never understood people who say what you just said," Wally responded. "To me you sound like a broken adding machine, one which is not being given the right figures to begin with. It's practically an insult to my intelligence."

"What do you mean?" asked Cindy.

"Well," Wally replied, shifting his body around to relieve his cramped sitting position. "You say you took drugs because they made you feel better. Better than what?"

"Better than I was feeling before," said Cindy.

"Fine, but what was bothering you before so that you weren't feeling so well?"

"I don't know," answered Cindy. "Life in general I guess. I'm overweight, my friends wouldn't like me if I wasn't stoned, I couldn't feel accepted if I was with them . . . things like that."

"Why didn't you go on a diet and get some new friends instead of tranquilizing yourself into fantasy land?" suggested Ed. "What you're saying is so stupid yet it's so common. Why didn't you do something constructive about those feelings?"

"I did. I did drugs. They make me feel good."

"I don't know how what you're saying strikes you," interrupted Sarah. "To me it seems foolish. Even a dumb chicken can fly out when the coop is on fire. You sound like you're waiting around for someone to take care of the fire for you — somebody else is going to get the fire extinguisher, somebody else is going to fix what caused the fire in the first place. What you do is take drugs and thereby ignore the problems. We've talked about this before, Cindy. You said to me that you didn't have much respect for yourself. How can you have any self respect if all you do is run away from problems and depend upon crutches like drugs and stoned out friends to support you, and give you 'love.' You'll stay a cripple for sure that way. You're not only letting the fire burn but you're letting the arsonist go free to set another one."

"Yeah," replied Cindy moodily, "that's it all right, that's me. But I feel so shitty inside that as soon as I feel uncomfortable I take drugs and get high. Then there is no problem. I can't see it, I can't feel it. I wish I had some shit here right now. I'd take it. I'd take it."

"Why?" asked Wally. "Are you feeling crummy now?"

"Yeah."

"How come?"

"Because of what Dan brought up . . . the conversation he heard in the bus."

"Why should that make you feel bad?" said Ed. "I mean it makes me feel bad, too, because people are so bottled up that they can't even talk about what's going on with them . . . even when they know other people know about it . . . even when it's been discussed with them and they haven't been punished . . . I feel bad about that but I wouldn't take drugs to do something about it. I'd rather discuss it and find out what's going on."

"Yeah," muttered Cindy. "I can see that. But I was one of the people who was part of the conversation Dan mentioned. I guess I might as well say it. I visited Arty and Dan over vacation. Arty and I went off and got stoned a couple of times. Mike mentioned that he got stoned over vacation at a party and so I told him what happened with me and Arty. That's what Dan heard. Jeeze it feels good to get that off my back."

All eyes turned to Arty. "I told Dan before and I'll say it again. Even though he's my brother I don't think what I do or who I do it with is any of his damned business."

"It is here!" exclaimed Dan. "You and I both came on this expedition because we were, in different ways, fed up with the horseshit which was going on at home and at school. If we let the same mistrustful, secretive stupidity take place here then we've just made here be the same as home and we're wasting another year. You can do that to yourself if you want to but I'll be goddamned if you're going to do it to me. I think this school is terrific. It's more fun and more honest than anything I've ever been through; and it is that way because all of us have made incredible efforts to make it that way. If you want to screw things up for yourself, go ahead. It's your life. But you're not going to mess me up by messing up the school."

"How did I mess up either?" asked Arty. "All we did was get stoned. People everywhere are doing that all the time."

"Right now I think you're full of shit," growled Dan. "The only thing that makes the school work is that we can take care of ourselves and make ourselves feel comfortable while we're here. That's why I brought this whole thing up in the first place. I was uncomfortable. You and Cindy were hiding something from everybody. How is that any different than stealing the doughnut? It breaks a trust."

"Baloney," fumed Arty.

"Do you think you like it here, that you're comfortable being here?" asked Dan excitedly.

"Sure, except when you do something like this," Arty replied.

"Arty, you're nuts! You're lying to me and you're lying to yourself. If you felt so friggin' comfortable how come you couldn't tell people what was going on? Why did it have to be a secret at all? Why didn't you bring it up? Why didn't you say something when I brought it up or when Jill asked about what was going on? Why didn't you say something when Cindy was talking? I think you must have been scared or guilty; you probably still are. If those kinds of feelings are comfortable then I'd like to hear about it. You're playing a great big game with yourself, I think. Go ahead and play it but don't ask me to play it with you."

"How do you feel right now, Arty?" asked Cindy.

"I feel like having a joint but I know I can't. Don't you feel that way?"

"No," said Cindy. "Strangely enough I feel pretty good. I guess that's because I talked about what was happening with me. I've got a big problem but right now I can at least see it as a problem so I don't have to get stoned over it."

"Why do you feel like getting stoned now, Arty?" asked Wally.

"Why not?"

"How do you see it being helpful or making sense?" asked Wally.

"I can't talk about that with you," said Arty. "You wouldn't understand."

"Why not?"

"You have to be stoned to know what it feels like. Then you'd understand it."

"You mean to say that you think I have to be in some other condition or some other person to be able to discuss it?"

"Yeah, that's it."

"I'll tell you what I think. It's just a guess. I think somewhere inside you know full well that you're hurting yourself by using drugs and you don't want to face up to your own foolishness. I think there may be all kinds of feelings you have about yourself that you've covered up by using drugs and getting high. To admit to yourself drugs are a foolish thing to do is to simultaneously bring to consciousness uncool, uncomfortable feelings. These feelings are now telling you not to discuss or try to make sense of using drugs. Unconsciously you're afraid of getting hurt. Whenever this situation has come up before, you've escaped it, you've escaped it by using drugs."

"What makes you think that?" replied Arty.

"Because you think I have to be stoned in order to discuss it. You want what happened to you to happen to me. It sounds like you want me to lower the efficiency of my thinking ability — to distort my rationality a bit — in order to talk with you."

"Oh no, it's not that. It's that you just can't talk about the value of being high without being high. You've got to have the feeling to know it."

"In other words I have to believe there's something wrong with me as I am? Well, I don't believe it. Evidently at one time or another you did and you got hooked on drugs as an escape from those feelings. You can't possibly tell me there's something wrong with me being me. What you're really saying is it would be convenient for me to be somebody else who's into the same difficulty you are in. Maybe you fell for that line because you had little self respect for your own thoughts and feelings. Most kids feel that way. It's part of growing up. You've been conditioned to feel badly when you've done things wrong."

"I have some self esteem in their eyes."

"Whose eyes?"

"The kids I hang out with; Cindy too."

"Not right now you don't," said Cindy. "I think you're avoiding a problem. I've been doing it too, but that doesn't mean I think it's a good idea."

Sarah interrupted. She was shaking, almost crying. "Wally, do you think we should let this conversation continue? Isn't this considered counseling or psychology or something? This is why they're hauling us into court and trying to close the school!"

"That's absolutely ridiculous," exploded Wally. "There's nothing wrong or illegal about a group of people going out on an expedition to explore the social and natural environment they live in. They have to successfully cope with each and every problem which comes up, or else be overwhelmed and give up. That's all that's happening here. That's all we're doing right now. We've dedicated ourselves to doing the expedition again this year and, by golly, I for one am going to do it. I'm not going to be controlled by the District Attorney in Augusta any more than Arty should be controlled by his friends who tell him 'we won't like you if you don't smoke or get stoned, or drink,' or some other such crap. I'm not going to let a stupid environment control me. I'll create or find a better environment to live in. That's exactly how this school came into being. I'll be damned if I'm going to cop out on my better judgement. I'm not part of the Nixon administration. The environment emanating from Augusta operates by punishment of those who might hurt other people. Punishment creates a healthy but misplaced distance from others because we unconsciously believe that everyone can and will punish us. This school has no punishment so we have to learn not to hurt other people or ourselves by understanding the effects of our actions and then acting accordingly. That's not illegal. Augusta may not like it because it threatens their system of punishment and frees people from foolish laws. But, in a free country our school is not illegal. To the contrary, it's the essence of freedom. Hey, I didn't mean to make a speech, but what Sarah said really got me upset. Arty, how do you feel?"

"I wish I was back home hanging out with my friends."

"We're your friends," said Cindy.

"My friends respect me," said Arty.

"I respect you," replied Cindy. "If I didn't I wouldn't even bother talking to you. I just don't agree that it's a smart thing to use drugs even though I've been doing it."

"Drugs, beers and my friends are a big part of my life," declared

Arty. "I think I can relate better with them."

"How do you know?" responded Al. "What do you have to compare with? Once I purposely participated in a reaction-time experiment. I had my reaction time measured. Then, I was given a shot of whiskey and they measured my reaction time again. They asked me if I thought it would be different and I was positive it was the same. The next day I repeated the experiment with two shots of liquor. I still was positive there was no reaction-time change. They repeated the experiment five times, each time with more liquor, and each time I felt for sure my reaction time was the same. Then they showed me the results of the test. Each time, my reaction times were slower and slower. I've read where they've obtained similar results using marijuana instead of alcohol. Now, I ask you, how do you know what your potential for happiness might be, creatively or relationship-wise, if your mind was not boggled or bogged down with alcohol or drugs? That's the hang-up and the self deception they create. They can leave you feeling you have to stay with them — keep involved with a good thing."

"They're like hypothermia: overexposure to weather," explained Bethany. "It decreases body temperature, withdrawing the blood supply to the brain. The brain stops thinking critically and falsely decides nothing is wrong even though the deadly symptoms of overexposure stare the victim right in the face. Unless the victim receives help he dies."

Dan declared, "Often kids become even more dependent on drugs by making money from dealing — selling the stuff to others. Crackpots. You could take the brain of a teenage pothead, stick it up a mosquitoe's nose and it would rattle around like a BB in a boxcar."

"Half of the problem is that some aspect of the environment *invisibly* causes the kids to feel uncomfortable," stated Sarah, "the other half is that we've never been taught to search for what is making us uncomfortable or even be aware that we are uncomfortable. We've never learned to recognize and respect our deeper personal feelings, so we're controlled by them. We take drugs to cover them up. The worst of it all is that real discomforting aspects of the environment are allowed to remain uncorrected — to hurt others as they have in the past — and thus continue the insanity. The incedible sale and use of drugs and alcohol in this country is undeniable testimony to the deteriorated, hurtful environment we have created and sustain. It hurts us. In the final analysis all drug use of any kind is a tranquilization of symptomatic uncomfortable feelings. Each time it takes place it reinforces the conditioned habit. That same energy could be used to obtain good feelings without using a degrading crutch."

"They're no good," sobbed Cindy. "Look what happened to me. I overdosed on pills twice — got myself so high that I lost track of how many I took. I had convulsive fits and passed out. A few days later I did it again. I used to have flashbacks, I'd go nutty without taking anything. But they let me drive a car. What a comforting thought to know a vegetable like me is behind the wheel of a motor vehicle. Here I'm learning to discover and change the environment which conditioned me to be so foolish. I'm learning to feel good without crutches. I sure hope they don't close down the school." There was a long period of silence.

"I want to think about what's been said," murmured Arty.

Wally thought about Cindy's statement and about closing the school. His mind began drifting back to the original subpoena, to last September in Charlie's office.

V

Sea water is a living thing. It is littered with miniscule plants and animals easily observed at night with the naked eyes like so many stars dancing in the water. Under the microscope, I have seen the algae, diatoms, protozoans, minute copepods, temporary larval stages of invertebrates, and fish eggs, which bob, swim and float along the surface. Only they can capture the energy of life directly from the plant life, minerals, and sun. Each and every sea and shore creature would cease to exist if one destroyed these pulsing, squirming, jetting, swimming ciliated little forms and the algae.

From a composition by Dan Miller, age 16.

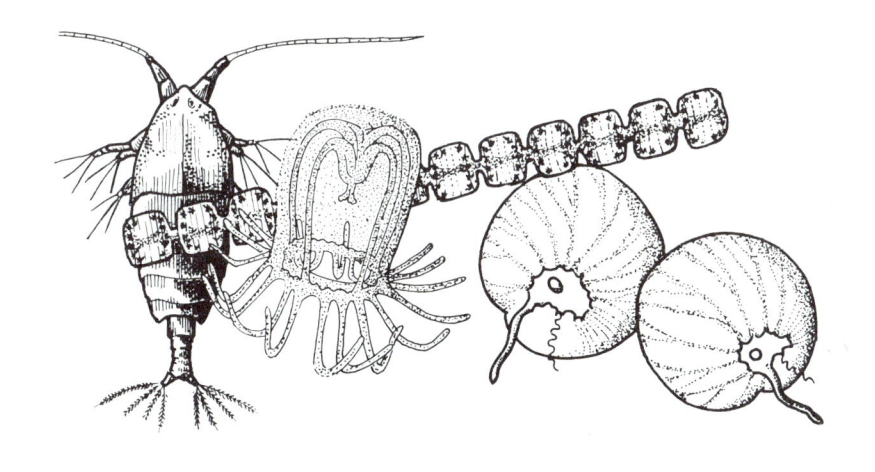

From "Refinery News" in *The Downeast Gazette,* April 18, 1975
In 1974 there were 26 major oil spills — one every two weeks. Oil taints, burns, coats, smothers and poisons; plankton is very susceptible. Oil can start cancers, affect reproduction and heredity, respiration, and natural plant and animal balances. Three days after a spill ninety-five percent of the oceanographic trawler's catch was dead. Life on the seabed was still dying a year later.

Berne Field, Director
Marine Biologic Research Laboratory

A week before the expedition got underway a September day was drawing to an end, but Wally and Sarah's conversation with Charlie continued:

"I see," declared Charlie. "After his suicide attempt almost twenty years ago Ben became a patient of Dr. Sullivan. Were you involved with counseling Ben after that?"

"Not much," stated Wally, referring to his journal. "That was the year I started the expedition school. I worked out of an office in Vermont and only returned to Whitehorse during vacation periods.

"Let's see here," Wally said, quickly turning the pages in the next notebook. "I had a conversation with Ben over Thanksgiving weekend when I was in Maine. Among several things he told me were that the most comfortable, peaceful moments he had ever lived were, one, as he was pulling the trigger and two, when he had taken the morphine overdose. Dr. Sullivan had put him on tranquilizers which helped his depression and he was beginning to understand some of the effects of his past through his therapy group participation at the guidance clinic. He seemed to be more in touch with his feelings and was doing something positive about them in therapy. He was no longer completely their pawn. He was also relieving depressing feelings by smoking pot and taking LSD or mescaline. He had friends for the first time in his life: some from the therapy group, others from the drug cult which had found and welcomed him with open arms.

"In retrospect, it seemed incongruous to me that a lad as bright as Ben could not 'correctly' commit suicide. Unconsciously, he must have known the gun had blanks, and that he needed to take more morphine to kill himself. His suicide attempts must have been a grotesque cry for help from deep within. I know Ben. Had he been operating up to par he could have easily handled the suicide in proper fashion. My discussion with him that Thanksgiving led me to believe he was also aware of this. He seemed happy to realize that his tortured feelings were not so uncomfortable that they demanded he kill himself. It was the first time I had ever heard him speak positively about himself, even if the subject had to be somewhat distressing. His suicide attempts had markedly changed his environment and the new effects were obvious. He was now being molded and sustained by an environment which he had selected because it was more caring about *him* and how *he* felt and acted.

"Ben graduated from high school and married the following year. His wife Carol was very supportive of him. They both attended college locally, the University of Maine. Ben became a medical technician. They had children, identical twins. Thirteen years ago, seven years after he graduated from high school, Ben gave me a very distressing call. Up to that time I had seen him only casually. He had appeared to be doing fine."

"Did you do anything like counseling with him?" asked Charlie.

"No, he was working only with Dr. Sullivan as far as I know."

"Then what happened?"

"Like I said, I got this incredible phone call from him."

"Hello Wally. This is Ben, Ben Miller — How are you?"

I knew from his tone of voice that this was no social call. He sounded scared.

"Wally, listen, maybe you can help me — somebody has got to help — Carol and I are in trouble, big trouble."

"God Ben, you sound desperate, what's happening?"

"I don't know exactly — nobody does. But we're in a hell of a mess. About a year ago I had some friends over to the house — old friends I hadn't seen for a couple of years. They were some of the kids I was doing drugs with back when I needed them." (My delight in hearing Ben use the past tense was overcome by the emotion pouring out of the receiver.) "Anyhow, they had brought drugs with them, you know, for old time's sake, and they decided we would have a party and get stoned like we used to. I didn't want to do it, so I didn't, but they decided to pop the pills anyhow — which was O.K. with me because it was nice to see them and visit.

"Well, while Nick was stoned he left some of his pills

lying around. It was mescaline, sitting in his shoes . . . he was barefooted . . . and . . . and . . ." Ben seemed unable to speak, "And Danny, one of the twins, well, we think he got hold of the pills and swallowed some . . . at least one . . . Nick doesn't remember how many he left in his shoe . . . Anyhow . . . nobody even knew it happened until we noticed that Danny was acting kind of strange . . . like he was drunk . . . then he started screaming and fell down and was having spasms; we didn't know what was happening . . . and some of them that were stoned were laughing . . . I almost killed them . . . we called Dr. Adams and told him what Danny was doing . . . I was in a frenzy. It was a madhouse, the doctor couldn't figure it out. By this time, Danny had passed out . . . he just lay there quivering and crying every once in a while. We tried to kick everybody out but some were in no shape to leave. Anyhow, the doctor figured it must have been something Danny ate and we tried to get him to vomit but couldn't . . . he was like in a coma . . . Doctor Adams got over as quickly as he could. He had already called the emergency squad and they came over. Doc pumped Danny's stomach and then we took off in the ambulance for the Machias hospital. Danny was in a coma for over a week being fed intravenously . . . we thought he'd die. Finally he came out of it as if nothing had happened — he seemed to be fine. But as time went by, we began to notice that he was acting differently than Arty, his twin brother. He wouldn't learn things as quickly, or at all. It was lucky that Arty was an identical twin. I mean, you could see the differences between them . . . it's been like a controlled experiment in science class . . . both twins have exactly the same genetic makeup, right? So as differences appeared, we could see them. Without Arty, who would have known that anything was even wrong? Not that it's made any difference because all the doctors and all the specialists have no idea what *is* wrong — and they don't know what to do. Anyhow, today a big-time pediatrician in Boston said that his tests show Danny to be mentally retarded and that we should start treating him as though he ... he were a vegetable — that he might remain just like a *three* year old forever."

"Jesus, JEEEZus," I murmured, "what are you going

to do?" I didn't know how to react to what I was hearing. I had only seen the twins twice since they were born. They were nothing special to me — I'd had very little contact with Ben, hardly knew Carol — so the whole thing was coming across to me like some kind of bizarre tragedy that you hear daily on the news reports. Like just this morning, I heard an interview with some woman whose husband had practically beaten her to death with a lead pipe about fifteen different times during the past three years. She was calling for help on some hot line interview show out of Boston. It really got to me as I heard it, but how close can you let these things get and how much can you let them affect you, upset you? In the long run, every single one of them does no matter how much you or I ignore or disbelieve them. They're part of our environment through the papers, magazines, radio, TV and they make up part of our image of the environment, even if they never happen to us. I've never even seen a person die. Yet if I watch TV for one evening I personally watch something like ten or fifteen people being killed in one way or another, delightfully brought to me by what used to be my favorite breakfast cereal, insurance company, or what-have-you. I know it's make-believe — what I see on the screen isn't happening to me here in the Maine woods. But it affects me without my knowing it. Last week I even bought two tear gas pistols to protect Sarah and myself in case some "fiend" happens upon our lonely little house. I don't want to kill the bastard, but I don't want to experience what happens an average of twenty or thirty times every night on the TV for those unlucky enough to have the electricity or inclination to watch. Crimes do reach me in my emotional impression of the environment, even though I know that most of them are fictional or distorted. But Ben's situation was closer than TV.

I murmured a bit and finally asked Ben how he was taking the whole thing. I knew Ben and I was genuinely concerned about his welfare, but in a distant way. It's not like he was my brother.

"Anyhow," Ben asked, "can I come over and talk with you? You're good at figuring things out. You really helped me a lot back in school. I think without our talks I might have really done myself in. You were the one thing that made life seem worthwhile back then. Maybe you could see some things a little differently than the doctors and psychologists. I've heard what you've been doing with kids at this environmental school of yours. Maybe you know something that will help me. I'm desperate — I don't want Danny to be retarded. He physically tests normally and has no brain damage, so why can't he learn?"

"Did you begin counseling Ben then?" asked Charlie.

"I didn't know what to do. Thoughts raced through my head as to how the environment molds people — especially kids. I was thinking out loud to Ben as they came to mind."

"You know, Ben, a doctor saying a kid is mentally retarded could actually make a kid mentally retarded even if he isn't. We tend to react to people the way we think they are, rather than to discover what they really are. People, everything for that matter, are really our images of them. I am aware that teachers who are told they are teaching retarded children will teach differently than they do if they are told that the class is made up of normal kids. They teach differently even if the kids who are supposed to be retarded are not retarded at all, but are normal! By unwittingly making a learning environment for retarded kids the teacher actually deprives these normal kids of needed growing experiences, thus retarding their growth! Students who don't fit certain teachers' prejudices often end up molded into the teachers' preconceived images of them.

"You know Ben, there is a simple experiment we used to perform in science classes. You'd put your left hand in a bowl of ice cold water and, at the same time, would place your right hand in a bowl of very hot water and leave them there for a minute. Unconsciously, your brain makes adaptations to the sensations it receives from these two different environments. It's conditioned by them. Then a new environment appears — a bowl of lukewarm water. Simultaneously, you'd place both your hands in the bowl of lukewarm water and would note what happens. Incredibly, the same exact bowl of water is experienced differently by each hand. The hot water hand experiences the water as being cold. The cold hand finds it to be hot. It's a vivid demonstration of the fact that our past experiences strongly determine and condition how we are going to experience a new situation. It's virtually impossible for us to be objective for we each come from different formative conditioning environments. The psychiatrist is conditioned to see Danny's problem as a psychiatric problem. The neurosurgeon may well see it neurologically. The plumber will see it as a leaky pipe somewhere. Perhaps you may be the most objective of all, Ben, because you're most concerned and you have a control, a measuring device — you have Arty, an identical twin. Ben, I guess what I'm thinking is if you think Danny is retarded because you believe the doctor, then you might really do Danny a harmful disservice. Why don't we get together and think about what things you have directly observed about Danny. I've got the summer off and maybe we could discover something which would help out in this situation. And for God's sake, don't get depressed — at least not yet."

"So you started counseling Ben at that time even though he was under Dr. Sullivan's care?" asked Charlie.

"I guess you could call it that. I was just being friendly and concerned, that's all. I was also very curious.

"Ben didn't seem quite the same as when I had least seen him. I at first attributed it to the pressure upon him from the mishap with Danny, but then I began to get the idea that something else was bothering him as well. There was just a hint of distance — perhaps it was the tone or the volume of his voice — it was like he was talking to me through a mask. I decided not to ignore it for it became bothersome. I found myself focusing some of my energy on whatever was causing Ben's moodiness. Often he would not look at me in the eye; and it struck me that as he was talking about what the doctors had said about Danny, he was acting like a frightened little boy who had done something wrong. I decided to ask if he felt comfortable discussing the situation and he said yes, but with some hesitation."

"You don't seem too comfortable, Ben," I told him. "Are you sure something isn't bothering you about being here? Do you feel perfectly comfortable?"

He was silent for a few moments and then said, "Well, I guess I feel kind of apprehensive about what you think about me and what I did to Danny."

"I am unaware that you did anything," I replied, trying to figure out what he was getting at. "What did you do that you think I won't like?"

"Well, I used drugs for years and I know you don't agree with that," he stammered. "I thought you might be mad at me, or think badly of me for having done that ... I mean, that's how I got to know Nick and that crowd — through drugs — and it was due to their visit that Danny is in the predicament he is in. I thought you might be holding it against me."

"Well, I'm really glad you told me what was on your mind," I replied with relief. "Why should I hold it against you — especially since you're not doing drugs now?"

"I don't know exactly," said Ben, "but you sure were adamant about drugs seven years ago, remember?"

"Yes, I do, but you're going to have to try to separate my impression of drugs as an institution in general from my feelings and thoughts about any individual and his or her particular situation. It's very important that you recognize that they are two related but entirely separate entities. I disapprove of the *concept* of drug use and its effects. But, for each individual I am aware that a series of environmental circumstances beyond his or her control or awareness have molded the individual into a drug-oriented relationship with the environment. In your situation, it's quite obvious what purpose they were serving — nobody knew it better than I did — so why should I hold it against you that you at times relieved your depressed feelings by using alcohol or drugs? I remember your slogan was 'I'd rather have a bottle-in-front-of-me than a frontal lobotomy.' What was and is important to me is that you were actively working on getting to understand and control or change the environment which was making you feel depressed. Without the depression, there would be no use — no need

— for drugs or alcohol. Isn't that correct? Isn't that what actually made you stop taking them?"

"Precisely," acknowledged Ben. "As long as I depended upon my father to give me security, I was unconsciously caught in having to listen and believe his ridiculous feelings that I needed to be a top competitor, to be as good as he. But he ultimately wouldn't let me compete because in his eyes I made him look second-rate to his own kid. So he competed with me in every way and I saw myself being worthless, a loser, and it depressed me. I hated his war stories for I completely disagreed with the concept of war. Yet, unconsciously I thought I was a cowardly queer for not being in tune with my own father. I felt worthless which made me feel even more depressed. In therapy, I began to realize that the whole relationship was really destructive. I was worthwhile in my own individual ways. The depression started going away and I was able to do well and feel better about things I wanted to do. I did things which were sensible to me and which made me feel even better about myself. Once I felt better I had no need for drugs or liquor, I was high on life. Carol helped a lot. She could see my strengths. My own virtues completely escaped my depressed outlook on everything."

"Yet, you've been caught up in the same bind with me since you got here," I replied. "You've actually cast me in the role of your father and have put yourself down for not meeting my expectations about drugs. You've done this even though you're actually no longer involved and even though I don't hold them personally against you or anybody that's caught up in their foolishness. It's not your fault that your inner or outer environment won't let you feel that good about yourself."

"You're right," said Ben. "Every once in a while I still get caught up in the same self-defeating trap. I can see now that I could have just asked how you felt about me and drugs from the start and squelched those feelings immediately. It's just like you said. I had an impression of you which I put down as being unimportant. I ignored my feelings instead of questioning or discovering if they were valid. I put myself down and projected it on you as if you were doing it to me — I made you into my father and then felt distant from you."

"How do you feel about me now?" I asked.

"Much better. It's not a problem anymore."

As he said it, I recognized that the distance and the hesitancy were no longer there and had not been for the latter part of the conversation. I pointed it out to him and he acknowledged with a smile. We felt warmly towards each other. I was happy that we were each able to make each other more comfortable in what might be a long and trying time with Danny.

"You see Charlie? It's a perfect example of what we were saying before about the environment being a powerful influence. For a few hours I was a major part of Ben's environment and had been turning him on 'uncomfortably'. Similarly, Ben was a major part of my environment, and did the same thing to me. Our respective environments were 'molding' us in an uncomfortable fashion. I became aware of my feelings and modified my environment by questioning and investigating it. Only then did I once again feel comfortable. Ben could have done exactly the same thing that I did. Since I was bothering him, he could have asked me what I did think or feel about him having used drugs and hanging out with Nick. Ben ignored his environment (me) and remained molded uncomfortably by my presence. He ignored his uncomfortable feelings and by doing nothing about them, remained uncomfortable.

"Quite obviously, Ben's feelings and his environment (me) were practically inseparable. Both were discomforting. Which was really the problem? Was it *me* doing something or *Ben* ignoring his feelings? Ahh, that's the question that makes the point."

"What point?" asked Charlie.

"About the impact of the environment and how we ignore it. We have all been so egotistically indoctrinated that we experience two entirely distinct, separate entities: one is ourselves and the other is the environment. But isn't it possible that there is only *one* entity which is nameless for it is unrecognized as such? Whatever you want to call it, we are it and it is us. Over the years, I've learned to call that entity *environment*. I am it. It is me. As it goes, so go I and vice-versa. We ignore the environment because we've never really learned that it, and therefore *we* are valuable in ourselves. We've learned all too well we're both just grist for our cultural, institutionalized economic and technological mill.

[margin note: ODD — THAT MARK WOULD REPORT THAT MICHAEL IS NOT INTO FEELINGS]

"The social environment, through language, can communicate within its own parameters; there is a vast language barrier between the social and natural environment which even made Thoreau believe the natural environment is a 'civilization other than our own.' The integrated social and natural environment is the real *environment*. Perhaps it should be called the universe. It is the same thing. It is what I mean when I use the word environment."

"You know this whole environmental interpretation of life that you guys have is rather foreign to me," said Charlie. "I think I'm beginning to see its importance in this conflict with the Attorney General. It's hard to completely understand it. I'm having trouble concentrating because it's getting late. Why don't we talk about it further in the morning?"

"Good idea," yawned Sarah. "Let's get some sleep."

"You go ahead to bed," suggested Wally, "I want to write in my journal. I'll be along shortly."

A new day began with the same old problem. It found the Bryces and their lawyer wearily seated in the kitchen.

"OK, what happened with the Millers then; what happened to Dan?" asked Charlie after they had finished breakfast. "That's what I asked them," replied Wally, continuing from his notes, "Carol said Dan couldn't learn right."

> "Arty, his twin, can learn just about anything when I teach him, but Dan is just about impossible. It bothers me so much that I don't even try anymore. Like if I'm trying to show Arty how to button his shirt, he'll watch and imitate me, and he'll do it right after a while. It's fun to watch him grow. He and Dan used to do things equally well, but now the difference is tragic. I couldn't teach Dan to button his shirt to save my soul. I give him his clothes and he'll dress himself or accept help but doing his buttons is past his comprehension. It's just about the same with most things. He's very inconsistent. One day he'll help me dress himself and will enjoy it, and the next day it's almost as if he's forgotten the day before — he doesn't help at all, even if I coach him."
>
> "That's another thing," interrupted Ben, "he doesn't eat regularly. Sometimes he will eat with us and sometimes he won't eat until an hour or two later . . ."

"... Or before," interrupted Carol. "That's what I meant when I said he was inconsistent — especially when compared to Arty. When the psychologist gave the kids blocks, they both played well together. As a matter of fact, Danny piled his in a way which was evidently quite advanced for his age — Arty tried to imitate him and couldn't do it. Then the psychologist went in the room and showed the kids new ways to pile the blocks. Arty did it fine, Danny happily started doing it, but then drifted off to doing something else with them. The psychologist told him that his were good, coaxed him, showed him new configurations, all to no avail. Dan wouldn't or couldn't learn them."

"The queer thing about it," continued Carol, "is that I have a hunch that Dan could do all that stuff if he wanted to, he just won't learn or cooperate in learning."

"On the other hand," said Ben, "when we got the tricycle, we tried to show Dan how to use it, but he wasn't a bit interested. Then we showed Arty who, after a while, was happily pedaling around the room. While he was using it, Dan came over and said 'Me want.' We took Arty off the bike. Dan tried to get on but didn't quite know what to do. He turned to me and started whimpering. He let me put his feet on the pedals, and his hands on the bars and then push him around. Pretty soon he was doing it on his own. We were delighted — and told him so. No sooner had we praised him when he got off the bike and started playing with the teddy bear. Meanwhile, Arty got back on the bike and Dan could care less.

"He never rides it while we're around, but when he thinks we're not watching, he plays with it and does as well as Arty. It's that way with a lot of things, but there's no real consistency to it. We've just about given up trying to teach him anything. It's frustrating and disappointing. We feel so guilty and miserable when we see Arty grow and learn while Danny won't just because of what happened with the mescaline.

"Sometimes Dan just stands and rocks back and forth for long periods of time, and nothing seems to be able to reach him when he's doing it."

"Sometimes he listens to you, other times he couldn't care less," said Carol. "It's such an unhappy thing, especially when we can see how responsive Arty is — and how we did all this to Dan."

There was a long period of silence which I finally broke, saying, "do you want to know what I think?" They both looked up as if I was going to give away money. "It seems to me that if you're going to get anywhere with this dilemma, the first thing that's got to happen is that you've got to stop kicking yourselves for what happened to Dan. You're part of his environment and he undoubtedly senses how you feel. If he senses sadness in you from his actions, he may very well be learning that his existence is painful to you and you're the part of the environment upon which he is most dependent — which feeds and clothes him, and gives him affection. I know it may be hard to do, especially with Arty around as a showpiece, but it seems essential to me."

"But it *is* our fault," said Ben. "Especially mine — Carol was never much into the drug thing. We were both responsible for not keeping an eye on the kids the day that Nick came over. It's easy for you to say we shouldn't feel badly about it, but you didn't do it, *you're* not guilty."

"Well," I replied, "it seems to me what's done is done. If lightning strikes a tree is it your fault because you planted it there? I don't think so; it's a phenomenon of the environment. Ben, is it your fault that your father and your family environment, molded you to what you were when you were a kid? I don't think so, and I know from our past discussions that you agree with me. You were depressed by your home situation and finally did something about it. You're in the same situation right now with the kids. What's done is done."

"I know," murmured Carol, "but you don't understand — *we* did it."

"You intentionally gave Dan mescaline?" I asked loudly, acting incredibly surprised (and it was an act).

"No, no, God no, not intentionally!" cried Ben.

"Well, then, why not live in your intentions. If you hadn't intended to hurt Dan, then why blame yourselves when he got hurt? I'm as aware of the situation as you are, I think, and I don't blame you for it in the least. It was an accident which involved drugs and you know, Ben, how judgemental I can be about that subject. I think you both might want to get some support or counseling help with regard to these feelings of guilt. Try to live in your intentions at the time. Maybe it would help to think that Dan was set back a year by having gotten the measles or something — so he can't be expected to be like Arty. Is it your fault that he got the measles? Why not let Dan be Dan and enjoy him for what he is — for that's what he is.

"Isn't that really what you wanted from your father? You are a powerful, dominant portion of Dan's environment. You are emotionally shaping him. Be as supportive as you can. Is there any reason to signal distress to Dan when he's not doing anything he should be distressed about? How do you think your misplaced distress will affect him?"

Ben, Carol and I sat quietly for awhile just thinking. I hoped I hadn't overwhelmed, frightened or alienated them. If I had been talking with kids in my school, I might have waited for responses to each of these questions, one at a time, so they were sure to be working with what was being said. If they could emotionally find it and live in it then let them do it at their own pace. But I really don't enjoy playing "teacher" or "therapist" with my friends in my private life. I just wanted to be me and to let them know exactly what I thought. As it was, I was purposely tempering my thoughts on this matter and conveying them in question form so that Ben and Carol could think about them and do something about the questions on their own. That is, if they wanted to. I couldn't see why they wouldn't want to act once they could view the problem in its environmental setting rather than as a personal fault. They had to move on from feeling unnecessarily guilty or anxious about it. It really upsets me that we're all trained by our society to see setbacks as being our fault, or someone else's fault, or morally good, bad, right or wrong. In my mind those are all manifestations of authoritatively being trained to be soldiers of our culture rather than free individuals in a sensible environment.

Carol was crying. "Listen, Wally," said Ben, "I can see what you're saying. I agree with it. If I was in my therapy group and somebody was putting themselves down like Carol and I have been doing I would tell them exactly what you've told me. But when you're sitting in the middle of these kinds of guilt and anxiety feelings, it's just easier said than done."

"I think I'll try to not feel so guilty," sobbed Carol, "and if I can't, then it would be best for me to get some kind of counseling help because I can see that this is really foolish."

We stared at each other for awhile. "I'd like to visit you guys in town and get a feel for what Danny is going through. I think you'd better know that I've had very little experience with young kids and I might prove to be more of a nuisance than a help."

"You've been helpful already," said Carol, a bit more cheerily. "Please come visit whenever you can."

"I see," said Charlie. "They asked for your assistance! What did you do?"

"I saw Ben and Carol several times during the early part of the summer, especially on the typical Bay of Fundy, wet-foggy weekends when I couldn't take the canoe out to go fishing. The visits were both fun and interesting. Danny kept right on with his inconsistent ways and it was impossible to really define what was going on with him. Sometimes, he'd play, other times not; sometimes he'd talk with people, sometimes he'd show no interest whatsoever and would just stand around and rock back and forth with his thumb in his mouth. Ben and Carol were taking the whole thing a lot more reasonably. Their guilt anxieties were quieting down.

"I remember a few interesting things about Danny," Wally reminisced, "that still stick in my mind — things which happened before the big discovery. I learned that for a few days after Danny came out of the coma he began to wet his pants, which he had stopped doing prior to the mescaline episode. He then stopped wetting them as mysteriously as he had started. Carol said he stopped because he seemed uncomfortable with the wetness. Arty had been 'dry' for close to a year, and remained dry.

"One day, while I was there, the kids had assorted toys scattered all around the floor. Carol asked them to clean them up and put them away and she started helping them. Both kids were involved in doing it, Danny kind of imitating Arty. Carol encouraged them, telling them they were good boys, and no sooner had she said it when Danny stopped putting them away and started playing with the little cars. Another time, they were playing 'London Bridge' with some friends. The kids would line up and circle around and then wait their turn when the bridge came down — all except Danny who would start moving past everybody on line to get through the bridge. The kids gently pushed him back and then he'd stand on the line. It was like he couldn't learn to wait his turn and had to be told each time."

Carol would ask Arty, "What's your name?" He'd answer, "Arthur Wayne Miller." "Good Arty," she'd reply."Wally you try it."

"Wally L. Bryce."

"No Wally, come on, ask Arty his name."

"Oh, O.K.; hey, buddy, what's your name?"

"Arthur Wayne Miller," he'd reply proudly.

Now in walked Danny. "What's your name?" I asked him.

"Danny," he said, "Danny Miller." Carol practically clapped with joy.

"That's the first time he's done that," she said and turned to him saying, "That was good — what's your name?"

"I just told you," said Danny, and he started playing with his blocks.

It was a few weeks later, early August, 1964. The mackerel were beginning to run, pollock were hitting and fin whales were in the harbor. A rainy Saturday brought me over to the Miller's, who were on their way to a birthday party next door. The kids played the usual party games, Danny having his troubles, but being accepted by the kids nevertheless and certainly not unhappy about making mistakes. They started to play "Simon Says", a game where you do what the leader, Simon, is doing only if he says "Simon says do this." The game is based on the idea that each participant receives two instructions simultaneously, a verbal instruction "Simon Says" and a visual one — the leader does something like clapping his hands. The player who follows the visual "command" without "Simon Says" being said is out. The winner — the last remaining participant — got a piece of chocolate as a prize. Well, Danny likes chocolate. And Danny won every time. Never made a mistake, never clapped his hands unless "Simon said" to do so. It was uncanny. He would flawlessly differentiate between the hypnotic repetitive "Simon Says" and when the words changed to just "Do this." Neither was he mesmerized by the leader's actions. Arty made plenty of mistakes. After a while, the chocolate prize was being given to the last two winners, because otherwise Danny would have been the only winner. As it was, he went home looking like a Hershey Bar. He actually did much "better" than Arty, the first time ever. Carol and Ben were delighted. So was I. Yet, in the middle of the game, it struck me while watching him that Danny was doing it not so much for the fun of winning, but simply because he liked and wanted those chocolate squares. I made my way over to Carol and Ben.

"I know this will sound crazy, and it's just a hunch, but maybe you shouldn't make a big deal over Dan being number one in the Simon Says game. Mention it matter-of-factly, but don't tell him he was good."

"Shouldn't we reinforce his good work in the game?" said Carol, so proud and happy she could burst.

"Ordinarily, yes," I replied. "It's the natural thing to do, especially in this situation. But I noticed a few things which might be going on and I want to discuss them with you before the evening's out. Praise him if you feel you must. Otherwise, wait — if I'm not mistaken, you and Dan may be happier if you wait."

"The kids finally went to bed. Dan took his teddy bear doll with him, Arty had given up bringing toys to bed. So had Danny but like everything else, it just depended upon his mood that evening — inconsistent was the word, and tonight just happened to be teddy bear night.

"Carol, who had enough self-control to just casually mention Danny's winning the game, returned from putting the kids to bed. "What's up, Wally? What was that all about this afternoon? What did you notice?"

"Well," I said, chagrined, "it might not be anything,

but then again, it might be. You can help me an awful lot by adding your impressions and observations to what I think may be happening."

"Let's hear it," said Ben.

"What was it about the game today which made it possible for Danny to do so well?" I asked them.

"I don't know," said Ben. "Ordinarily, he wouldn't play, or would get it wrong, or who knows what — that's the usual Danny thing."

"Beats me," said Carol. "He sure does like candy, though."

"I think that's part of it," I said. "He didn't seem proud or happy to be a winner and he doesn't ever seem to experience competition as a factor in anything. Today was no exception. But today he won — all the rest of the time he's a loser."

"Maybe he's forgotten what competition is or something," said Ben. "Before the accident (I was really glad to hear that word instead of the 'we screwed him up' of two months before) he and Arty would compete in many ways: take toys from each other, race to places, things like that."

"O.K.," I said, "but the thing that really hit home with me is the dynamics of the game — the trick which he was able to master without making an error. The trick to that game is to not get overwhelmed by the repetition of doing something right, over and over again, so that when the command slightly changes (and it's only the vocal command which changes), you're so conditioned by what's already taken place that you follow the leader even though the rules say not to follow. What it boils down to in my mind is that *Danny can not be conditioned by the environment* when everybody else can, including Arty, his genetic twin."

"Yeah," said Ben, "that's a way of looking at it. But why all of a sudden is that happening?"

"Ben, Carol, listen: Maybe it isn't all of a sudden, maybe it's been happening since the accident and we haven't recognized it. For instance, Danny used to be competitive with Arty until the accident. Is competitiveness something which is conditioned into a youngster through repetition? Doesn't the environment reward the winner in that he gets the toy or the attention each time he wins? After a while, it's like 'Simon Says'. You compete for the good feelings of winning at first, and the behavior is repeated until it's done unconsciously. Competition is acceptable behavior in our culture, and is, therefore, reinforced."

"I'm not sure exactly how conditioning works," said Carol, "but what you're saying makes sense to me. Competition is like a habit, is that right?"

"Exactly," I replied, "and the environment — social or natural — is the conditioning agent. That's what's so amazing about what seems to be going on with Danny. If our assumption is correct, the mescaline has somehow frightened Danny so that he may not be able to be conditioned by the environment. Or, to put it another way, Danny has become so sensitive or aware that the environment can be hurtful, can put him in a coma, and can kill him, that *he avoids any kind of rewards which will condition him to the seemingly hurtful culture or environment which surrounds him.* He only gets rewards by *choosing* what he wants for himself — he rewards himself instead of falling prey to conditioning by the environment."

"Jeez," said Ben, "that might well be. That's a little bit how I felt after I took the overdose of morphine. I was totally encompassed by my own feelings — living in their radiance — and didn't even know the 'environment' was there. Until I passed out, it was like I was living in a big cave full of my own feelings, with no interference or static from the environment outside the cave. While I was in therapy I began to realize I could have those kinds of feelings without drugs. As I began to understand the effects of past and present environmental situations I had been in, I was able to cope with those situations or ignore them. I would roll them back and create a cave, a place for me and my good feelings. By getting to know, and to be aware of the environment and its effects, I was able to deal with it, make room for my feelings and stay high on life. That's when I dropped out of drugs — who needed them?"

"You know," said Carol, "when I think back on the times when Danny has acted peculiar, there is an element of conditioning in each one. Like the time he'd say his name when asked, but not when I tried to get him to repeat it for mommy's praise. He shied away from that. Or when he's putting away his toys, and I tell him how good he is or how well he's doing, he immediately stops doing it. Maybe it's like you say: he's allergic to rewards from the environment because either he has enough rewards from himself — like being able to win chocolate — or he's afraid of getting close to the environment because it damn near killed him with mescaline."

"Or like in games," said Ben, "he's never been conditioned to waiting his turn in line, he's been exposed to it many times but has never made it a habit, so he has to learn it, or be told each time he plays."

"Wally, do you know much about conditioning and how it works?" asked Carol. "I'd really like to know a lot more before I'll believe this whole thing."

"Not that much," I replied, "and what I do think I know is somewhat out of phase with just about every area in psychology, so I'm a renegade. I never even studied experimental psychology, I've never read anything by B. F. Skinner, who has done a lot of research about this. Most of what I've picked up has been from first hand observation of the teenagers in our traveling school."

"Yeah," said Ben, "but you achieve results there which are completely unique in the education world — you get kids off alcohol, drugs, dropping out, dishonesty and vandalism — lots of asocial stuff like that. That's why you're on the radio, that's why all the papers keep writing articles about you. Whatever you do know seems to work plenty well, so there's no need telling us you don't know much. You're just being modest, Wally. Ever since I've known you, I've had a secret motto: 'The Bryce is right'."

"It's not modesty, Ben," I replied. "Frankly, it's just that when I talk about the environment being a conditioning agent, people think I'm nuts. We've all been brought up so distantly from the concept and values of the environment, especially the natural environment, that a lot of it is just invisible to the ordinary person who was brought up living in a house, protected, and fortressed from the energies of nature and society. We're so blind that I really think our society, and everybody in it, is almost totally insane — a nut house — I live on its outskirts. I've camped out all over this country at least nine months of every year for the past nine years, winter and summer. I've taught others to do the same and to learn directly and first hand from the environment and each other — none of the interpretative garbage of republicans vs. democrats, straight vs. hippy, Jews vs. Catholics etc. We use direct observation, direct evidence, and real life encounters with the many facets of nature and people. That's like living in another culture and although I know it's applicable here, who even understands it except the students who come with me?"

"Hold it right there," said Charlie. "I've got an idea!"

VI

It would depend upon where I sat as to whom my companion would be. On this particular grey day I was high on the granite rock where the pounding surf would reach only in extreme tides or storms. At my side was a species of periwinkle, a long way from the sea water crashing below. It has found a habitat which has practically made it a land animal, although its cousins remain in the intertidal zone. I really wished I could have spoken with it and found out how it felt to be right in the middle of evolving from living in the water all day to being splashed maybe twice a month. In years to come, it might become a land animal.

From a composition by Dan Miller, age 16.

The Downeast Gazette, October 16, 1974
It's exceedingly dangerous to float tankers as large as the Empire State building down the swift, rocky narrow entrance channel. It takes a tanker 17 miles to stop and five miles to turn 360 degrees. An oil slick would be fifty miles long and five miles wide under normal circumstances. The rapid tides in this area would greatly increase the pollution potential.

Thomas Randolph,
Marine Engineer

Charlie's eyes brightened a bit, a smile hinted that something was popping in his mind. "I think we're getting somewhere now," he exclaimed. "I'm beginning to see the light as to what this is all about."

"What is it?" asked Sarah. "What's going on?"

"I'm not positive yet! Let me ask you a few questions and then make a phone call, I'll be able to know a lot better then. First and foremost did you start treating Ben and Carol and Dan at this point?"

"What do you mean treating?"

"Well, did you start teaching them the things you teach on the school, the concepts you describe in the book you did about your school, *The Trailside Classroom,* all that stuff about environmental conditioning?"

"Why yes," Wally retorted, quite surprised at the question. "What else do you think I would tell them? I live and breathe it both at home and school, what else *could* I tell them? If they wanted somebody else's point of view then they should have gone to talk to somebody else."

"As I said, I think I can see what the problem is. You've been approached by some people who are really troubled, and you've snatched them out of the hands of qualified medical help by telling them that if they become Eskimos they'll be O.K. You've done it right under the professional nose and pocketbook of Dr. Sullivan, and he's undoubtedly fighting mad about it."

"What do you mean, become Eskimos?" asked Sarah.

"I mean a foreign culture. There is no recognized, valid therapy or institute in this country that understands, no less recognizes your concepts of environmental conditioning or education."

"What do you mean," queried Sarah, "the school has been around for a long time! We've worked with over a thousand students!"

"That's quite true," agreed Charlie, "but you're not legally approved nor recognized by the State. As a matter of fact you're in violation of a few of their laws. You exist only because they have not enforced them."

"There are plenty of other types of cults and therapies which exist and are not in trouble. Why pick on us?" demanded Sarah.

"They're all approved for operation in one way or another," Charlie explained; "or if they're not, nobody has issued a complaint; or, if a complaint has been issued it has gone unheeded. I think the two of you had better get a grip on the reality of this situation. You're illegal and, for whatever reason, the state is actively doing something about it."

"We applied for approval," fumed Wally. "At the time they said we didn't fit into any classification they could approve. They approved only school houses, not school buses. We can't obtain approval."

"Correct!" exclaimed Charlie. "The only way to fight this thing at this point is to either get rid of the complaint or prove beyond a doubt that it is not legitimate. That's why I have to know exactly what you did with the Miller family, exactly what you taught or counseled. Sooner or later I've got to call the psychiatrist who will testify on his investigation of the nature and legitimacy of what you do. His opinion of this whole thing is critical to whatever the Attorney General and the grand jury will do. Do you think you can make what you're doing appear to be legitimate in the eyes of a psychiatrist?"

"Hell, I've got no idea what any individual will think about it. Like you say, it's so different from our mass culture that it sounds like I'm trying to make everybody an Eskimo. But that's not really the idea at all."

"Why don't we go over some of the major aspects of what the school does," suggested Charlie. "Perhaps I can tell you how they sound from a legal point of view, and maybe even from a medical one. Why don't you tell me what you've been telling the Millers and we'll see what we come up with?"

"It's really quite simple," answered Wally. "We've observed that any individual recognizes two basic entities in the universe. One is the individual himself, and the second is the environment. The environment produces the individual. His substance consists of atoms passed down over the millennia — perhaps utilized before by dinosaurs, trilobites, trees, ferns, etc. The environment also molds and forms the individual. It gives him his characteristics and makes Bushmen look and act like Bushmen; Frenchmen, French, etc."

"So far, so good," noted Charlie while taking notes. "What's so controversial about that?"

"Well, how does this strike you?" asked Wally. "We also fully realize and appreciate that the reverse of what I just said is also true: that is, the individual helps produce the environment. He shapes the environment, and he is everybody else's environment; one man with an idea and power can dam up two hundred and fifty-five miles of shoreline in Glen Canyon or can prevent another similar dam from being built on the St. John River."

"Are you including the emotional environment in the word Environment, such as the charged atmosphere of my courtroom dilemmas?"

"Absolutely. The word Environment means everything in the biosocial universe; all the relationships between living things and their world. Everything!"

"Go on."

"People receive and imprint impressions from the environment: other people, animals, lightning, noise, the works. These images are at times 'irritating' to the organism. At times they trigger off or arouse tension. We are really just overdeveloped, complicated bags of protoplasm anyhow, just like a one-celled amoeba. Irritability or reactibility is an attribute or function of protoplasm. So the environment is a stimulus which always elicits a response — consciously or unconsciously, positive or negative. If you shine a bright light in somebody's eyes, his pupils will close as an unconscious response. If the light is irritating, the individual will yell, 'Shut it off! Or, he may close his eyes. Both are conscious responses.

"It is obvious that there is a counterreaction fed into the environment from the individual whenever any interaction takes place. If a person is shining a light in your eye, then yelling 'shut it off' will affect them.

If you're feeding a fish to a porpoise, the fish is the stimulus to the porpoise. The porpoise responds and the individual in turn is affected by the porpoise's response. If it eats the fish the individual may stop feeding the porpoise. But if the porpoise did not eat the fish the individual might try to feed it again. The porpoise's *response* affects the *stimulus* (environment) and this is just as important a part of the interaction as is the stimulus response phenomenon. It is so often overlooked because we are so self-centered and egotistical we just think about what happens *to us*. We are not taught to be concerned about what happens *to the environment*. It is considered to be our 'resource', playground, garden of Eden, or whatever! But for each action there is a reaction in the environment *which in turn always affects the action. This is very important:* Most of our problems are caused by our lack of recognition of this phenomenon. We train the porpoise and simultaneously the porpoise 'teaches' us to feed him by acting in certain ways. But if you ask what the individual is doing, he will tell you he is 'training the porpoise.' Period. We fail to recognize that the reverse is also true."

"How does the environment 'train' us?" questioned Charlie. "I can't see that."

"If you remain in contact with a certain stimulus or environment repeatedly for a period of time, you unconsciously go on 'automatic pilot' while your conscious mind becomes occupied with confronting new phenomena. The *response* to repeated stimuli becomes unconscious."

"Hold on a minute, I'm not sure I understand. Run through that again."

"It's like — umm — like an airplane. Let's say your feelings and perceptions are the fuel and engines of an airplane. Your conscious mind is the pilot. It regulates the fuel, engines and direction of the plane."

"So far, so good."

"The pilot directs the plane's take-off and then flies a familiar, repititious direction. That's when the pilot switches on the *automatic* pilot. It automatically adapts to the atmospheric conditions and takes over the airplane's operation. It is similar to the unconscious mind of a person. The pilot is now free to fulfill other duties. He is no longer in contact with the fuel and engines which are 'automatically' coping with the environment. He is unaware of the plane's automatic operation unless he checks it or is confronted by the plane doing something it shouldn't."

"OK. I understand that."

"That's basically all there is to it. Any aspect of a person that operates under 'automatic pilot' is called conditioning. The feelings and perceptions which motivate or operate the individual *are still there full force,* as are the fuel and engine of the plane. But they are *unconscious.* The pilot is not in contact with them. All the conscious mind can perceive is their effects.

"The automatic pilot is set and locks on to prevailing environmental conditions be they good, bad or indifferent. That's what I call conditioning or training by the environment. For instance I see a stop sign. I can be trained to put my foot on the brake. Repetition of the 'stimulus-response' interaction makes it unconscious and automatic; it can happen without me being aware of it, especially if the response is rewarded. I'm sure you've had it happen to you; a car appears from nowhere while you're driving and you 'instinctively' slam on the brakes before you even have a chance to think about it. It's not 'instinct', it's automatic. It is a conditioned response. It's rewarded by not crashing into the car ahead. It was rewarded thousands of time in the past by avoiding a traffic accident at each stop sign, by not getting punished in the form of a traffic ticket from a police officer, by being given a driver's license.

"It can be seen in all animals just as obviously as in people. Take bats. Bats, through their natural radar, can precisely detect items in the dark but once they enter their home cave they are in familiar territory; an environment where they have had repeated contact. The repetition conditions them to that terrain. If you change around the inside of the home cave they bump into newly placed blocks and obstacles which they could have otherwise detected easily. It's a universal phenomenon. The individual behaves automatically, unconscious of ordinarily experienced, repeated stimuli.

"Let's say I shine a light in your eye and every time the light goes on you agree to clap your hands. If we did this a couple of hundred times repeatedly, chances are you'd be conditioned. The next time that I'd shine a light in your eye, you'd clap even though nobody asked you to. That's classic conditioning on a behavioral level. I could make it happen even faster by giving you an irritating electric shock before the light went on and make the shock stop as soon as you clapped your hands. The clapping would be rewarded in that it stopped the shock."

"The whole thing reminds me of hypnotism," said Charlie, "post hypnotic suggestion."

"I think it is the same thing, but let's not confuse the issue. I want to get into rewards and punishment and where they fit in.

"The process of life consists of a series of feelings which are either comfortable or uncomfortable, tense or relaxed, depending upon the environmental stimuli. Some people call it the pleasure-pain principle. Life itself is a pleasurable feeling which one would not want to lose or threaten. Punishment is a pain, it's uncomfortable. At all times, an individual is living in either one feeling or another, whether they think about it or not. They are either consciously or unconsciously comfortable or uncomfortable at any particular time. There is no 'middle ground' as long as you're living, for living is a pleasure, that is . . . when it isn't a pain.

"Before you act or while you act you have feelings: tense or relaxed — comfortable or uncomfortable. Most people, when they talk about conditioning are talking about *behavior*. They ignore and overlook feelings—typical for our society. But what I've seen time and time again is that *feelings can be conditioned in exactly the same manner and more readily than behavior can be conditioned*. If a kid sits on a hot stove, he/she may be conditioned on a feeling level to avoid stoves, even cold ones. If teachers give you a hard time, your feelings may be conditioned to avoiding school. If marijuana, liquor, or food makes you feel good, your feelings may be conditioned to continue to use them as a pacifier even though you agree that it's foolish to do so. In addition, and this is very important, your own thoughts, actions or perceptions — accurate or inaccurate — can act as stimuli for your feelings. The *thought* of a luscious ice cream sundae (stimulus) can make you *feel* hungry (response).

"Personal thoughts, actions, and perceptions are stimuli. They are part of the environment of your feelings. Your feelings respond to them as well as to the outside environment. Most thoughts and perceptions are really internalizations of the outside environment. They are like fantasies or images of the outside world and, in similar fashion, they can act as stimuli and elicit responses. If repeated and reinforced, thoughts, actions and perceptions can be conditioning agents: stimuli. The *thought* of a lemon can unconsciously make you salivate each time the thought comes to mind.

"That's what Nationalism is, that's why you retain your culture when you move into another one — you have conditioned feelings. That's why friends can turn a kid on to drugs — or cigarettes — even if he decided to quit. You can become conditioned by your environment and your internal images of it. It's unconscious and out of your control."

"Why did you tell all this to Ben and Carol?" asked Charlie.

"Because it's all especially true in kids, and Danny seemed to be immune to it. Because childrens' reasoning powers are so limited and so underdeveloped that they're easily and overwhelmingly conditioned to their childhood environment, religion, lifestyle, etc., whether it be rewarding or punishing. That's what was so amazingly interesting to me about what happened to Danny. You see what I mean? If he couldn't be conditioned anymore, then he'd have to live on a conscious, awareness-only basis. Lots of times he'd be different than everyone else. He'd only have his immediate unconditioned thoughts, perceptions and feelings to fall back on and that could be a big problem."

"What would the problem be?"

"He wouldn't feel or act like other people."

"Is conditioning so important in our society?"

"Charlie, it's unbelievable what conditioning can do, how it shapes us. Sometimes it's downright bizarre. PSYCHOLOGY TOMORROW reported an experiment in which a number of reliable top rate scientists were put in an experimental situation where a brilliant light was shined in their eyes, immediately followed by a loud siren. Following the siren, the light went out. They wrote down what they saw and heard, i.e. saw the light, heard the siren. I think the light was so bright that it was mildly uncomfortable. The light, followed by the siren, was repeated many times. Each time they'd write down what they saw and heard. Towards the end of the experiment, the siren was, at times, *not* sounded but many of the scientists wrote down that they *did* indeed hear it. They had been conditioned into believing they heard a siren which did not sound although they had previously been trained as impartial observers."

"That's amazing," said Charlie.

"Another time an experimenter would say the word 'Now' and a light was directed into a person's eyes. Naturally his pupils would close. This was repeated many times. Then the person was given the light switch button. The experimenter would say 'Now,' the person would push the switch and the light would shine in his eye. The experimenter then didn't use the light after awhile, he'd just say 'Now' and the person's pupil would close anyhow. It had been conditioned to a new stimulus — the word 'Now'."

"That's like Pavlov's dog and the bell ringing before the dog was fed," remarked Charlie. "After a while Pavlov noticed the dog would salivate when the bell rang even though there was no food around."

"Right," Wally continued, "but after a while the experimenter would let the person himself say 'Now' and then push the light button. Pretty soon the person would just say the word 'Now' and his pupils would close. Then it got to the point where the person had to just *think* the word 'Now' and his pupils would close. They then took him to a doctor saying they had found a freak, a person who could at will close the pupils of his eyes. The doctor was completely convinced that the phenomenon was real.

"Just think about the number of physical ailments people may be conditioned into thinking they have. It's no wonder that the faith healers work for the ailments they heal are probably conditioned into existence in the first place; they just break the conditioning."

Charlie added, "I remember reading an experiment where teachers were pushing switches which would shock people in the next room. Although they could hear people in the adjoining room screaming in agony, they'd continue to push the button for long periods of time whenever they were told to do so. It turned out that it wasn't people in the next room, it was tape recordings; however the switch pullers didn't know that. They were conditioned to obeying orders."

"It shows just how much we're conditioned to obey authorities," gasped Wally. "It's incredible, it's just like Watergate burglars; it must happen all the time. It's so common. If Dan was immune to conditioning he'd be a freak who needed a special environment. I thought Ben and Carol should know that. Why not?

"When you think about it, conditioning is the classic epitomy of dictatorship," continued Wally. "It's fascist in nature. The conditioned person, especially if he's a child, is being directed and doesn't even know this is happening; nonetheless conditioning is a major form of education in both family and school. We are god-damned foolish to think we can have a free country or be free when we've been brought up conditioned to economic technology, competition and exploitation. That's not freedom for the individual. The individual is a puppet-slave to the stimuli in the environment to which he/she has been conditioned. Money is a perfect example. The almighty dollar is almighty because we're conditioned to it. Every time we receive money we're rewarded with what it can buy: rewards like food, clothes, shelter and admiration. People unconsciously will do practically anything for money, even theft-murder-violence-no matter, it's happening all over. That's what's happening across the bay where we live; in Northpoint where they want to build an oil refinery. The damn fools are willing to risk the pollution and destruction of an oil spill for money. They're completely conditioned by money. Right across the border, the Canadians have no financial interest in the proposed refinery, so they won't let the tankers come in because they know it's insane. But they'll be bought off. Money will win in the end. It always does and will until people realize that they've been conditioned to it.

"So that's what I'd told Ben and Carol. It's no big deal.

"What we've done on the school is to design an environment which educates an individual to deal with his or her conditioning. We help students become consciously aware of all the factors involved in conditioning. They learn to recognize the environment: the stimulus, the response and the rewards past and present. Once aware of these things, they can consciously change them around or eliminate them. If the student so chooses, rationality and reason can take over. That's what education should do — help people decondition themselves from the foolish aspects of our economic, social and political system. Instead, education too often reinforces the system. Why not? Look who's on the school board, look who's teaching!

"Not *our* school, though. We help kids discover how they basically feel. We make them as aware of their feelings as we possibly can. If they feel uncomfortable, they may be motivated to discover a multitude of factors: their environment, the stimuli, their response, the reward, how they effect the stimulus by their response, how to avoid the stimulus or perceive it as unrewarding, how to substitute new stimuli for old ones and how to avoid conditioned feelings. Even if they feel comfortable they are still confronted by the stimulus which is making them comfortable. Through somebody else's viewpoint, they get to see the effects of the stimuli upon them, their effects upon it. Then they can consider if the relationship is rational. So even though drugs and alcohol may make one feel comfortable, they get nowhere in our school. In our school environment the conditioning syndrome can begin to be broken overnight and can be rearranged for the rest of the students' lives if they so choose.

"I just got a letter from Sally, one of last year's students. She's chosen to obtain counseling help instead of getting drunk. Joe called me yesterday. Before he joined the school he'd been stoned for four years since his parents were killed. He'd gotten "turned on to drugs" and was wasted all through high school. He called me from his house to tell me the house was full of his friends, that they were all stoned, or drunk, and he didn't even feel like getting high — he's completely immune to his conditioning. He's got it beat, he's just been accepted by a good school, and is a different, happier person. So are those who know him, or will know him."

Wally was practically shouting. "Very few people even understand that their conditioning is the cause of most of their personal problems and our society's social and natural environmental problem as well." He lowered his voice and looked intensely at Charlie. "People are unconsciously scared blue that they're going to lose the rewards or will experience the punishment of their conditioning, thus they intellectually talk one way and emotionally live another. What in God's name can be wrong with showing people something about that? It's not illegal. It's common sense!"

"Hold on Wally, relax. Let me get this straightened out in my own mind. It sounds like you're saying something like — like — what's a good example?" Charlie thought a moment, "OK, here it is: we have difficulty switching over to the metric system because we've been conditioned to the system we were born into. The old system has been part and parcel of our childhood environment."

"Exactly," replied Wally. "As kids we learn from many sources that a foot is twelve inches long. We accept it. It remains in the environment. It imbues our senses. We can judge it physically, relate to it, and can use it for communication and understanding with other people. We depend upon it as an entity in common with others, a tool with which to cope with the environment and all the while never need to be conscious of where we learned its meaning or value. It's automatic. Unconsciously it's become a conditioned part of us — our heritage if you will."

"You believe that's why it's difficult to switch to metric," continued Charlie. "Metric activates unconscious feelings of inadequacy and unfamiliarity usually covered up by 'automatic pilot.' They are mildly uncomfortable so we resist. Metric appears to be detrimental — a punishment of sorts — a loss of rewards gained from being on automatic pilot. In addition, metric is an encounter with the unconscious rewards and punishments which may have originally conditioned us to the old system. For example: receiving praise or good marks for knowing there are twelve inches in a foot, or being considered stupid for not knowing the number of feet in a mile. They've been under 'automatic pilot' since childhood.

"That's the idea precisely," exclaimed Wally. "Now we're being confronted by the government which insists that we switch to metric. The confrontation suddenly makes us realize our past conditioning. We have to make efforts to break it if metric makes more sense and if it will be our new environment in years to come. Confrontation becomes the key to discovering past conditioning as well as to being more sensible in the future. Without confrontation our normal lives are hardly different than a rat in a cage which is being conditioned by reward or punishment to learn established behavior. Potentially we can be a great deal more but our social environment does not ask us to achieve. Society simply asks us to conform most of the time."

"That's why our school works in areas where others can't make headway," said Sarah. "The expedition is one confrontation after another. It's great for those who can handle it and choose to do so. What's illegal about that?"

VII

The 30 foot tides of Fundy are attached to the phenomena of the solar system. The moon, the sun, the centripetal force of the earth in its orbit, the land forms of the planet; all affect the rising and falling water. I could feel its chains to the heavens. It was with constant amazement that I would watch the water slowly retreat over a mile out to sea only to trickle back across the mud flats six hours later. The unique funnel shape of the bay makes the tides so extreme here. They, in turn, affect each creature living in their time table. Here I could touch the connection of the common clam to the motion of the stars.

From a composition by Dan Miller, age 16.

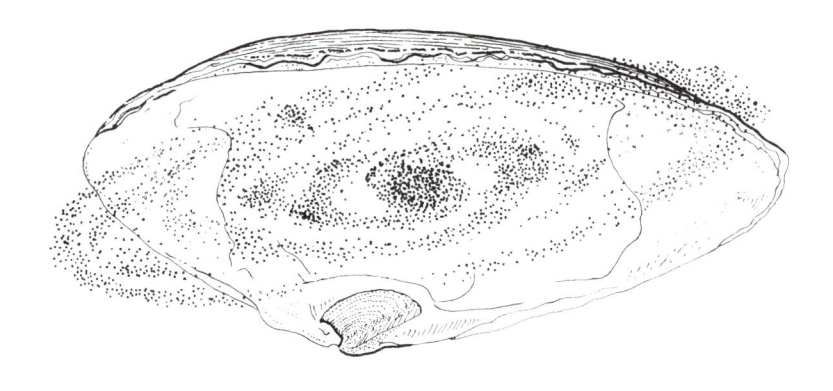

From *The Downeast Gazette,* March 6, 1975
The Richton Corporation today settled a sixty-four million dollar negligence suit out of court. The settlement of 13 million dollars went to the relatives of the 125 persons killed in the Bison Creek flood disaster which also left thousands homeless. Richton is planning to build a supertanker port and oil refinery here in Northpoint.

"So, Charlie," quizzed Wally, "you tell me. Is sharing these kinds of ideas with the Millers considered practicing psychotherapy?"

Wally carefully thumbed through his notebook, scanning four or five pages, then turning ahead some more.

"Ben and Carol took Dan to see Dr. Sullivan for a check-up. They asked him if he could test Dan to see if he was immune to conditioning. Sullivan asked why and they explained to him what I had said. He was evidently quite upset about my hypothesis that Dan was immune to operant conditioning. He told them that there was no such known disease, and that there were no tests for such a condition. They told me that he had advised them to keep away from me and to ignore what I said; that I sounded like some kind of a crackpot."

"Perhaps that was the beginning of the situation you're in now," said Charlie. "Then what happened?"

"He evidently tried, to no avail, to get Dan to repeat an action just to see if he could be conditioned. Dan would not do it. He'd lose interest, he didn't appreciate the praise which was being given for doing something. My recollection was that it had something to do with blocks. Anyhow, Ben and Carol kind of shied away from me after that session with Sullivan. But my curiosity was really aroused about what was going on. Here, I've found it. On August 13, 1964, on a rainy afternoon I went over to visit them, and without Dr. Sullivan's permission I tested both boys to see if they could be conditioned. Carol and Ben were there. I've got it all here in my notes."

Charlie interrupted: "Hold on. That sounds important. There's no reason to go over this whole thing twice. I think we should present Dr. Gitman with as complete a picture as possible. Steve Gitman is investigating this case for the Attorney General. There's no reason to hide anything from him, he'll find it out anyhow from the Millers, or Dr.

Sullivan. Why don't I call him and see if he can come over and hear this stuff."

"Go ahead," declared Wally. "I've got nothing to hide."

"What happened after you tested Dan?"

"The Millers and I had a lengthy bull session with Dr. Sullivan so all points of view could be considered and maybe a course of action agreed upon."

"Do you have notes about that session?"

"Better than that," said Wally, smiling, "I taped the whole thing!"

"Did everybody know it was being taped?"

"Oh sure, it was no secret, the recorder was right in plain sight on the table. It consists of two tapes, so I must have changed them right there in front of everybody. Dr. Sullivan has a copy of them. It's no secret."

"It might be very important for Steve Gitman to hear the tapes. Maybe they'll help our case, in fact, how can they hurt it? Have you listened to them recently Wally?"

"Last week."

"Do you think they'd be harmful?"

"Not at all. I think they will shed a great deal of light on what this is all about. Dr. Gitman could get them from Dr. Sullivan anyhow."

Dr. Gitman arrived a little after noon. He was a fairly young fellow, in his early thirties, and had a very pleasant air about him. He was wearing informal clothing and sneakers. Sarah had expected some kind of detective with an Austrian accent. Wally thought Dr. Gitman might be in disguise, appearing friendly and interested in order to throw people off their guard. That way they might reveal more than they should for their own welfare.

Charlie briefed Dr. Gitman as to the discussions which had taken place so far, offering to give him a copy of his notes on the matter.

"Now let's get down to business," said Charlie. "You were saying this morning that you tested the boys for their condition-ability without the consent of Dr. Sullivan. You also conveyed that Dr. Sullivan had attempted to do this previously with Dan and had been unsuccessful.

"Right," acknowledged Wally returning to his notes. "On August 13, 1964 I went over to the Miller's house with a whole bunch of little pieces of chocolate and sat with the twins through a rainy afternoon."

"Hey Arty, look what I've got here ... hey, hey, it's chocolate ... mmmmmgood. Real yummy. Would you like some, Arty?"

"Yes, give me one," he said. So I gave him one free for starters and he ate it.

"How about another?"

"Gimme," said Arty with his hand out.

"Wait, Arty, you've got to be polite. Here, put your hands at your side and say, 'Please give me a piece of chocolate' like a little gentleman."

"Please give me a piece of chocolate?" asked Arty without hesitation.

"That's good," I said. "You said 'please' and didn't grab. Very nice," and I gave him a chocolate bit. "Want to do it again?" I said.

"Please give me a piece of chocolate," said Arty with his hands by his side, and I gave him the chocolate bit, which he ate, and then said, "Please give me."

I gave it to him as soon as his hands reached his side. He ate it and before he was finished chewing, had his hands in position and was saying, "Please give." I slipped him another piece. By this time, he was like a little ol' wind up tin soldier doing the manual of arms: one, hands at side place, two, say 'please give', three, take chocolate, four, eat chocolate, five, go back to 'one' as quickly as possible. I ran out of chocolate after about thirty-seven pieces had disappeared down the hatch, each in the same manner.

"All gone," I showed him. "I'll get some more after supper. You go play now."

I counted out thirty-seven pieces of chocolate from the bag in my pocket. "Hey, hey, Danny," I said, "Hey, look what I've got there. Real yummy, would you like one?" I gave him a chocolate.

"Can I have another one?" asked Danny.

"Wait. You have to ask right and not grab. Put your hands by your side and say please ('Simon Says', I thought)."

"I don't wanna," says Danny. "Can't I have another chocolate?"

"Nope," I replied, sticking to my guns, "Hands down and say please."

He did it and he loaded up with thirty-seven chocolates in record time.

"That's fine Danny, maybe you can have more after dinner."

"Goody," said Dan and he went to play with Arty.

"So there it was. Stimulus: Chocolate.Unconditioned response: get a piece; Reward: eat chocolate. And I changed it to Stimulus: Chocolate.Conditioned response: Hands at side, say please; Reward: eat chocolate.
After supper Arty and Danny were in the living room with us. I casually put my hand in my pocket and came out with — why, of all things, a piece of chocolate."

"Hey, hey, Danny and Arty, look at this — chocolate!"
Arty turned to look at it. His hands slapped to his side. "Please," he shouted.
Almost instantly Danny cried, "Ohh, can I have it?" and excitedly took it out of my hand, gobbling it whole.
"It doesn't prove anything if you don't want it to," I told Ben and Carol later that evening. "Who knows how ten other kids would have reacted. And you've got to have a lot more than just that one situation to prove my conditioning hypothesis for sure. If you did it with ten kids would they all react like Arty? Would Danny have been conditioned if it was repeated one hundred times? How about two hundred? Might Danny be conditioned in some other kind of experiment?"

My own thoughts were that the situation was suspiciously predictable. The coming years would undoubtedly be stressful and chaotic. He was bound to have trouble, and lots of it. I didn't know if anyone could handle it. The thought that Danny might not survive crossed my mind. There's a great deal of survival benefits gained by conditioned learning: 'Cross at the green, not in between.' But I didn't want to alarm Ben and Carol. It was not a pretty thought to know that if Dan was daydreaming and the light was red at the street corner, he could walk across the street and be hit by a car because his conditioning did not take over when it should have.

"Dr. Gitman," interrupted Charlie, "Do you mind if I ask you a question with regard to this case?"

"Go right ahead, I'll answer it if I can."

"What is your role in this whole procedure?"

"I've been hired by the Psychiatric Division of the Public Health Department to prepare a report on their behalf for the Attorney General."

"What is your report supposed to convey?"

"It's to be the results of my findings while investigating the allegations of the complaint filed with the department, a complaint which is now in the hands of the Attorney General for a hearing."

"Do you have any idea why Dr. Sullivan is filing the complaint at this time? The tape we are going to hear is the last contact my client had with Dr. Sullivan, and that was twelve years ago."

"I have no idea of exactly what is going on. I do know that Dr. Sullivan is not one to fool around with. He's being considered for the position of Director of the Psychatric Division which is a very powerful office among the medical professionals here in Maine."

"Perhaps things are becoming a bit clearer," exclaimed Charlie with a look of surprise which changed to a critical shaking of his head. "Maybe he is somehow using Wally, Sarah, and their school as a proving ground or trumped-up issue to insure himself of getting the office."

"I'd have no idea about that," declared Dr. Gitman sincerely. "I'm not part of the department so I have no idea what's going on there. But if this tape is what you say it is, it should expose Dr. Sullivan's reasons for making his allegations."

"It will certainly show our areas of disagreement," acknowledged Wally. "I note from my journal that I went to the get-together with serious doubts about its outcome. I was obviously very prejudiced about Dr. Sullivan's ability to come anywhere near grasping or understanding my point of view. I note that I expressed this to Carol Miller on August 21, two days before the meeting. It certainly explains why we never hit it off at the meeting."

"Could I hear what that was all about?" asked Dr. Gitman. "It would provide me with some background material which could prove to be very helpful to your situation."

"What do you think, Charlie?" said Wally.

"If it's accurate, go ahead and read it. We're not going to get to the truth of this matter by hiding anything. If your preconceived prejudice is going to help Dr. Gitman better understand the situation then why withhold it? I'm quite sure the Attorney General could subpoena your tapes and journals. If they can get them from Nixon, don't worry, they can get them from you."

"I agree," murmured Sarah.

Wally began to piece together the conversation with Carol:

"Ben, Carol and the kids dropped over to the farm unexpectedly about a week later. They were on their way back from visiting Dr. Sullivan.

"He thinks you're a crackpot," said Ben. "Maybe we didn't tell him what you told us correctly, but he didn't go head-over-heels for all this environmental conditioning stuff. He's never heard of anybody with the kind of disorder which prevents conditioning."

"Well, neither have I," I exclaimed. "I've only explained to you what I thought from my point of view. I'll be the first to admit I live a very unorthodox life, run a very unorthodox school, and have a very unorthodox outlook. You'll have to take that into account; in addition, remember I have no license, nor do I want one, so I may not even speak the same language as those fancy dudes in their offices. That's their environment, it's man-made. My environment is out here in the wilds so naturally I'll see things differently."

"I'm getting confused," wailed Carol. "What are we going to do?"

I was alarmed at her distress but could certainly see why she was upset. I surely wouldn't have wanted her problems nor responsibility as far as Danny was concerned. I was beginning to feel nervous. After all, I was leaving in a few weeks, going back to teaching and learning about ecology in the fullest sense. On the school I was going to live it. If a picture is worth a thousand words, being part of the picture is worth a million. Ben and Carol were going to live in town, cut off from interaction with the natural elements, protected by walls, roofs, lawns, heaters, lights, plumbing, floors, media, automobiles, jobs, and economic outlooks. That was their world — a fortress against the world of nature. Was it fair to expose or inflict my values, my outlooks upon them in their time of trouble? Maybe my conclusions would only be valid in my environment, and they should seek answers only from others who were living in similar situations to theirs, from people who had the same conditioning. For example, I once met a man who was a popular preacher out in a remote area of Appalachia. He had a big following. He baptized people, was well-respected, ... the whole bit. Then, for some reason, he gets a "calling" to preach in the city to those in need there. He set himself up on a street corner and gets thrown in jail for causing a crowd to gather. He then tells the cops that it's God's calling and they send him out for psychiatric examinations. The diagnosis is that he's psychotic, living in another world, and should be institutionalized. Maybe that's where I'm at. Maybe I should tell Ben and Carol to keep away from me. I'd already suggested it, but they keep coming back for more. Is that my fault? No wonder Carol was confused.

"Carol, I can understand your confusion," I said. "Maybe you'd better leave my environmental conditioning approach out of the picture. It's not real to you, you don't live in it directly. The psychiatrist can talk from today to tomorrow about me being a crackpot. He is perfectly right for his city-world lifestyle. But he doesn't use an outhouse; he probably wouldn't be at all comfortable squatting in the woods. He's right at home with a sewage system which pollutes, while I utilize the top six inches of soil to naturally, safely, completely dispose of and recycle my excretions, at no cost. Now you tell me who's the crackpot?"

"That's unfair," said Carol. "Good sewage systems don't pollute."

"Maybe good sewage systems don't pollute in front of your eyes, but the natural environment is being destroyed to make them work. Dams are being built, oil and coal are being burned to provide the materials and power necessary to build and operate the sewer system. Oil, coal, quarrying, steel, transportation: all pollute, so one form of pollution is being replaced by another.

"People's minds are being polluted, too, and not only because they're deluded into thinking they're solving a problem. Good Lord, a sewage system in a one family house must cost well over a couple of thousand dollars — where does the money come from? Four to eight-hundred hours of work, work which is ofttimes energy put into our polluting, exploitive economic system.

"It's so stupid that all these jobs, pollution, and environmental deterioration exist because people have been conditioned not to poop in the woods. They rationalize it by saying they're 'civilized' but all that really means is that they're avoiding the unconscious punishments, or obtaining the unconscious rewards, of their childhood conditioning, toilet training and the like. There's a civilization in nature that's taken eons to evolve, and it's being ignored by those of us who are 'civilized'. Nature may damn well be the *only* civilization that exists. Ours is just a temporary fantasy world drawing its life blood from nature."

"OK, OK, I got the point," said Carol. "I've heard that idea before. I', familiar with it, anyhow."

"Then answer me a serious question. If you know how your personal lifestyle is screwing up the natural environment, then why haven't you changed your lifestyle? Why haven't you done anything about the situation? Why let it go on if it's foolish?"

"I don't know. I'm busy with the kids, raising a family, keeping a household. We have to meet the payments on the house, on the car, on the freezer. There are the bills to pay. You just can't forget your responsibilities."

"That's one answer. It's the same as mine, but different."

"What's your answer?" she asked curiously.

"Conditioning," I said. "Plain old conditioning, fear of losing the rewards or feeling the punishments of a childhood which was molded by the environment, by the American way of life, by parents and by an addiction to living the way you're living now."

"I'm not so sure of that," said Carol, somewhat defensively.

"Why don't you live in a teepee?" I asked. "Seriously."

"I'm comfortable in a house. I'm used to it, I know what it's like outside, cold and wet, dirty and buggy."

"Comfort is a reward," I said, simply. "Cold and wet and buggy are uncomfortable. They're types of punishment. Dirty is a punishment from when your parents tried to keep you clean as a kid. Ask Dr. Sullivan next time you visit and see what he says about that."

Carol snapped back. "You ask him. Let's all get together. He says he can meet with us Friday evening! Coming?"

VIII

    The anenome and the barnacle were neighbors, but they lived in different worlds. The anenome would be in the water 22 hours of each day, giving it plenty of time to catch small animals in its poisoned tentacles while others hid amongst them for protection. The barnacles' home high on the rock shoreline twenty feet above afforded it only 7 hours of ocean time and 17 hours of air. Although they were neighbors living next to each other, they could never change homes, for twenty feet up or down the sea wall would mean death to either of them. I loved the barnacles' feet which combed the water like a fan, picking out bits of plankton and feeding the animal within its little white fortress from the waves.
From a composition by Dan Miller, age 16.

From *The Downeast Gazette,* May 2, 1976
We are insanely licensing what amounts to a major attraction — a free money dispenser. Each tanker delivering its payload profits about four million dollars. It cost $50,000.00 per day to operate. While the safety record at seas has been deteriorating steadily and the collision rate increasing alarmingly we have approved a refinery; a tide swept convention hall for these floating disasters. It's stupid to wave money in their faces and believe they'll behave themselves while waiting on line to grab it.

                                              Thomas Ives, member
                                              Environmental Protection

Wally explained the tape to Dr. Gitman and Charlie while loading it onto the recorder. "This is the tape of our meeting with Dr. Sullivan, who began by explaining his reasons for wanting to see me. He felt that I had made rather large impressions upon Carol and Ben. He wanted to be sure he understood what I was talking about and to see if there might be any validity to my perceptions in this matter. Wally thought about it while walking across the room. He turned and said, "He also wanted the Millers to be aware of conflicts, if any, which might influence their thinking. Charlie, why don't you play it?"

Charlie pushed the button and Dr. Sullivan's voice, from twelve years before, echoed from the speaker:

"Mr. Bryce, there are a few bothersome things about Danny's situation which we don't know how to handle. Danny is extraordinary because he doesn't seem to care whether he takes our tests or not. Sometimes he quits right in the middle of them and rocks, sucks his thumb, or does something completely different. So we have no idea what has happened to him as a result of the mescaline."

"Neither do I, Dr. Sullivan, I'm no psychiatrist. I just have some impressions and experiences which lead me to come up with an idea as to what might be going on."

"Yes, as I understand it, you think Danny is immune to conditioning. But that is unheard of. And your ideas about the environment being a conditioning agent are sensible but not common — none of that is disconcerting. What is perplexing is your lack of respect or identity with the culture which we live in. You're like a foreigner here, and you perceive things with a foreign point of view."

"I guess that's a way of looking at it. Even what you've just stated sounds inaccurate to me although it's perfectly reasonable to you."

"What seems inaccurate?"

"Well, I don't want to make an issue of this, but I don't think I'm a foreigner here. I think you are — we all are. As I see it, 'here' is North America. 'Here' is an ancient community of plants, geology, animals, soils, climate, weather, clouds, sky, etc. That's what 'here' is in an empirical sense. The life community here has squatter's rights of something like two hundred and fifty million years since it separated from Europe and came here through the process of continental drift and plate tectonics. Now, isn't that true? This continental mass settled here way back then, and established an intricate interdependent, interrelated living community which had its own unique, workable plan and rules about the way things would get done. Each entity had its reason for being. Then, we came along, a scant two million years ago — maybe only 100,000 years ago here in North America. So in that sense, we're the foreigners, we're the strangers. The only thing which makes me seem 'foreign' is that I've found I can enjoy living in the old, natural world, to some extent I can enjoy its ways, and appreciate its integrity. So I do that. The difference is that I make attempts to live *with* it, while you spend your time living *off* of it. But other than that, you're perfectly right about me being different. So, please continue."

"Well, I understand that you try to get students to learn about this ancient process and apply it to themselves — and by understanding it and the natural protective process of conditioning in our culture, you obtain remarkable growth and maturity in your students. I read that in *The Trailside Classroom.*"

"Thank you."

"What are you anyhow? What's your profession? A doctor? A naturalist? A teacher? Travel agent? Musician?"

"That's an interesting question. It's actually two questions, the one you asked and why you asked it. The answer to the second question is the answer to the first, really."

"I think I'm missing something. Why is there a question about why I asked the question? Are you trying to hide something? Trying to confuse me? Are you experiencing me as being threatening in some way by asking you what your profession is? Isn't it a legitimate question to ask a person how they make a living or what they are trained to do?"

"Maybe I make a living by questioning people who question me. What I'm getting at is that too often we think in these occupational levels. If I told you I was a professional pervert, your impression of what I say might be completely different than if I was a noted historian. I've met a couple of noted historians and some of them impressed me as being perverts — so where does that leave us? The point is that our society is organized into subpockets of expertise and experts. The cobbler fixes shoes, the lawyer handles legal affairs, etc. That's our social environment — and it conditions us into experiencing people as gears, cogs and switches in the great economic machine which gobbles up nature. Your conditioning, Dr. Sullivan, has unconsciously rewarded you into viewing society *as it is;* so hidden in your mind, a person is not just a person, he is in addition an occuperson, I mean occupation. When confronted by your question, an *individual* might just not feel that they have any status; they won't be accepted by you or others if they don't have an occupation of stature — or money to substitute for stature. So one individual conditions the next into seeking status or money, unconsciously herding them into our giant economic machine which then rewards them socially and financially for being a cog or a gear. It makes it very difficult in such an environment for an individual to discover that he is an individual person, or what it's like to be one, and very difficult for him to act like one. Hell, it's damn near impossible to find a person, anymore. It's getting mighty lonesome living alone, surrounded by experts and occupations. Perhaps that's why God invented the dog, man's best friend, to replace all the people who've disappeared into the machine. In any case, Dr. Sullivan, what I've just done is what I often do. I confuse people and some of them even pay me to do it — imagine that! I just happened upon what I do as I discovered that most of us are living in an insane society which we've invented. It conditions us into being insane and we feel uncomfortable about being that way, acting that way, and playing that game. I wouldn't join it. I wouldn't join any organization which would accept members as confusing as I am. So people at times seek me out to help them find their sanity."

"I see. You're a nature boy living in Fantasia!"

"I live in the natural world as much in fantasy as in real life. However, there's no possible way I could become the 'nature boy' you perhaps think I am. My conditioning is much too strong for that. How could I even define a goal for myself when goals are conditioned by the culture or environment long before one becomes aware that there are such things as goals?"

"You know, your natural environment concept is undoubtedly your escape from reality, and from the anxieties of your childhood."

"How nice of you to say so, but I strongly disagree."

"You're nobody's fool, you're well aware that retreating to the natural environment could be an escape from feelings stemming from toilet training, religious prejudice, your short height, feelings of inferiority, wanting to be different, rationalization of anxieties, and many more. Perhaps you're actually running away from contact with people which you find frustrating and overwhelming. That must have crossed your mind."

"I don't want to be rude, but you can't make any inferences until you've made the natural environment into your home — done it, mind you, not vicariously, I mean the real thing. On the school, we camp out all year long. I've done that for nine years now. It hasn't hurt me a bit. There's nothing that I've been able to discover which has not become more meaningful or enjoyable since I found that I am, in reality, independent of most of the crap which Madison Avenue has conditioned people into believing is a necessity. The only drawback I've found is that when this particular subject is discussed, I can't find an ear that is not deaf — which is nothing short of incredible when you come right down to it."

"You've got to admit that living in the woods in this day and age is sort of abnormal."

"I'm sick of that kind of thinking, I think that kind of mentality is what's abnormal — not me, and I'll tell you exactly why. Your only measuring device for what is normal is the *people* in your society. What's normal for cannibalistic tribes is not normal here. There's no objective measuring device for normality. I can measure a yard, describe a yard or communicate a yard, and have a yardstick to precisely demonstrate what I'm describing. But there is no yardstick when it comes to measuring people's behavior, attitudes, or feelings. So, 'abnormal' means nothing."

"Science can measure how people will react in a certain setting and can determine what is normal in that setting. That's our yardstick."

"Absolutely not, because the yardstick you're talking about changes its size in different *environments*. A real yardstick measures 36 inches in the U.S.A. as well as in New Guinea. Can't you see the point I'm making?"

"I see it alright, but you don't live in New Guinea. Neither do Ben, Carol or Danny. So why get them involved with New Guinea?"

"You're missing the point, Doc, you're missing it because you're blind as hell. You can't help it but your conditioning and education have made you blind."

"How am I blind, I give up? What can't I see? Name it."

"You can't see the yardstick which *does* measure people objectively, no matter where they reside."

"It exists? What is it?"

"*The environment*. The long term effect of any action or attitude upon the natural environment is what determines the ability of an individual or his society to survive. The quality of survival is purely and simply determined by nature in the long run. Nature is the only objective measuring stick of people. If the environment is healthy, the individual it molds, maintains, and supports is healthy. If the environment is deteriorated, so is each individual in it. We go as it goes. That's what I've learned to use as a measuring stick for just about everything I do. And it works. It provides direction when none seems apparent. It's a terrific guide."

"It sounds like foolishness to me, I'm perfectly content to do things for money and help people at the same time."

"That works fine but you have to admit that helping a murderer feel comfortable while doing his thing is a crummy way to make money. So is making money while polluting or destroying the environment. The two are identical. They're both idiotic because they're hurtful in the long run. Actions must be measured by their effects and considered accordingly — and nature is the ultimate measuring device. That's why it's so delightful to live directly in contact with nature and the elements. It preserves sanity — I know because I've done it."

"If it's so terrific, Wally, why doesn't everybody do it? Why has progress always led away from living in the woods?"

"I'm stunned, Dr. Sullivan. Stunned! You're a psychiatrist and you are asking that question? How can a person do what you do and not understand the connection between our distance from nature and mental disorders, social ills, and our insane destruction of the natural environment which keeps us alive? It's so obvious to me — but then, my perceptions have come out of the wilderness, the maternity ward of mankind. You have not yet been there.

"Dr. Sullivan, some of the kids on the school asked that same question this past year, and I attempted to answer it by writing a paper on the subject. It was published in *Natural World*. Would you like to read it? Basically, the concept is psychiatric in principal, so I think you'll enjoy it."

"Mr. Bryce, how could you ever write a paper about something which went on while nobody was there to observe it?"

"It's easy. First of all, the same process is still going on today so it can be observed; secondly, the effects of such a process remain long after it has taken place: for example, a cinder cone can tell you that a volcano erupted even though there was nobody around to witness it.

"Ah, here it is."

Wally stopped the tape and passed copies of the article to Charlie and Dr. Gitman.

IT'S A DOG'S LIFE
by Wallace Bryce

The Black Hole exploded once again, slinging out into space the cosmic dust which makes up the universe. Quarks, neutrinos and hundreds of other atomic particles flowed and reacted to create the night sky. All was in motion, and remained in motion. The energy flow took different courses, producing different forms which interacted with each other. New forms were created, each with an integrity of their own, each integrated with the total energy flow.

Near the rim of one galaxy of energy was an inconspicuous star around which orbited planets and asteroids. On the third planet from the star, the energy field warped in an unusual fashion for the area, creating a combination of atoms and energy which not only could gather their own kind from the environment, but which displayed irritability. They would respond to stimuli from the environment. In the latter days, the compound received the name protoplasm. The energy which formed the universe continually formed protoplasm into new life forms, experiments which supported and depended on each other and had protoplasmic qualities. A great chain of life evolved: each organism sensitive, each sustained by the other, each attempting to survive in the milieu, each exhibiting the life process, be they of one cell or many.

Red Dog and Grey Dog were links in the three billion year old chain. They had just arrived into a new area where rabbits abounded. They moved into a leaky cave which gave them minimal protection from the elements of nature. When it rained, they got wet. When it was warm, they were warm. Whatever happened in the environment happened to them, but not enough to deprive them completely of their life energies. With minor adaptations, they survived, but always under the relentless pressure of the environment. A tighter cave reduced the discomfort of wetness and chance of death, but death was always present, always attempting to make energy for others from the energy of the two dogs. That was the name of the game of life. Discomfort was a signal that death was increasing its pressure. Vigilance was the watch word for all. Anything providing shelter or energy from the environment was treasured.

One fine day the two dogs went hunting and chanced upon a rabbit which ran through some cactus in order to escape. Both dogs ran into the spines and yelped with pain, but sped on. The next week, the same incident was repeated in a different area. That was how the rabbit survived. The cactus was its protector. After many months, the dogs ran into and located many of the cactus plants. Those they repeatedly ran into, they learned to avoid.

Food became scarce in the immediate area and again the dogs moved. There were new cacti in the new area and the repetitive learning process started again.

Nobody can be sure exactly how the change took place. Perhaps it was a mutation, perhaps it was from selection or inbreeding. But something had changed. For when the dogs returned from the hunt, Red Dog said, "Grey Dog, you don't get spines in you anymore. How do you avoid them?"

"I noticed that," said Grey Dog. "I don't rightly know how to convey it. All I can tell you is that I can see the plant which has the spines, I can recognize it by its smell, I know which plant has the spines. I can see it right now, and I avoid it. It helps me catch those rabbits, too, you'll notice. I'm way ahead of you."

"Wait a minute, hold on, did you just say you can see it right now?" said Red Dog. "You're out of your mind, there isn't a spiny plant anywhere in this cave."

"That's just the point," said Grey Dog. "I can see it anyhow. I can see it behind my eyes even though I can see through my eyes that it isn't there. I have no idea how it happens, but I see it, or an image of it. I carry the image around in my head. When I see a plant that looks like the image, I avoid it, and end up with rabbits instead of spines. Let me tell you, it's so fantastic and so rewarding, that I find I rely as much as I can on my use of the image of the plant. It avoids discomfort, it provides pleasure. Why, shouldn't I do it?"

"Can you teach me how to obtain images?" said Red Dog.

"I'd like to, I really would," replied Grey Dog, "but I don't even know how I do it myself. It just happens, it's a gift, I was given a gift, but I don't know how it's made. All I know is that I can relate and respond to the internal image of the spiny plant, and it helps me survive better than before. I can expend less energy to obtain more energy from the environment. Boy, am I lucky."

A few days later, both dogs returned from the hunt. Grey Dog had gotten the rabbit, but Red Dog had no spines in him.

"Hey," said Grey Dog, "now it's happening to you. You have no spines in you."

Red Dog looked happy and replied, "Yes, it's happened to me but in a different way. I'm following you. When you avoid a plant, so do I. So now I, too, don't get spines."

"But you don't get rabbits either," said Grey Dog, "although you do help by limiting their choice of where they can go."

"I'm happy with it if you are," said Red Dog. "I'm avoiding those spines and I'm eating better because together we're catching more than ever. It's terrific!"

"A few new things have happened with me," said Grey Dog. "I've met some other dogs who can do the same thing that I can do. We're cousins. We all had the same grandparents. We've discovered that not only do we have images in our heads, but we can convey these images. I can describe the spiny plant and put the picture behind my cousin's eyes even though he never saw a spiny plant. I can draw a picture of the plant and he can get the image. I can tell him to avoid it and he sometimes can do that. And we're able to produce images of practically everything we can sense. We can remember them. We call it symbolizing. We relate to the images as if they were real. It works so well that at times I find I'm relating to the symbol and think it's real and vice versa. It gets confusing."

"Gee," said Red Dog, "I've met a lot of dogs who can't do that. They're just about starving cause you guys are getting all the rabbits. I'm sure glad I'm your friend and we get along. Otherwise, I'd be full of spines and hungry, too."

Many years passed and many things changed. One day, Grey Dog returned to the cave after playing chess with his cousins. He had no need to hunt that day because he had used an idea from his cousin and had borrowed a rabbit from him so he could play chess for the day. When he entered the cave, he could not find the rabbit he had saved.

"Hey, Red Dog," he said, "have you seen the rabbit I saved for today?"

"Saved? What's saved? What does that word mean? Each time you come home from your cousins, you have some new thing. I don't know what in the name of Rin Tin Tin you're talking about."

"Where is the rabbit I left here?" demanded Grey Dog sharply.

"Oh, that rabbit," said Red Dog. "Don't worry about it. I ate it this morning after you were gone."

"You stole my rabbit," said Grey Dog. "You took it without my permission."

"What the hell are you saying," said Red Dog. "Stole? Permission? What does that mean? I never heard of them."

"Bad dog, bad dog," said Grey Dog, and he charged at Red Dog.

"Hey, Grey Dog, don't bite me," said Red Dog. "I can see you're angry and I don't know why. But I do know what's been going on because this is not the first time this kind of thing has happened. Last week you came back with the idea that I was bad because I disobeyed you, whatever that means. The week before I didn't respect you, whatever that means. Before that, I was a bad dog because I ran into a spiny plant and you couldn't get the rabbit because you were depending on me to be up with you and to scare the rabbit your way. Before that, I was a dumb dog — stupid, because I didn't obey the rules or whatever. What rules are, I don't know. Each time you're angry and try to punish me you bite, you push me in the spiny plant which you now call a cactus. You've just about used up the inept part of the rabbit population; the rabbits that are left are much harder to catch, so you're not even getting food with less energy — you're back where you started. And you're always angry or unhappy about something. You're not even as happy as in the good old days. And I know why, too, because I've been watching it happen right in front of my eyes. It's downright disgusting."

"Red Dog, I'm not sure I will tolerate this insolence. Tell me what you've seen. Stop keeping secrets from me. That's wrong, you're not even honest. Bad Dog, Bad Dog."

"Insolence? Secrets? Wrong? Honest? What does that mean?"

Grey Dog grabbed Red Dog's neck in his jaws.

"O.K.," said Red Dog. "I'll tell you what's going on. You think you're different than me — that you've changed. But you haven't changed one little bit except that you can symbolize. That's the only change."

"Out with it, why am I so unhappy?"

"Because you're scared — afraid — terrified of what's inside you. You're so scared you won't even let yourself see it. That's why you have to ask me now. Otherwise when it shows up, you automatically switch to other, more pleasant symbols, even though you still feel uncomfortable, and are therefore obnoxious and anxious."

"What is inside me that is so terrifying, so upsetting?" asked Grey Dog, scowling.

"Your feelings! Your feelings about discomfort and death in the environment. You're at their mercy. Oh, that's what's doing it all right. When you first were able to avoid a cactus by avoiding its image behind your eyes, it was obvious to me that the pain, the discomfort of the cactus spines was also behind your eyes. But you could switch it off by thinking, dreaming, fantasizing that you could avoid the cactus, avoid the pain. You've been doing it ever since. You've conditioned yourself. You conditioned yourself into believing, knowing, that you could avoid the feelings of death and discomfort by manipulating their images in your mind and shutting them off. You fantasized rules, you fantasized that the things which would possibly let your hidden, hurtful images appear were bad, wrong, distasteful. To escape the painful discomfort within you you've created schemes of good, bad, right and wrong. Bad things are anything which makes you feel your hurtful images. You now live by the rules of these hurt-avoiding schemes rather than by the laws of nature. You think you've escaped the discomfort of nature by making your real environment conform to your schemes. You've swapped a world full of rabbits for their images. But you can't eat images and you know it. You've got the discomfort of nature burning inside of you — and rather than realize it, you're beginning to destroy your environment because you think it's hurtful. That's why you're unhappy, Grey Dog. It's actually the unconscious images inside which are hurtful. You're living in a fantasy world full of distorted anxieties, fears, misapprehensions, rules, tensions, punishments, and ignorance. It hasn't happened to me because I can't symbolize — but I'm doing OK. Members of the great chain of life can't symbolize... and they're doing OK. But they were better off before you were able to symbolize and utilize them as dirt to extinguish your fantasy world fires. Just yesterday you were chewing down bushes and bringing them in the cave so you could lie on them to protect yourself from your inner fear, your fantasy, your image of being cold. I sleep in the same cave, I feel the cold of nature, I find it's nice to know that nature is still there, 'cause that's where I get my food. That cold is a comfort because I don't know anything else. But you've killed bushes to protect yourself from something which is harmless. Will nature ever forgive you?"

"Are you finished?" asked Grey Dog harshly, keeping his hold on Red Dog's neck.

"Just one more thing. The greatest hoax which you play on yourself and the environment is the distortion that your images are accurate reflections of the environment. It's a cruel hoax. You never realize that your image is as false as water is dry. A cactus plant is a lot more than just a hurtful pinprick. Cactus is what protects the rabbit from getting caught, so there are still rabbits around to be eaten. The wild pig eats the cactus. His feces fertilize the grass, his diggings aerate the soil so grass can grow, the rabbits eat the grass and the rabbits are our food. The cactus plant is part of our survival. Is that part of your image? No, not at all. There are hundreds of other things going on with a cactus plant. Are they all part of your image? No, you know they're not. You're not even aware of them ... I've already heard you say to your cousin that it would be great to somehow remove all the cactus plants so the rabbits couldn't hide and you would not get stuck. You were also talking about destroying an aspect of your life which keeps you alive — your environment — just because your image lies to you."

Red Dog's discourse had inadvertently activated Grey Dog's unconsciously learned inner fears of being hurt by being wrong, rejected. Grey Dog could feel them, but they appeared as Red Dog being obnoxious.

"Red Dog, roll over!" barked Grey Dog furiously.

Red Dog rolled over. He lay there, thinking, "What the hell am I doing here on my back at Grey Dog's feet and command? Rats! He's been part of my environment and has conditioned me. And I've become dependent on him. Screw this. When I get up, I'm leaving, only because I don't know how to do something about being conditioned. I don't have the tools. Now, if I could symbolize, I could fight conditioning tooth and nail and still live with nature. I'd use my ability to symbolize wisely. I'd use it to maintain myself by maintaining my environment, and fighting irrational conditioning and ignorant, false images through awareness."

Today, casual observation of dogs, wolves, coyotes and their genus, reveals that Grey Dog is no longer to be found. He somehow became extinct — a victim of some devastating aspect of his environment. But the ability to symbolize again appeared in the great life chain, at a later date, this time in an anthropoid ape. It was assisted by this ape's ability to pick things up with an opposable thumb, to verbalize and to make and use tools to increase its power over the environment. One need only look in a mirror to see that anthropoid today. What do you see? Yourself? No, that's only an image of yourself which your images imagine to be yourself.

What is your self image? Grey Dog? Red Dog? What do you do with the uncomfortable feelings you carry around inside you? Which dog will you be most happy being? What will you do about it?

THE END

Wally switched the tape back on.

"I take it you see yourself as being Red Dog," said Dr. Sullivan.

"No," I replied. "I'm just trying to be like him. I've been brought up like Grey Dog and I'll never lose it, it's too strong. But Danny, he might be Red Dog. Danny might be what Red Dog was talking about becoming because Danny won't roll over, so it seems."

"That's your opinion. I think it's your projection of your own desires."

"Time will tell."

At this point Carol broke in, "Meanwhile what should we do, Dr. Sullivan?"

"Carol, one positive thing you could do is not take Mr. Bryce's ideas too seriously. After all, you're running a home, not a kennel. Danny is being brought up in the world of people, in a culture. Even if Mr. Bryce is correct in assuming that Dan can't be conditioned, he's still going to end up being a person, not a dog. Don't start buying stock in Purina Dog Chow. Maybe there is no big problem. Dan may just be different and will assimilate into our culture."

There was a sudden silence in the room as the first reel of the tape abruptly ended. Charlie proceeded to put on reel two.

"Anybody for coffee?" he asked.

IX

I thought I was a goner for sure. The seventy foot finback whale had surfaced less than 100 yards away from my small boat. He turned and dove directly towards me. It was a fantastic sight to be so close to the animal. I could see barnacles growing on his skin. What incredible voyages they've had, I thought, as the whale passed underneath me and surfaced on the other side. Eddie told me later he'd seen them jump clear out of the water, landing with an immense noise and splash. Their blowhole expelling air is plenty loud — looks like a geyser.

From a composition by Dan Miller, age 16.

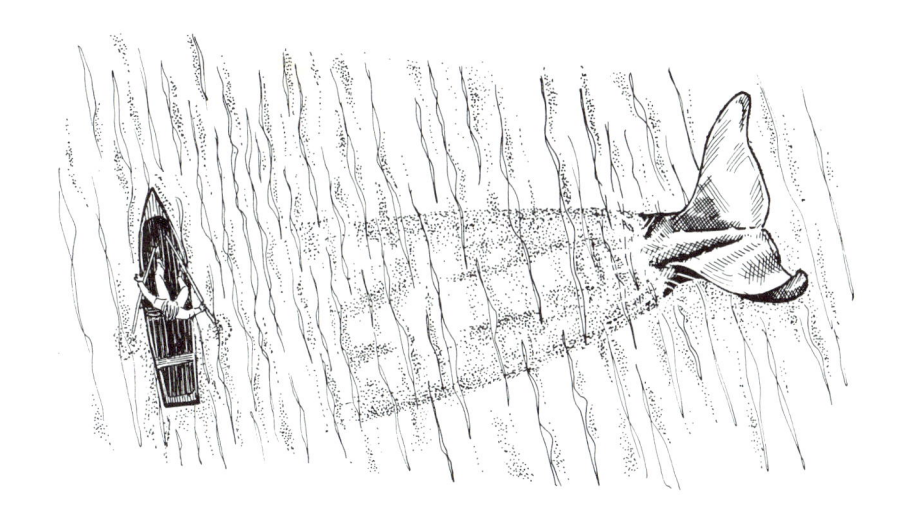

From *The Downeast Gazette,* Dec. 6, 1974
The biggest moving thing ever built by man is the supertanker. Brimming with oil, the largest of them weighs over 400,000 tons. They dangerously migrate around the world sometimes carrying extremely heavy but legal summer loads from tropical areas into storm filled winter seas. This can strain an overloaded vessel's plates and frames, springing leaks. In the interests of safety a tanker may release tons of oil to become more seaworthy. This has been the cause of many slicks. Yet it is the empty tanker which is the most dangerous for it is more susceptible to explosions.

Dr. Gitman finished his coffee, and looked up at Wally. "It's easy to say this in retrospect, but did it ever occur to you that since Dan is alive he couldn't have the condition you thought he had?"

Wally looked surprised. A sheepish grin came over his face. "You may not believe this Dr. Gitman but I still think my thoughts in the matter are accurate. I've yet to be convinced that Dan can be conditioned. I've also thought about the fact that Dan might not survive. I even talked about it with the Millers and Dr. Sullivan on this second reel of the tape."

Charlie took the tape and began to lead it onto the recorder.

"The fact that he has survived proves very little," Wally continued. "Dan has been living in a protected home situation. What will happen to him when he leaves home? Will he survive that?"

Dr. Gitman looked a bit bewildered. With a note of suspicion in his voice he said, "Let's hear this next reel."

Charlie clicked the tape on. Ben's recorded voice caught their attention as the discussion twelve years ago continued:

Ben: "Wally, what are you mumbling under your breath?"
Wally: "Forget it."
Ben: "I take it you disagree with Dr. Sullivan."
Wally: "To the contrary — he may well be right. Dan may actually acculturate."
Carol: "You don't seem too happy about that."
Wally: "I'm not! Dan might be better off being a dog; with any luck at all he would at least be sane. At least my dog knows what nature is for; he can sense it, experience it, enjoy it, and be tail-wagging happy about it on a continuing basis. It is part of his hourly, *now* life; nature runs in

his blood. My God, think about it. People spend most of their conscious life in the past or future, resolving anxieties from their past conditioning and distance from nature. How many of us really live in today — without being dragged down by the worry or concerns activated in us by our contact with our culture. How many of us are happy most of the time?

"I'm in no way convinced that Danny is going to make it in our culture. As a matter of fact, and I've been avoiding saying this, it may be that unless he's protected from himself, the culture will seriously contain, hurt or kill him. He may need to be institutionalized."

Carol gasped.

Ben: "Don't be so upset, Carol, I've thought about that. I didn't want to unnecessarily worry you, so I've never mentioned it. But what Wally says is true: much of what we call culture is nothing more than conditioning. Home is where the heart is, and the heart is where it was conditioned to be during childhood. If Dan is going to resist conditioning, it seems possible that he's going to mess up the 'home' of the people in any community, and they'll act accordingly."

Dr. Sullivan: "Mr. Bryce, you're unnecessarily misleading and frightening Carol and Ben. There are many misfits in our culture who survive quite well. Several of my patients are social outcasts who somehow manage to maintain themselves."

Wally: "I can easily think of a specific situation which, had Danny been there, could have led to disaster for him and others. Our school group was camping in a forest area in Wyoming while studying alpine glacial geology. I started to back up the bus when I heard the sound of breaking glass and people yelling, 'Stop, stop!' I had inadvertently backed into the protruding branch of a tree which did not show up in any of my three rearview mirrors. The branch had come through the back window almost a foot by the time I stopped. Nobody was back there — that's our equipment storage area — but the seriousness of the situation was all too apparent. It was possible to back up the bus and hit or run over anything there because of blind spots, even with three mirrors.

"Through discussion, it was decided by all the staff and students that we would no longer back up the bus unless we had somebody in the back looking out the rear window to avert a similar accident. That was the beginning of a cultural change because the driver and passengers had to begin to relate to their environment in a new manner. A week went by and one day Sarah was backing up the bus when the same thing nearly happened again, this time with a parking meter. The problem this time was that even though the student in the back was watching, everybody else was talking so when Chuck was saying 'Stop!' Sarah couldn't hear him. She didn't stop until the last moment when, by luck, his voice got through.

"Another meeting was called, this time by Chuck, and after due consideration, it was agreed that when the bus was backing up everybody would keep quiet ... another adaptation, this time to the social environment. But it wasn't enough, for oftentimes students were occupied with other matters and overlooked the fact that we were backing up.

"Through a meeting, this problem was reconciled by either the driver or anyone else yelling 'backing' when we were going to back up, and the driver would not back up the bus unless it was quiet. Still that was not enough because there were some students whose voices did not carry from the back to the front; they were not loud enough and they were looking towards the back while yelling towards the front. Finally, it was agreed that communication would have to be established and tested before the bus was backed up. Within a month it became habit, or conditioned cultural behavior — a total community effort if the bus was to go in reverse reasonably and safely.

"Believe me, after a while, the reprimanding of students by other students was quite harsh and severe if they talked while the bus was backing. It started out being a loosely knit agreement, a folkway. It became reinforced as conditioning took place, becoming an unwritten law that was enforced by group pressure. One did not want to be talking when the bus was backing. That person would appear to be an unreasonable, stupid, inconsiderate, asocial, unthoughtful outlaw if perchance his / her involvement in conversation superceded the cry of 'backing' and the silence which followed. Talking rarely happened though, for the stimulus of the yell of 'backing' was conditioned and one usually stopped talking automatically. The response was rewarded each time, for we could proceed without an accident or reprimand. But if a person like Dan couldn't be conditioned, it could be a serious physical and social matter. People would be harsh with him. It could emotionally scar him, right?"

Dr. Sullivan: "I suppose that could happen."

Wally: "It was extremely interesting to observe what would happen when an individual from outside of our 'culture' was on the bus when backing took place. Sometimes a guide, a friend or parent might be visiting. If they had not been forewarned, (and who would remember to do so?) they would remain talking after 'backing' was shouted. Sometimes it was ignored, sometimes they were embarrassed by being the only ones talking and often loudly to overcome background noise — and they'd be overheard by everybody when all of a sudden everybody except them was quiet. Sometimes they were told to be quiet, sometimes it was explained. No matter what happened, the visitor could sense that they had entered a new cultural setting, a foreign country.

"At school some students would shout 'backing' to make people be quiet, even when we were not on the bus. After leaving school, students have reported back to us that they have felt uncomfortable when sitting on a Greyhound or another bus when it starts backing. Some say they have automatically said shhhh, and others near them have in turn stopped talking. Some say they can hear the word 'backing' being shouted as the Greyhound bus backs out of the station. Truly, cultural conditioning had taken place.

"And what happened in following years when the original experience of the tree branch through the window had not taken place, but the school bus still had to back up? Did we adults, as experienced members of the past year's group, wait for an accident to occur so all could learn from it? No, we did not. We utilized images and told the kids what had happened in previous years, and what we had done about it. We asked what they wanted to do about it each year. And was passing on this vital information effective? It was not. You could have a full hour speech and discussion about backing up the bus and what to do, and until these students had gone through the process of backing up the bus for a few weeks some people could not behaviorally learn to be quiet. And some would think that the staff was giving orders, and get so mired down in anti-authority feelings that they would feel differently about the staff, unhappy with them, afraid to talk to them. The instruction about backing had indeed aroused conditioned feelings from past teachers, parents, and learning situations. Some kids would feel the anxiety of these conditioned situations and would react accordingly. They'd block out half of what was being said due to preoccupation with anxiety. Some students would obey immediately and would direct others, only to discover they never fully realized the rationale for being quiet while backing: after all there were no trees in the New York City parking lot — where the discussion originally took place. Some thought it was stupid because an electric button signal system could easily be set up between the back and the front, but never expressed their ideas at the time; they just obeyed 'orders.' Interestingly enough, Danny would probably be able to handle these kinds of planning situations well. He would not be bogged down in conditioning which boggled the mind."

Carol: "Right. So the thing to do is to steer Danny towards situations which are like that."

Wally: "Fine, but where are you going to find them? Once behavior is established it remains established through conditioning of action or feelings. Will Danny be able to handle that? Carol, think about what society really consists of. It's basically institutions such as governments, the church, corporations, the family, police or schools. Each of them is a grouping of conditioned responses. They're nothing more than bunches of situations similar to backing the bus. In their own way, they each give us the stimulus. They yell 'backing', and we respond positively or negatively, depending upon our conditioning with regard to their stimuli. That's what they're set up to do."

Ben: "What stimuli are you talking about, Wally? I can't think of any."

Wally: "Yes, but while you can't think of one, you and I are responding to them all the time. For example, each institution has a value symbol which represents it and its 'power' over us. People fight and die for the flag of their country, or split in disagreement over what they have been conditioned to believe it represents. Each institution has a value symbol of some kind and we recognize it. We salute it, kneel to it, bow to it, obey it, conform to it or respect it in one way or another. People actually wear school and corporate value symbols on their 'T' shirts. The cross, the corporate seal, the school colors or flag, the wedding ring are all stimuli. Each institution has many such stimuli: rituals, uniforms, a dogma as to why it exists, rule enforcers, a hierarchy of people who operate the institution, taboos: the things the institution says you're not allowed to do. The ultimate example of institutional conditioning was Nazi Germany. Fantastic conditioning to the swastika and Fuehrer led people to 'Heil Hitler' even though he was preaching race hatred. They accepted a dogma which had little foundation in reality, ethics or morality. Conditioning to rituals, rule enforcers, hierarchy, taboos were all powerfully there. People were helplessly caught in an institution which their own apathy had helped create.

"Our culture, like any culture, is based on its institutions, its conditioning agents, their stimuli, and the unconscious conditioned feelings, behavior or attitudes that they elicit and reinforce. That's why you can't just bring two cultures together geographically or economically and expect it to work out. Black vs. white, Indian vs. settler, pothead vs. straight. Much of what holds a person to their culture is unconscious conditioned responses. No matter how much you talk or act, you never really reach it. How will Danny survive in any society? When he wipes his ass with the flag, he's a goner.

"We're so wrapped up in our conditioned images, our symbols, our ignorance of their power and distortion that we can no longer even see the real environment which they represent. All we are conscious of are the images. Unconsciously, we are slaves to their conditioning. Danny might just become the only free man on the face of the earth and he could very well be killed for it. He could be a threat to each person and institution which he meets for he'll activate the hurtful feelings each carries within. We're each a bag of unconscious hurt due to the punishments of conditioning and our removal from the natural environment. Danny's actions or thoughts could unintentionally make that hurt become conscious and painful. He'd be a living image of it. That's what most criminals are to those who just hear about them.

"An interesting example of exactly this kind of thing happened last year on the school. We went to visit and watch some of the ceremonies of the Hopi Indians, a pueblo tribe of Northern Arizona. Their dance ceremonies are completely unique. While the costumed men are dancing and portraying spirits who are asking for rain, crops, and good weather, other men are acting as clowns. The clowns make fun of the dancing spirits. They annoy them. They portray the irreverent behavior of the village 'sinners' and are part and parcel of the ceremony — much to the amusement of the villagers. It would be like attending Mass in St. Patrick's Cathedral and while the services are taking place, some stark naked guys are stealing the golden candlesticks, and painting the archbishop's nose green while goosing him under his robes. In Hopi dance ceremonials that's the approved role of the clowns.

"After the dances, we went to a small Mormon community where the discussion turned to the subject of weddings, because Ernie, one of the staff members, was getting married in June and had invited the school to attend the informal, untraditional wedding. One of the Mormons described a 'shivaree' which takes place sometimes before the wedding. At a shivaree, all the friends of the bridegroom harass and make fun of him and the upcoming marriage.

"We decided, with Ernie's consent, that clowns would appear at the wedding and would have a shivaree as part of the ceremony. It would be a multicultural wedding. Oh, you should have been there. It was quite something. The clowns asked the bride and groom if instead of an untraditional wedding, didn't they want it done 'right'. Ernie and his wife said sure, and the clowns proceeded to get all involved in having them go through a spoof on a traditional, typical, institutionally conditioned wedding ceremony. Ernie was Italian and the clowns brought out a special wedding cake which was a cold pizza with toy cartoon characters making love in the middle of it. They read fake obscene telegrams of congratulations from famous people. They had a toy getaway car marked up obscenely like a real wedding car would be. They had everybody kiss the bride, but with chocolate kisses. They had wedding guests throw rice, but it was sticky, cooked rice. They had wedding rings. The rings were bells that the bride and groom would ring. They had a wedding procession in which everybody holding hands were wound into the center of a circle and couldn't get out. It was fun, but people who were conditioned into traditional weddings were really offended. Those who were outraged were given buckets of water to throw at the clowns. They did it with a vehemence, but it didn't relieve all their tension. We had hit their institutional conditioning where it hurt. Their conditioned fears of punishment for institutional disobedience came right out. Brother, they could feel them. They called the whole thing disrespectful. Some were close to infuriated. They said the clowns were distasteful, insane imbeciles. Yet, all that was actually done was to combine some typical rituals of various American subcultures and perform them in another subculture. It hurt. Tears were in everybody's eyes either from laughing or crying. It depended upon who you were and where you were coming from. Either way, it was certainly unforgettable."

Dr. Sullivan: "It's getting late, and although I can understand what you're saying, Wally, I can't find any evidence for Dan having the ailment you describe. All you're working with is your own observations in an incredibly unique situation which is close to being another reality."

Wally: "That's because you live in a world separated from that reality. But you're correct, for that's where most people live, no matter the consequences."

Dr. Sullivan: "What consequences do you mean?"

Wally: "What consequences? Dr. Sullivan, it is fascinating to talk with you. You remind me of a little kid who's never seen a lion before except maybe on television. I remember taking some kids to the zoo for the first time. They thought a lion was really small, like a foot or two long, for that's how big it was on the television screen. They were amazed and frightened to see the full-sized animal. It was a shock. Frankly, you come across to me that way, like there's an area in your mind that's never had any exposure to the concept or reality of the environment as an integrated entity."

Dr. Sullivan: "What makes you say that?"

Wally: "Because you seem so distant from the interrelationship of an individual's actions and the world he lives in. You understand it conceptually, but the actual impact on a feeling level, on a total living level, on a long term basis, just seems to escape you. It seems like a blank area. Your personal world consists of contact with isolated parts of the environment. Like your kitchen stove. It's isolated. It's like Grey Dog's concept of a cactus."

Dr. Sullivan: "What do you mean by that?"

Wally: "Your kitchen stove undoubtedly has a pilot light. Over a third of your stove's gas consumption goes towards keeping that pilot light lit. One of the consequences of that is an energy shortage, an overuse of natural gas. Another consequence is your need to earn money to pay for your pilot light. Still another is how you'd feel if your stove didn't have one and your neighbor's stove did. Yet another is the CO_2 content in the air from millions of burning pilot lights. Still another is why the pilot light is there in the first place. That's the most important one. That's why I'm really discussing the pilot light. It saves you time, so you won't have to strike a match. The 'saved' time is used for some other contact with the environment. Time is a vital part of the environment we just take for granted. The whole energy shortage and pollution problem is a large consequence of time. Like drying clothes. If you dried your clothes directly in the sun it might take more time than in an electric dryer, but the efficiency factor is incredible. Either the sun does the drying directly, with 100% efficiency, or, to save time the sun's energy must first become wind and water evaporation, which becomes clouds, then rain, then a river. The environment then must provide polluting, energy sucking cement factories, steel mills, copper smelters, fuel, aluminum mills and labor to make both electric dryers and the electric power to run the dryers off of running water. The actual difference in environmental efficiency between drying clothes one way or the other is nothing short of ridiculous. Yes, time is saved but look at the consequences to the environment. That's the dead area in your mind, Dr. Sullivan: The interrelationships. To me you are Grey Dog's ultimate successor; when you go to the store and buy an electric clothes dryer, the concept of environmental effect is practically not there. Which makes more sense: direct sunlight or the dryer? Which has the most reasonable long term consequences? Long term — that's time. Time is a vital part of our environment. Do they generally require courses in school about the significance, role and effects of time? No! Why is it less important than economics? My school teaches 'environment' which includes all these things. And you're foolish enough to say that *I'm* unrealistic. I'm living in a separate reality! Whose reality is really separate, mine or yours? Whose will stand the test of time?

"Dr. Sullivan when you get right down to it saved time is really nothing more than button pushing. They're identical, they're basically distance: the ultimate removal of people from contact with the environment; the ultimate end to what Grey Dog's images began. That, Doctor, is reality. And I think you know it.

"I can't disagree more strongly that my school or myself is a separate reality. If we are so separate, we would be teaching and training students to adapt to another culture. Overwhelmingly substantial facts prove that our students are more vital, are stronger, are more active and are happier citizens in this culture because of their contact with the school: the school you call 'another reality'. What we work with is obviously real — real people and the real environment. Otherwise, the school just wouldn't work. I think the undisputed constructive carryover from one to the other proves the point."

Dr. Sullivan: "That may be correct but it's not relevant to Dan's ailment. There is no evidence for your diagnosis other than your single experiment and observation of the twins which is completely unsubstantiated. No one has ever discovered that a malfunction such as you describe can even exist in an individual. As best as I can find, we might be working with an unknown disorder, or a special kind of mental retardation. It is far too suspicious for me to even consider that Danny's special disorder has just coincidentally been correctly diagnosed by a layman — a teacher who specializes in interpreting and explaining all mental disorders as being the result of conditioning by the environment."

Wally: "Is that what you think I've said? I guess we haven't communicated that well after all. I think conditioning is the basic process by which all psychotic and psychoneurotic tension and anxiety is generated. What is 'treated' by psychotherapists and the like are the conflicts *resulting* from foolish conditioning. Conditioning is not responsible for certain types of mental retardation or brain damage pathology.

"Your work consists of getting people to reasonably adapt themselves to a social setting which in the long run is self-destructive, stupid and criminal. It's a setting which conditions people to ignore their basic thoughts and feelings and depend instead on authorities other than nature.

"Conditioned unconscious fears lock a child into uncomfortable behavior, thoughts, and feelings. I help young people discover the effects this process has in their own lives. I help them create a more comfortable 'no fault' environment of self discovery. I teach individuals to help both themselves and their environment because they're one and the same thing.

Dr. Sullivan: "Aw, come off it. The most incredible and unbelievable aspect of your hypothesis is that in order for it to be true, a three and one half year old child has to be able to understand himself and his surroundings. Danny has to be able to discern his natural from his social environment, his instincts, or drives as you call them, from his learned behavior. He has to have a sense of self that most adults are unable to obtain in a lifetime. How completely absurd!"

Wally: "Absurd to you, because you don't see them in yourself due to your own conditioning and training. It seems absurd to me to refute that a child, a baby, can't feel, can't on a feeling level experience hunger, pain, pleasure, fatigue, heat and cold and the effects of the environment on these feelings. To the contrary, I think a baby can experience his real environment better than an adult because he has not been overlayed by years of cultural conditioning, such as 18,000 hours of public school attendance. Even a microbe can experience its environment and be conditioned by it. Furthermore, you'll find that environmental detachment starts early; babies have been conditioned while in the womb. I know of some experimenters who sounded a loud noise to a pregnant mother and the baby did not respond to it. Then they sounded the loud noise and poked the baby by lightly pressing the mother's stomach. The baby would react by moving. After this was repeated a number of times, the baby would move after the loud noise was sounded — though he was not poked. As for Danny, he had only 3½ years of normal environmental conditioning. Today, if I'm correct, he experiences the environment more realistically than any of us can, for what else can he experience if his images can't be distorted by conditioning? He is not old enough yet to be seriously misled intellectually."

Dr. Sullivan: "This is going nowhere. Perhaps we should call it an evening."

Ben: "Just one question. What do you think the result of all this will be on Danny's personality?"

Dr. Sullivan: "Any youngster who has some deficiency or abnormality may feel its effects in that he can't compete. He feels different, is different, and is treated differently than 'normal' kids. A student with a reading deficiency which is not discovered, like nearsightedness or dyslexia, will learn to think of himself as being inferior or stupid or unscholarly and will have tension and therefore perhaps further unproductiveness, in that and other areas. He or she will be scarred by their disappointing performance and its effects."

Wally: "— Depending upon the environment and how it conditions him to perceive himself. A student may learn to sublimate his reading inability with mechanical ability. By choosing to stay in a machine shop environment and social setting, he may happily maintain himself as a worthwhile machinist and citizen. In any case, to my way of thinking, Danny won't develop these types of personality difficulties unless he already had them instilled before the accident. It is usually conditioned feelings which cause them. He may well be a highly academic, somewhat erratic, isolated type of person who is not swayed by praise or punishment but seeks genuine love and companionship on a 'now' basis."

Ben: "Well, thanks a lot guys. You sure have been helpful. You don't agree on anything and leave us in the middle. Frankly, I didn't expect much more than that."

Carol: "But it does help, for at least we know what to keep our eyes out for."

Dr. Sullivan: "Mr. Bryce, maybe you should lay low. Your environmental outlook and conditioning hypothesis may not be a positive contribution, since they are not the norms in the environment where Danny will be living. You might just become an escape for adaptations he might otherwise learn to make."

Wally: "Perhaps, but I completely disagree with the judgements you place on my values. I also think that you're shamefully naive with respect to your relationship with the environment. I guess we'll just have to think about what's been said here this evening. Good night."

X

Each fish and mammal in the sea is a host for many different species of parasites. I found a load of tapeworms in a dead shark I cut open. The cod has worms imbedded in its muscles. Each animal is a hotel for others — somehow they have all learned to play life's game together. Indeed, I believe they must strengthen each other, for they could not play the game alone. The parasitic worms are passed from one predator to another and live in different forms as part of their life cycle. There are more parasites in the fish up in the northern bay because the pollution from the paper plants weaken the fish's resistance to them.

From a composition by Dan Miller, age 16.

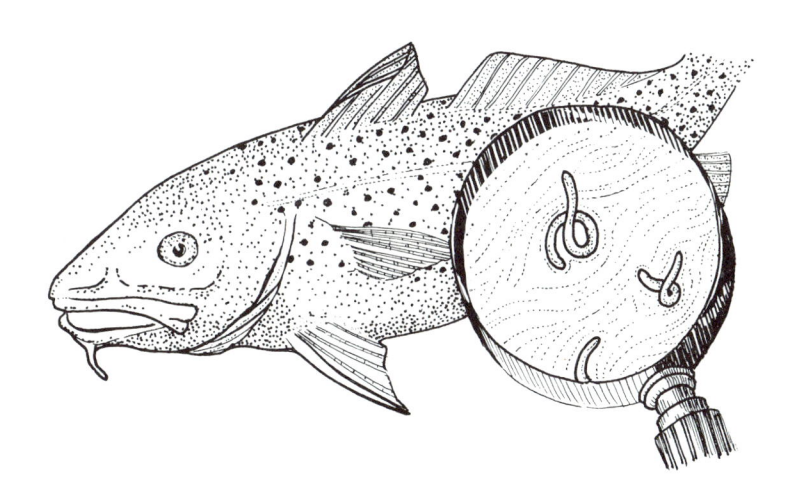

From *The Downeast Gazette,* June 8, 1976.
I don't understand why my government tolerates the refinery. We Canadians are on the leeward side of the prevailing winds. We'll bear the brunt of the fumes, the sulphuric acid fogs, the damaged soil and air quality, reduced fishing and oily waters.

Kenneth Robb, Selectman
Crystal Beach, New Brunswick.

Charlie shut off the tape machine with a loud snap. After several seconds Sarah broke the silence.

"What's your reaction to what you've heard, Dr. Gitman?"

"I suppose I shouldn't tell you, but I will," he said earnestly. First of all, what's happening to Dan is absolutely fascinating. It's clear as a bell what the differences are between you and Dr. Sullivan. I don't even want to attempt to comment upon who's right or wrong. But, I will say this. There have been other therapists in this state who have had equally radical ideas. They have been prosecuted, jailed, and fined. One of them died in jail in the fifties. Many people in the field felt he had gone off the deep end, that he was psychotic, even though he had been a licensed practitioner. A precedent has already been set, and it may well be that you're going to have to prove beyond reasonable doubt that what you do and how you do it are valid, that you're not a mental health menace. I may have to testify to that allegation in one way or another. I'll want to get as much information as I can about the effects of your school on your students and their families. I'm happy to tell you that I've only heard highly complimentary enthusiastic reactions from former participants including the Director of the State Mental Health Association and the University Center for Psychotherapy. I'll tell you something else as well. If you can clearly demonstrate that Dan is indeed immune to conditioning, Dr. Sullivan might have to drop his complaint because he can't afford to look foolish in his present state of candidacy for the Directorship."

"How would I go about proving that?" asked Wally.

"If you can present me with some conclusive proof or an irreproachable case history of Dan, I'd be able to contradict Dr. Sullivan's allegations in my report, . . . and at the hearing if necessary.

That might be of considerable assistance to your case. Part of Dr. Sullivan's position is that you have proselytized an unproven 'medication' if you will, while counseling people to refute legal and licensed therapy. It's exactly what's happened to Laetrile and cancer therapy. I don't envy your position. I must say that professionally I'm extremely interested in your findings with reference to Dan. I'd like to hear and see what else you have in your journals."

Wally seemed a bit heartened by Dr. Gitman's interest and offered to be of service if he could. He picked up the twenty-two remaining notebooks and sought those marked with bright red bookmarks. He eagerly opened the first one and from its pages withdrew a letter postmarked "Whitehorse, Maine, October 9, 1969." It was written to him from Ben. Dan was 10 years old at the time. Wally gave Dr. Gitman and Charlie two copies:

Dear Wally,

I thought you might be interested in keeping up with the latest with respect to Dan and his problems. Dr. Sullivan decided that we should try to get Dan's I.Q. tested to see if part of his problem lay in that area. You'll perhaps be amazed to learn that Dan has an I.Q. of 27. That's right! Of course it's meaningless. I think you would have enjoyed being there when they gave the test. It was the Stanford Binet. I was allowed to watch the whole procedure through a one way mirror. I was told I had to keep very quiet. I nearly burst. It was in some ways incredibly funny but I was caught between laughing and crying.

Dan's biggest problem is the same as the one we face. He knows that he's different and neither he nor we know what to do about it. When they tried to give him the I.Q. test, he would only do the parts of it which were interesting to him no matter how much we tried to tell him beforehand that it was very important that he do everything. He would be completely preoccupied with the total environmental setting he was in, and not just the test. It happened each time he took it. The examiner would tell him that he would like to discover which words Dan knew.

Wally interrupted the reading. "The examiner was obviously checking to see the extent of symbolization which had already taken place in Dan's brain. How much of the environment had Dan put into images? How able was he to maneuver or manipulate these images and communicate or impose these manipulations upon the environment. If he was real good at it, he'd have a high I.Q."

"Why do you want to know what words I know?" Dan would ask. The examiner would then have to create some explanation right on the spot or Dan wouldn't proceed. He told Dan it was to find words which he didn't know. Then he would know which words to learn. That sounded interesting to Dan, so they asked him to define orange.

"What does 'define' mean?" asked Dan

"Glad you asked. It means, 'Tell me the meaning of.' "

"You want me to tell you the meaning of orange?"

"That's right. Very good."

"Why is that good?"

"Well, you understood what I was trying to say."

"But I understood what you were trying to say before. I just didn't understand the word 'define'."

"Oh, I see. Do you understand 'define' now?"

"Sure, it means tell you the meaning of something."

"OK, can you define 'orange'?"

"Which orange?"

"What?"

"Which orange do you want me to define?"

"There is only one word — orange — what does it mean?"

"You think there is only one orange? I can think of several oranges. Are you sure there is only one?"

"Yes, one word: 'orange'."

"There's more than one that I can think of — you name one."

The examiner thought for a while. Danny sat silently, waiting expectantly. Finally the examiner said resignedly, "OK. An orange hanging on a tree."

"You see! More than one orange hangs on a tree. Which one do you want me to define?"

"Maybe we should go on to a different word," said the examiner.

"What's wrong with 'orange'?"

"Well, we're having a little difficulty with it."

"*We're* having difficulty?" queried Dan, genuinely confused.

"I'm not having difficulty. You want me to define the word orange, but you won't tell me which orange, so I have to ask you. I even have to tell you that there's more than one on a tree. Which part of the tree?"

"Which part?"

"The orange you want me to define, where is it in the tree?"

"Uh — on the branch."

"Which branch?" said Dan earnestly.

"I don't know, an upper branch."

"Which upper branch?"

"How about a high branch," replied the exasperated examiner.

"Is the tree in Florida?" asked Dan.

"I don't know."

"Is this a trick? Is it a trick? You ask me to define orange and you don't know which orange or where it is," said Dan, earnestly impatient. "How can I do that? Give me a hint please, is the tree in Florida?"

"OK, OK, it's in Florida."

"Where in Florida?"

"What choices do I have?"

"I thought you were asking me to make the definition. You've got to tell me. I'm really trying to get this test right."

"Which tree would you like? You pick the tree and the place."

"You mean you don't care?"

"It's your answer," he said, pulling his hair.

"It's your question. Don't you care, ... *don't you?*"

"No, I don't," he said, breathing heavily. "Whatever tree you desire is OK."

"How about the tree I saw in the backyard of the motel in Orlando when we were there after visiting Disney World last year?"

"Fine, I'm sure that was a nice tree."

Danny suddenly became upset. "This isn't fair — this is a trick question."

"What are you talking about now?" screamed the examiner.

"There is no top branch in that tree. I remember climbing it and breaking that top branch off. Arty ate the orange on it. There is no orange! Why are you trying to confuse me?" cried Dan, hopelessly.

"For God's sake, don't cry, cut it out. Use a tree in Miami."

The crying got worse. "There was a blight in Miami. There were no oranges there last year. Besides, now you're changing the questions, how can I get them right?"

"I insist that we do a new word," said the examiner. "Let's try again."

"No."

"Try a new word. Maybe it won't be so confusing. Please. What can you lose?"

"Oh, OK. What's the word?"

"Define 'top'."

Danny looked at him with amazement. "Does this have anything to do with the last question?" he asked.

"No, nothing! Define 'top'."

"I've got it! This one is easy. It sits below or underneath something else. Isn't that right?" said Dan.

"I'm not supposed to say," said the examiner.

"How am I going to learn if I don't know what a word means, if you don't tell me if I know it or not. That's why I'm taking this test, right?"

"Well . . ."

"That's what you said when we started," said Danny. "Otherwise, why do this?"

"OK, your answer is not correct."

"How do you know? Did you see it?"

"Top refers to a place."

"I know. I know the place, underneath."

"That is not correct."

"You moved it?" said Dan, incredulously.

"It was never there."

"It was so, I put it there. Underneath!"

"What are you talking about?"

"Top. My top. I left it underneath the table."

"You left your top underneath the table?"

"Yes. Why did you lie to me? You lied, you lied!"

"Now, just a minute, sonny," said the examiner. "I did not lie to you. You better watch out who you're calling a liar."

"You did lie, you did!" exclaimed Danny.

"How?"

110

"You said just a while ago that this question had nothing to do with the last question."

"That's true too," said the examiner. "It doesn't."

"Lies, lies, all lies," said Danny. "My top is orange. You're trying to confuse me."

You can see why he only got twenty-seven. He took the test to be specific — too specific — but, that doesn't mean he can't generalize. It's just that he does what he wants to, when he wants to. He's so peeved by being tested that he just somehow came up with another point of view. I guess that's not surprising, especially if he has not learned anything by conditioning. His associations are not going to be the same as everybody else's for he's not pressed into them by the mold of the people around him.

There were plenty of examples of this and I'm surprised that he got anything right at all. Here are some more examples from the I.Q. test.

IF X
COMES BEFORE U
IN THE ALPHABET
CROSS OUT
A
BELOW
OTHERWISE
CROSS OUT
B

His answer was, 'If I put an X through B, then my 'X' sitting over the B will come before U in the alphabet.'

CROSS OUT THE GROUP OF LETTERS WHICH IS DIFFERENT:
CCZO   ACBC   SCLC   RCMC

His answer appeared:
CCXX   XCXC   XCXC   XCXC

IF PENCILS ARE FOUR FOR A QUARTER, HOW MANY CAN YOU GET FOR 75¢

Dan's answer was '20'. They are cheaper, he said, when you buy the whole box full, which only costs 72¢ plus 5% tax which comes to 75¢.

WHICH INSTRUMENT DOES NOT BELONG IN THE FOLLOWING:
PIANO   DRUM   VIOLIN   GUITAR   BANJO

Dan's answer was "Piano! It's the only one we own."

PLACE THE BLOCKS IN THE HOLES SO THEY FIT EVENLY.

Dan took his pen knife and whittled down the square block to fit perfectly in the round hole.

PICTURE VOCABULARY: 18 3" x 5" CARDS WITH PICTURES ON

THEM.

The cards were shown one at a time. Dan was asked to explain what he saw.

In each case Dan said, "It's a 3" x 5" card with a picture on it."
HOW IS IT DIFFERENT THAN THE LAST CARD?
"This card has a different picture on it."
"WHAT ELSE?"
"This card came after the one before it."

The following statements were read to Dan and he was asked to explain what was foolish about each of them.

(1) THE JUDGE SAID TO THE PRISONER, "YOU ARE TO BE HANGED AND I HOPE THAT WILL BE A WARNING TO YOU."

Dan responded, "It's foolish 'cause the judge never learned that it's not right to kill people."

(2) A WELL-KNOWN RAILROAD COMPANY HAD ITS LAST ACCIDENT FIVE YEARS AGO AND SINCE THAT TIME IT HAS KILLED ONLY ONE PERSON IN A COLLISION.

Dan answered, "It's foolish for the railroad company to have collisions on purpose. I'll bet they do it for the insurance."

(3) WHEN THERE IS A COLLISION, THE LAST CAR OF THE TRAIN IS USUALLY DAMAGED MOST. SO IT HAS BEEN DECIDED THAT IT WILL BE BEST IF THE LAST CAR ALWAYS IS TAKEN OFF BEFORE THE TRAIN STARTS.

Dan said, "That's foolish because they could put the last car in front and get some use out of it."

IN WHAT WAY ARE THE FOLLOWING GROUPS OF THREE THINGS ALIKE:
1. SNAKE, COW, SPARROW
Dan answered, "They all live on the ground, except for the sparrow."
2. WOOL, COTTON, LEATHER
"They're all fuzzy if the leather is suede."
3. KNIFE-BLADE, PENNY, PIECE OF WIRE
"They all can be like this test — dull!"

WHAT DOES EACH OF THE FOLLOWING PROVERBS MEAN:
1. STRIKE WHILE THE IRON IS HOT
"How to get a raise in pay in a steel mill."
2. LARGE OAKS FROM LITTLE ACORNS GROW
"Plant little acorns if you want big oaks."
3. THE MOUSE THAT HAS BUT ONE HOLE IS EASILY TAKEN
"You can easily sell that mouse a faulty hole he doesn't need."

4. YOU MUST NOT THROW PEARLS BEFORE SWINE
"You'll get stronger by throwing the swine first."
5. DON'T COUNT YOUR CHICKENS BEFORE THEY HATCH
"Count your eggs before you pay for them."
6. OUT OF THE FRYING PAN INTO THE FIRE
"Charcoal broiled tastes best."

It seems to me that Dan summed up his situation when he took the projective technique test. In this test a picture was shown to him of a man who might be climbing down a rope. He was asked to make up a story for the picture. His story was about a little boy who was trying to escape from all the people around him who kept saying he was different. The rope goes down to a new group of people and the same thing happens there so he escapes down that rope only to find that it ends up with the first group of people who were around him.

As you can see, things are just about the same. Thought you'd want to know.

                        Love,
                        Ben

"That's absolutely incredible," said Dr. Gitman. "It says so much."

"Wait until you see what's coming," said Wally, with a growing sense of confidence.

XI

The herring that swarmed through the bay were not more than an inch long. Last year there were so many that they were followed in by squid, which occasionally grounded in the ebb tide. As the fish grew, they made for deeper water where the schools could be seen at night as highly glowing areas in the sea, for they excited the sparkly little dinoflagellates with their presence. This was the signal for the fisherman to spread his nets. Often the cod, squid, and pollack would swim into them and occasionally a porpoise or whale as well. The silver sided herring schools were the feeding grounds of the sea world.

From a composition by Dan Miller, age 16.

From *The Downeast Gazette*, July 8, 1974
The bay area has been identified as being the production ground for the world's greatest population of herring. It is an important, viable Canadian fishery. The American refinery will risk the loss of a renewable resource for a non-renewable one.

Paul Wesson, President
Fisherman's Association

"Wally," said Dr. Gitman, "do you mean to tell me that you've been in contact with Dan for how many years? Twelve? Twelve years and you've never seen or heard any evidence of conditioning in him?"

"During that period . . . that's exactly what I'm trying to tell you. Now don't get me wrong," continued Wally, with a concerned glance. "I'm not saying that Dan has *never* been able to be conditioned. He showed plenty of effects from the conditioning which took place before he overdosed."

"What do you mean? How do you know?" asked Dr. Gitman, intensely curious at this point.

"Well, obviously Dan can talk, read and write. He had developed elementary language skills and known their rewards before the mescalin accident. When he was only four months old Carol had begun reading to him while he was happily sitting on her lap. He would enjoy looking at the pictures in the books she read aloud. Since then he has kept increasing and improving his written and verbal skills even though they are basically learned through the conditioning process."

"Doesn't that seem contradictory?" asked Dr. Gitman.

"Not really," Wally replied. "Since Dan had already experienced rewards from language and its use he is, even now, still responsive to them. Dan is therefore able to continue to improve his written and verbal skills through a relatively normal conditioning process. The only difference is that the rewards for improvement today come from early childhood memories and feelings. He is otherwise immune to any normal conditioning which would take place after three and one-half years of age."

"What other carry-overs did you observe from his pre-accident conditioning?" Dr. Gitman queried.

"Well, there was one thing which Dan really craved. It was friendship. Perhaps he desired it so strongly because he had such an extremely difficult time obtaining it. He knew what it was, he knew its value. Even though inter-personal relationships were not a part of his everyday life, he could want them. Feelings of warmth, support, protection, and sharing were not out of Dan's experience parameters. To the contrary, they were probably more of a desire and more of a need in him than in you or me. I looked up my thoughts about this in my journal after Dan applied for the school. Let me see . . . here they are. I'll read them if you'd like."

"Go right ahead," said Dr. Gitman.

Journal entry: February 25, 1976, Whitehorse, Maine. Chilly, Clear.

Why is Danny in the situation he is in right now? What is his status today with respect to conditioning? Perhaps the learned rewards of conditioning have passed Danny by, but that didn't happen until he was three and one-half years of age. Until that time, I take it that his response to conditioning was normal. Unconsciously, on a feeling level, he could remember the warmth of the womb and the trauma of birth. He could remember the protection from that trauma through the loving, concerned hands and hearts of Ben and Carol. He would depend upon his parents. These feelings remained intact in his memory bank. They could be stimulated by attention from others, from acts of human kindness or the promise of those past rewards becoming tapped, active and flowing from interactions with those who surrounded him. Dan was not brought up by wolves in the wilderness, although there were those who acted as if they didn't believe it. He *would* respond to kind people. Among Dan's peers, the conditioning process continued past the age of three. Their environment dictated the graces of their culture which they accepted and demanded from each other. It's too painful any other way. Conditioning to the American Judeo-Christian, capitalistic outlook is nothing short of brainwashing. To a child it is simply the fascist game of do or die, except that die in this case means rejection. Rejection means not only loneliness, but the unconscious frightening feeling of losing the approval of adults, the people who supply you with the necessities of life.

To Danny (before his accident) and his peers, nature is not experienced as the source of life. The source is their parents. Parental approval means life and the conditioning process quickly takes its course. The natural stimuli are hunger, thirst, cold, uncomfortable sights and sounds, pain and discomfort. The natural response is to suckle, to eat, to drink, and to seek the protection of the gods of the day, the parents who provide food, water and protection. The conditioned stimulus becomes the perception that these goodies for life obviously come from approving people. The conditioned response is to eat, drink, excrete, and act all in a manner which wins the approval of parents and authorities. That behavior brings the rewards which only they can provide.

Within such an atmosphere of slow but sure brainwashing, children quickly learn the culture and ways of their parents. Eskimos create Eskimos. Americans create Americans. Indians create Indians. Wolves create wolves — even if, by chance, they are nurturing human babies.

Danny's problem was that an overdose evidently stopped the conditioning process after three and one-half years. His conditioning to that point taught him that approving parents brought vital rewards. But evidently by the age of three and one-half, he had not been strongly conditioned to understand that disapproving parents can bring discomfort or pain. Criticism or rejection was not unconsciously implanted as being uncomfortable, something to be avoided. Instead, Dan was trapped by time after time, with person after person, learning the hard way that disapproving people can hurt you, that most people are not as supportive as your family, and that criticism or rejection of cultural phenomena is hurtful to others. Danny knew this intellectually by the age of ten, but his repeated findings never conditioned him to automatically restrain his criticisms or rejections of the habits or ways of others. He would make this blunder constantly; outspokenly, but unintentionally, hurting others with ideas and value judgements which were painful. If someone criticized him or made fun of him, he took it without being threatened, for he had never been conditioned into learning that criticism might be hurtful. He could only think intellectually about what was being said and would not understand its emotional ramifications. Therefore, he was always surprised when a potential friend would suddenly begin to avoid him. It was always a puzzle. He was left with a deep longing for friendships.

Perhaps the greatest difficulty his lack of conditioning presented was that he could not automatically locate and filter out the thoughts which would be taken critically by others. Danny consciously lived, breathed, and rejected the foolishness he perceived in the world around him. He could not be himself, with his real thoughts and feelings, if his "critical" outlook was thwarted. In addition, the effects of conditioning were all too clear to him because of his own immunity to it. This, combined with his lack of fear of being critical or outspoken, made Danny into a rather obnoxious individual. Actually he was a very nice person to get to know. He would desire your company, and would greatly appreciate it, but it was virtually impossible to get close to him. Danny appeared to be too hurtful, too perceptive an individual. He would stimulate too many negative feelings within those who came into contact with him. They would not stick around to discover his true intentions or the real source of their discomfort, which invariably turned out to be their own past conditioning. It was easier for them to find someone else, or flee to the movies, T V , hi-fi, sports or whatever. Even doing homework was often times preferable to being with Danny.

Since Danny had a difficult time satisfying his needs and desires for people, he resourcefully learned to obtain good feelings from the non-people environment. There he had no difficulty. He could love animals and gain their affection without being rejected. He could fill the hours of each day gaining good feelings from the energies and sensations around him. He did not completely depend upon people and their rewards and conditioning to discover gratification . . . or to discover himself. Instead these discoveries came from the physical environment, from nature itself. The rich world of plants, animals, geology, time and motion were the vital substitutes for the stimulation other kids were getting from their culture, from their civilization, and from each other. Danny was in touch with a civilization which was not created by man. Fate gave him little other choice. It was more pleasant and rewarding to watch seals or to feed them fish than to chase after some schoolmate who would be embarrassed if you became excited and wet your pants, even though you were eleven years old. This rarely happened, but when it did, word got around and distances increased. It was fortunate for Danny that his mescaline accident did not happen when he was younger. There's no telling how much loss of bowel and bladder control would now be plaguing him in a society conditioned to shun such accidents.

The list of Danny's trespasses during his days of elementary and junior high school would fill a book. When Ben and I would run into each other or occasionally go fishing together, it would not take much coaxing to get him to talk about what Danny had done most recently. A personal conflict was evident in Ben's tales. He was somewhat critical of the American way of life, our foreign policy and our economics; so he would almost take pride in what he considered to be the maturity or perceptiveness of Danny's observations. On the other hand, he was greatly concerned about Dan's loneliness and his lack of friends. His stories would unveil a mixture of pride and sorrow. One in which Danny, at the age of nine, lost a friend comes to mind:

> Danny, Arty and a friend were sitting over by the sea wall in the rose garden. It was a beautiful day and evidently Bob, their friend, was taken by it.

"It's such a beautiful day today. Nothing like it. I feel great today," Bob said to the twins. "You know, I feel so good and so happy today, that nothing could bother me, nothing."

Perhaps it was a challenge or maybe Bob was just overtaken by the scene down there and how he felt. In any case, Dan said, "I can make you upset."

"No you can't. I feel too good."

"I know I can."

"How?"

"He could kick you," said Arty.

"It wouldn't do any good. I'd ignore it today 'cause I feel so good."

"I can easily make you upset," said Dan.

"Go ahead and try."

"No, cause I know you'll hit me."

"I won't either. Go ahead."

"O K ," said Dan, getting ready to run away, "are you ready?"

"Yep," said Bob, "let me have it."

"I can't do it," said Dan. "I know you'll get mad."

"Go ahead, go ahead. I won't, I promise."

Danny looked at Arty who said, "Here's your chance to do something wrong for a change because you're being asked to do it. He says he won't get mad — why not find out? You do it all the time, anyhow."

"I dunno. Why should I hurt him?"

"Please do try," said Bob. "I really mean it. I feel too good. Nobody can get me mad. Really."

"O K ," said Danny, up and running, "SHIT ON GOD!"

It didn't take a second for the words to sink in when Bob jumped up, madder than blazes, swearing mad, and tried to catch Dan who was way ahead and locked in the house by the time Bob got there.

That afternoon Mrs. Hitch complained to Carol in no uncertain terms that there are some things a child should not be allowed to say, and that she didn't want Bob to play with the twins anymore.

"The thing that . . . amazed Ben . . . and me was that Danny somehow knew exactly where Bob's conditioning lay, exactly what button to push. Arty had known Bob much longer and he had had no idea what was com-

120

ing or what he could actually do to get Bob mad."

Journal entry: June 16, 1973 Whitehorse, Maine. Warm, Overcast.

"Here's an incredible story," said Ben today while we were out in the boat. "Dan was playing baseball during gym. He's not good at it because he keeps losing the purpose of the game. He keeps forgetting he's supposed to be competing, to be trying to win. Anyhow yesterday he got a hit and was passing first base towards second when he screamed, 'Look — an eagle — a bald eagle!' The first baseman looked up to see it just as a throw to first came from the pitcher. The ball went into right field. The team yelled for Dan to run, but he just walked, watching the eagle which was attacking an osprey carrying a fish. Everybody started watching it. The throw came in from right field to second base and continued right on past because the second baseman was watching the eagle. Danny walked past second and was on third before they discovered what had happened, for they were all watching the eagle. They were all mad and Dan said he'd be glad to return to first base if they wanted. There was a big argument about it during which Dan walked back to the plate to get his binoculars which were in his jacket. Since nobody had called time out, it was considered a home run by Dan's team. Then the argument really got going. It was still going as the period ended.

"Later, the boys were discussing it at lunch and Dan infuriated them by asking what difference it made if he scored or didn't score. 'How does it affect anything?" he asked. 'It just seems to me that you're all getting something out of winning or losing. What is it?'

"Nobody could explain it to Dan, he just couldn't feel any better by being a winner, and he said so. 'It all seems like a joke to me,' he said. 'You guys are all really thinking you're big shots. You think that people will like you better if you win. Even if they do like you better because you're a winner, isn't that stupid? What good is winning? What are you winning? Affection or attention from others? Maybe you're just trying to make yourself look big or feel better, but why do you need to be a winner to do that? Does that mean you feel like losers all the time until you win a game? Why do you feel like losers? Is that really what you are?'

"Well, some kids were ready to hang him, others just ignored him, and some agreed with the idea, but said they'd always try to win anyhow. Finally Danny said, 'Being a winner is just a trick you play on yourself to make you and others think you can overpower the environment or make more money, or be self-sufficient. But hell, let's face it, it's a trick. You may win a baseball game but you can't pass math. So what's the good of it, are you really a winner? It's a trick.'

"As I understand it, his friends were not very pleased to hear that, but that's Danny for you. He can see people and relate their actions to the total environment. He can clearly see the environment because most of the time that's all he has. And don't they dislike seeing the games they play! ... They take what Danny says and feel like he's making fun of them — is turning them into losers — as if he had the power to do so. No wonder he has no friends. They experience their feelings and associate them, transfer them, to Danny, the person who's bringing them out. It's a funny thing though, some kids are beginning to listen and understand what he's talking about. Even though he's only thirteen some are actually turning to him for advice, or quoting what he says to others when it suits their cause."

I remember when Ben and Carol came over one evening last year and told me about the party Ann, one of Danny's classmates, was having. Ann said she was going to have a homecoming party at her house for past and present Whitehorse students. She asked if Dan would like to go. Dan's sixteen years old yet nobody's ever asked him to a party or anywhere else. Dan said it was only because they wanted Arty to come that they asked both of them because he was standing there at the time.

Ben had a long talk with him about going, and it wasn't easy. Dan just was thinking it was going to be a waste of time, and people were going to get mad at him so why should he go and spoil their fun.

"What about your fun?" Carol asked, "isn't there any fun in it for you?"

"I don't know. If it's like school, I guess it would be OK. But I don't know what they're going to do, or if I'd like it. I'm strange that way and I know it. So why should

I go?"

"Why not go and find out?" Carol urged. "You can always leave."

"Yeah, I guess that's true."

So he went, maybe because Carol wanted him to go. He and Arty had a long talk about what they were going to wear. Arty was planning to get dressed up a bit, but not Dan!

"Screw it," he said, "if they don't like me the way I am, then why bother trying to make myself look like what I'm not? I'll just end up being me anyhow."

"Yeah, but what is really you?" said Arty. "If you are somebody who wants to appear nice to other people, then you are the person who appears looking nice, right? That's you, isn't it?"

"But what's wrong with me the way I am?"

"I don't know. Nothing, I guess," said Arty, "but are you happy with the kind of friendships you have?"

"I hardly have any."

"Maybe that's because you don't try to please others like you could if you'd a mind to."

"I always felt it was intruding," continued Carol, "when you start asking sixteen year olds 'what happened' and they respond with vague platitudes. Dan just did not want to talk about the party. A few days later I found an article he wrote about it for the school paper. He never submitted it. He just left it lying around. I spoke to him about the article and got his permission to make a few copies. I thought it was important since Dan assured me it was true. Want to read it Wally?"

I sure did, in fact, I duplicated a copy for myself.

"Dr. Gitman, Charlie, do you want to look at it?"

"Sure thing," they replied, almost in unison. Wally gave them each a copy.

THE PARTY
by Dan Miller
"Beware of all enterprises that require new clothes."
— Henry David Thoreau

Last weekend in an effort to overcome my supposed anti-social attitude, I attended my first (now last) party. It's unfortunate that I didn't stick to my immediate impulse of avoiding this gathering; I'd have been a lot better off, but I originally thought that it would be a good proving ground to demonstrate that I, the school freak, was not a total cynic or cop-out nature lover. However, it wasn't a proving ground for me, but more of a disproving ground which I'd like to describe in hope that some individuals may avoid the worthless exposure.

I didn't think I had any strange ideas of what this party or any party would be like. I thought I'd get a chance for some conversation, refreshments, maybe just an interesting evening is all I hoped for. I didn't feel I had an innocent image of these gatherings, yet, after my peek into a party, I've realized how innocent my preconceived view really was. I could not have imagined the situation, even if I entertained the most bizarre thoughts.

The evening started out on a high note. And I knew my preconceived image was quite inappropriate when they charged a dollar for beer at the door. After insisting for five minutes that I didn't drink, and still getting nowhere, my brother paid the buck and shoved me through so we'd "avoid any argument."

When we stepped in, I was hit by the blare of intensified electric noise (music), the pungent smell of spilled beers and clouds of cigarette smoke, accented, of course, with marijuana.

With all that it was hard to walk any further in, and I felt like running out. But this was new to me, very, very new and worth examining. I thought so; I stepped in.

I waded through the crowds of people, each crutching — I mean clutching their beer or joint in one hand and their cigarette in the other — and I found myself a spot in the corner where half empty beers and overflowing ashtrays piled over me.

This was quite a circus in front of me I remarked to myself. I couldn't help but feel that I was an anthropologist observing a little-known cultural ritual because it was so alien to me.

However, as I looked around, I spied my classmates intermingled in the crowd. They were no different than the others; they were wasted, costumed, and into it. Mike, my old lab partner, was right in the middle of the floor, lying flat out with the headphones on full blast. No one moved him, they just walked over him, as if he was a dog.

At least half of my class was there (physically) though they weren't in their regular clothes. Oh, no, I couldn't even recognize some of them in their new outfits. I was one of few people there graced in the regulars — jeans and a T-shirt. I thought it was ridiculous for Arty to try to convince me to go scurrying through the dark corners of my closet to find another piece to add to my outfit or more appropriately, my costume. I didn't paint my face to look older (?), prettier (?). Hell no, I only do those things when it's Halloween, but by the looks of these mannequins, it's Halloween every weekend.

It was a sad sight, the girls had enough shades of colors to paint the most brilliant landscapes of Maine, the guys had combined every shade of corduroys ever sold — everyone was spotless — there wasn't enough dirt to home a blade of grass, it was a sterilized scenario, a ludicrous facade.

One kid told me he spent $40 on his suede boots, "And they're for parties only." My brother's friend paid his sister to iron his non-permanent press shirt and to wash his flares so he'd have "a girl-catching outfit." Good old 'Susy C. Plastic' must have taken hours to paste on her eyelashes and I bet you 'Ann Knotme' had washed her hair at least three times that day and changed her clothes even more. All for the sake of falsifying their image so they could attract boys.

Half the girls there were sitting on the edge of their seats, staring red-eyed at the bearded college seniors. The only thing to keep them from ripping a poor guy's pants off was that they were too drunk. They had that grungy smell of puke radiating from them which kept everyone at bay.

There were quite a number of fellow classmates there, my age or younger, who just stumbled around the room aimlessly, colliding with any stable object which would just send them on a new course. It must have been their first party also, by the looks of how drunk they got themselves. Either that, or they enjoyed bruising their heads on corners constantly.

I decided to get out of my secluded observation point and to explore this ritual gathering. I ventured into the living room, which was then designated as the smoking room. There sat a group of at least twenty people, all cross-legged in their costumes. There were about five pipes of dope circling the group — it was a smoke-in. Everyone would contribute what they could out of their sacred cellophane stash bags to "keep the bowls going." It was a hilarious spoof on the old peace pipe gatherings of the Indians. I mused to myself that there sat before me a perfect picture of your "ozoned," materialistic, 20th century Indians.

I went to the bathroom, expecting to be alone. I found myself company in the form of a class president (I won't mention any names). He couldn't speak for himself, for he was passed out in the bathtub, with his dinner remains smeared all over him. Pleasant Pres I named him right there.

Well, as the night rolled on, I continued my anthropological observations. I turned to vocal participation; I decided to ask my fellow (cl)assmates why they insisted on doing this.

One guy, who I didn't know, burped out that "It's fun," and he took hold of his beer and chugged it down, only to gag on a cigarette butt someone had extinguished in his bottle.

"Fun," I sarcastically questioned him, as I moved on. Most people I spoke with were so out of it that they couldn't even tell me why they party. They'd just stumble back, offer me a joint or would chug another beer. Others just remarked that I sounded like their folks and I should fuck off.

No one could sensibly tell me why they partied:

"Oh, it's fun," (wasting my time with a bunch of no minds).

"It's a way to meet people," (when they're unconscious).

"Something to do," (I have nothing better to do, I feel so low about my possibilities).

"A good place to get a girl," (sure is, they're so drunk, they won't know what they're doing. Neither will you . . . Abortion #34615).

"Everyone else does," (Yeah, why not? Everyone's jumping off skyscrapers. Let's go).

They all were pitiful responses — because it was a pitiful thing. There is *no* sensible answer, because it's *not* a sensible thing.

Halfway through the night, as if to really demonstrate the effects of parties on individuals, a frightening situation exploded. I was totally unaware of LSD or acid, but I quickly realized its power and potential for damage.

The ordeal involved a girl who I later learned was given a "hit" of acid without her knowing it. People (?) thought that was funny, even entertaining, and some thought she deserved it because she didn't get high. Sick? I think so; it was the icing on the cake. These asses who play with people's minds, I'd kill the bastards if they did it to me. It could change your whole personality, it's mind altering. Maybe I'd be like them if I was drugged. Maybe they were all drugged or maybe I was. I'm the school freak, right? And we all know why, right? Anyway, the whole situation is worth full coverage; a sad but true demonstration of the dementing powers of partying.

I was sitting on the stairs, viewing the whole party of no-minds, the music was blaring and the smoke bellowing. It was quite a circus. Suddenly, this "hit" girl jerked into the room. I could tell at a glance that this girl was far from any normal condition – even semi-normal. She gazed around the room slowly looking as if she was peering through each person. She'd cock her head and start following something, then she'd stop and reverse her direction. It was obvious that she was watching something – but it was invisible to me.

Her attention switched to her own body. She limply flung her arms out, watching them as if they were totally unfamiliar or unattached. She'd examine them intensely, peering ghoulishly at each pore, then for no reason, she would fling her arms out and watch the after effects, which clearly weren't visible to me.

A guy approached her, speaking in a mystical tone, "Trails, do you see the trails?" He waved his arms around as if producing a lingering design for the girl's amazement.

It wasn't long until others joined into the "fun" of teasing this tripped-out girl.

"Are you tripping?" said one guy spookishly, as he opened and closed his hands quickly in front of her eyes. Others poked away at her, pulled on her pants or pinched her breasts when she was distracted by someone else's stimulant. She'd jolt around, trying to catch the prodder, but she never could – much to the poker's enjoyment.

Her eyes began to search for a way out of the crowd, but she was surrounded. She started to tremble, the teasing (torturing) was too much. She let out a hideous scream and fell to the floor limply. Not many heard the scream because of the music, but mostly because of their condition. Those who did just glanced over their shoulder to see the familiar sight of a passed-out partier. It was nothing new, nothing to worry about.

The girl started to roll in place, she heaved and twisted, cocking her head from side to side. She looked like a poisoned rat in convulsions. Sweat poured from her, her clothes were sopped, her eyes bulged, her body shook. No one did anything. The circle of morbid observers just watched, smirking, glaze-eyed at the spectacle beneath them. It was a sickening sight, one which I couldn't stand.

Just then, as if to add to the whole sickness of the situation, a new album was put on and ironically, the lyrics, "Get High, Everybody, Get High" pulsated out. People began to jump for joy in affirmation of getting high. Joints were lit, beers opened, both were held high in the air as if to salute their actions. This was their anthem, "Get High, Everybody, Get High." The words belted out and the crowd recognized it.

It was too much; the girl was still freaking out, to the enjoyment of her sick onlookers. The whole situation had become too bizarre, it was no longer an anthropological observance. It had gone too far. People were too out of it. They needed a very, very cold slap, a breeze of reality. They needed a goddamned gale of common sense.

Obviously, nothing was going to change unless I acted. I decided to take revenge for the sake of this poor deranged girl who, because of "Getting High was for Everyone" was now rolling on the floor. I had plenty of ammunition surrounding me, at least 10 half-empty beer bottles. With my bird's eye view, I let them fling. The bottles ricocheted against the walls like hockey pucks, only to smash at the opposing wall, showering glass and stale beer down on the fools below — 1, 2, 3, 4, 5 — bottles were bursting all over and it wasn't long until I had everybody looking my way. Ah, but there still was music. That God-forsaked anthem "Get High Ever- - - - - - - "scrrchhh I landed a bottle right on the record player, and smashed the album to bits, thank God!

The room was dead silent, all eyes fixed on me, the school freak. The jibberish of the girl was the only sound, a grim reminder of the glazed-eyed group assembled in front of me.

Immediately, before anyone could utter a word, I yelled out for someone to call an ambulance for the girl — and some did.

The owner of the now destroyed stereo started to curse at me, but I quickly silenced him by threatening to smash more if he wouldn't shut up. I had a few things to say, I told him and everyone. And I didn't want to be interrupted. They thought I was nuts — mentally insane and God knows what they thought I'd do. My brother just stared at me, mouth open, unable to utter a word. Suddenly, a feeling of total disgust swept through me, and in the midst of dead silence, I walked out the door.

If this is your social event — your activity to prove that you are not anti-social — well, I'd rather be a hermit, solely conversing with slugs because it would be far more stimulating, sane and healthy."

Dan "the Freak" Miller

XII

There are not many creatures who delight in living in the soft oozy mud of the mile long flats. Some have adapted by being able to hold oxygen for long periods of time. I often thought that all these animals had it easy. They would just lie there and the ocean would bring them their food and then remove their garbage as well. I wondered if they were bored, or if they had something to look forward to. Did the tide differ so that one day it might bring ice cream and the next day spinach?

From a composition by Dan Miller, age 16.

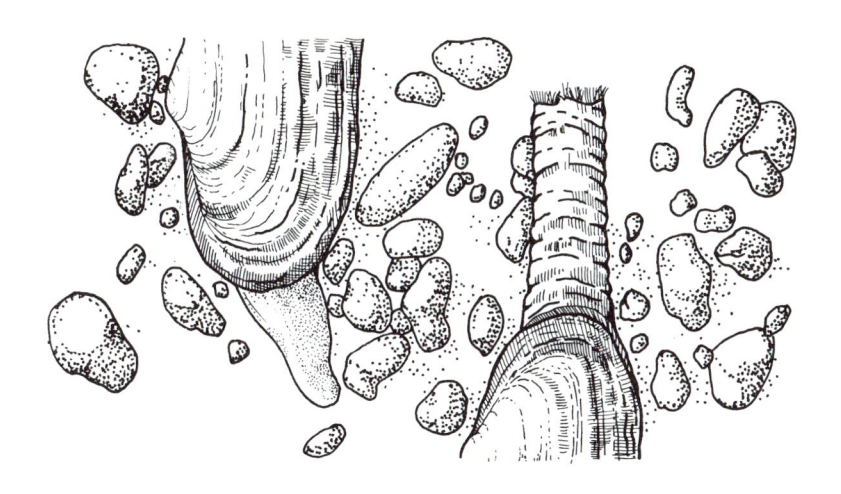

From *The Downeast Gazette,* February 11, 1976
Take your pet dog or cat. If you have none, then use your mother or son. Pour oil on their food for a week and make them eat it or starve. Pour oil on their hair, skin, in their eyes, ears. Force their heads in a bucket of it for days at a time. I refute those who say this is an unfair example to use. Just because we are not sensitive to the plight of wildlife caught in oil spills does not mean what I'm describing does not take place. Have you ever worked with animals after an oil spill?

Dr. Robert Davis, Biologist
Wildlife Study Federation

Dan's unsubmitted editorial just about left Dr. Gitman aghast. "Wally, do you believe that this all really happened?" he sighed remorsefully. "Did you ever check it out to see if it was true?"

"No," replied Wally. "Like I've said, I'd had very little contact with Dan since he was a little kid. But to be honest with you Dr. Gitman, I do believe the story. Frankly, it's almost mild compared to some others I've heard which I know are true. It makes me sick to my stomach to think of what kids grow up with nowadays. I've only had contact with Dan since last February when Ben sent him over to talk to me about an incident which took place with some girl."

"Does Dan have a girlfriend?" asked Dr. Gitman quite surprised.

"Not a chance," said Wally with a shake of his head. "He doesn't have any friends from what I can gather."

Suddenly Sarah started to cry. There seemed to be no apparent reason, nothing had changed to suddenly make her upset. For awhile she would not, and could not, say anything. Wally just sat there unable to do anything, tearfully and helplessly watching Sarah. Dr. Gitman became uncomfortable and thought perhaps he ought to leave. Wally pleaded with him to stay. The sobbing was the only sound in the office. Finally it lessened, then ceased. Sarah blew her nose, wiped her tears and apologized. "I'm sorry. It just got to me, Dan having no friends and all, no matter how he tries. It his me so hard because I feel exactly the same way right now." She started sobbing again, "All we've tried to do is to put together a school where people and the environment can support each other. What's wrong with that? But now that the impact of what's happening is first beginning to really hit home, it's overwhelmed me. I must be feeling exactly how Dan feels, how he felt last February when he came over to talk to Wally. Oh, what could Wally or I do other than try to offer whatever help we could. I can see now that we did counsel him, we did give him advice even though he is under Dr. Sullivan's medical treatment. I'm finally beginning to realize on a feeling level why Dr. Sullivan is making an issue out of this. He must see our concern for Dan as being a way for Dan to escape from him. He must feel unsuccessful and threatened by his lack of success especially since he knows he's being judged for an important position. I'm beginning to think Dr. Sullivan can only make himself look good by making us look bad. He's going to try anything to stop us and he has the law on his side. Dr. Gitman, I'm so afraid that by telling you we encouraged Dan to come on the school we'll be doing ourselves harm." Tears began flowing from Sarah's eyes again, "At the same time I'm so positive that the school will help Dan and so many other kids that I'm compelled to talk about what happened, how it happened, why it happened. It just all caught up with me at once."

"What did happen?" questioned Charlie. "Do you think you can tell us?"

"I'll try," sobbed Sarah. "It had to do with a girl named Gail Rogers.

"Gail was one of few who would have much of anything to do with Danny. She was somehow able to not be completely repulsed by Danny's questions and comments. There was a sadness in her which somehow recognized a sadness in Dan's situation. While others often ran in embarrassment, laughter or fear, Gail recognized how that would hurt. Her good Christian attitude kept her from running away from Dan quite so quickly.

"The day that Dan walked into class with his fly open for the umpteenth time was not a very pleasant one. It was the eleventh grade math class. At first, nobody said anything, but soon the snickers started, and while some were sharing secretive smiles with each other, others could not refrain from laughing outright. As it began to crescendo, Gail yelled, 'Why don't you all shut up!' then walked over and whispered to Dan, who began to button his fly.

"Dan liked Gail because she did not find him obnoxious. He decided that he might get to know her better if he spent some time with her. He bluntly asked her how that would be possible. She was quite taken aback with the forwardness of the question, especially since it was asked out loud in front of everybody during a social studies discussion. Gail was interested in Dan, but not *that* interested. She suggested that since she spent a great portion of her time at the Christian Fellowship Club of her church, maybe he should come to some of the meetings there. It was Dan's first encounter with Christianity and the Bible. Ben and Carol had long before decided to let religion take its natural course, if it had one."

> Dan was a bit suspicious when he walked in through the church portals with a cross on each door. He knew he was entering foreign soil and, although suspicion filled his mind, he looked forward to seeing Gail, and what might take place. Although everyone was neatly dressed and there was a party atmosphere in the room, it was a different kind of party than before. A record player was turning out some music, and a few kids were dancing. Others were gathered around refreshments, talking. Gail greeted Dan with a smile, said hello, and shook his hand, then said, "Hey, everybody, I want you to meet Dan."

It was all smiles, kids coming over to shake Dan's hand as if to congratulate him on somehow arriving in this situation. Dan couldn't understand it. They were all so damned friendly, so welcoming. There were many of the same kids who would have nothing to do with Dan at school. Some had been at the party.

"What the hell is going on?" he wondered.

Then the minister came over and shook his hand, patted him on the back and welcomed him. By this time, Dan was sure that a rumor had gone around that he had inherited a million dollars and was giving it away. He thought to himself: I may need that much to pay the medical expenses incurred to repair my hand — it's just about been shaken off, then pausing: hey, I didn't say that out loud. Good move Dan. Maybe you're learning something.

After a while, the minister sat down and the kids arranged themselves in a discussion circle. Dan sat down next to Gail. The minister began the discussion: "I thought this evening that we might share our ideas about the Godlessness, the immorality we see all around us."

"Oh brother," thought Dan, as he glanced at the kids who had been at the party.

"That's a good subject since we know that God does not approve of it, yet it's close by," Gail agreed.

You don't know how close, thought Dan looking two seats to his left. "It is an appropriate subject," he said out loud, "especially since the town has put a 9:15 p.m. curfew on people under 18 years old — too much vandalism."

It was quiet for awhile. People were thinking. A thought crossed Dan's mind which seemed exciting and interesting — it carried him in its flow — and the words came tumbling out.

"How do you all know the god which wants things to be moral is your god? There are gods of other peoples who see morality differently than we see it like the Indians across the bay. In some religions, like the Aztecs, it was moral and right to kill people, to make human sacrifices. Maybe you guys know which god to worship, but I've never been here before." It was an honest question, and its honesty cut through.

The minister responded, "We know that because the Bible tells us so. The first great commandment God gave to Moses was 'Thou shalt have no other Gods before me!'"

"It sounds like you need training to know your god and what he wants you to do. How does he train you to know him and his desires?"

"He has given us the Bible," said Gail with conviction, "and it contains answers to all our questions."

"It also sets down the rules of morality, especially in the commandments. God makes the whole world work in his infinite wisdom," said the minister conclusively.

"I thought nature did that?" asked Dan, earnestly. "Is god nature?"

"God must have made nature. Genesis in the Bible describes the process. You should read it," suggested one of the students.

"I'd really like to. Do you have a bible handy?" asked Dan.

"Seek ye the truth for the truth shall make you free," said the minister giving Dan the Bible.

Dan began reading, while the meeting was going on. About ten minutes later, he let out a whistle of concern while he was reading, right in the middle of the meeting. Then he said "Wow!" a couple of times, then, "This is unbelievable." By that time, the meeting had stopped. All eyes were on Dan, inquisitively, wondering what was so exciting about what he was reading — somehow the Bible had never seemed exciting. This was something entirely new. Maybe he had found something sexy.

Unaware that all eyes and ears were on him, Dan muttered out loud, "Jesus Christ, this is a load of shit."

"What's goin' on Dan?" interrupted Gail quickly, while the others gasped. "What did you find?"

"This is unbelievable," explained Dan, "Unbelievable."

"What?"

"What it says here about the origin of the earth. It says god made everything. He made people in the image of him. I guess he is like us or vice versa. Then it says here 'God blessed them and God said to them be fruitful

133

and multiply, and replenish the earth and *subdue it*, and *have dominion over* every living thing that moveth upon the earth.' He put *man* in charge of *nature?*"exclaimed Dan in disbelief. "He told man to subdue nature? Hey, that can't be, can it? How can man live if he subdues nature? That's not the way the world works, is it? What's going on? And it never says what god is — just what he does — and he seems to do exactly the same things as nature does. Is god nature?"

"God is the guiding light of the universe."

"And are we like him?"

"Yes."

"That's really saying that the universe is run by a power which is like us. It sounds like we run the universe, that we've made god in our likeness instead of him making us in his likeness. That sounds more like it. That would explain why we say god told us to subdue nature. God is just our egotistical image of our own fear of nature. It sounds to me like he's been created by us to explain or give power to our own man-made rules and stupidity, when it comes to our relationship with nature. God is just a glorification of ourselves and our hang-ups. How can we obey his commandments if we've created him to create them? We're really just obeying our own man-made rules and rationalizing them by saying they come from god. It's a trick we play on ourselves."

"I'm lost," interrupted Bernard. "Let's talk about morality."

"How can you?" asked Dan. "How can you if god's commandments are actually man-made. What's to discuss? It's just 'business as usual'. No wonder nobody respects the commandments in the middle of the week. They don't respect them deep inside 'cause they know they're made and enforced by people. And I must honestly say that I don't have that much respect for people. They've not thought much of me. None of you have at school. You see and treat me like a freak, not a person."

"But we invited you here," Gail.

"I'm beginning to realize that all your welcoming and handshaking here have been to get me to obey man-made rules. That's why there's refreshments and music and fun and both peer and parental acceptance for being here. Those are rewards for coming, to unconsciously make us have good feelings and associations about obeying restrictive laws which are basically man-made. The laws are dressed up to look like they come from god. You know, it strikes me that if god is merely an image of man, then nature is actually god — the real God. Nature is the guiding power from outside and within. Nature seems to meet all the requirements and definitions of God. God is not a man. God is an all-encompassing process called nature. While I was reading I rewrote the bible, substituting the word 'Nature' for the word 'God' to see how it reads. Here, let me read this page that way:

" '*Nature* formed man of the dust of the ground and breathed into his nostrils, the breath of life, and man became a living soul.' That sounds right to me," said Dan. "The next passage works that way too, listen. 'And *nature* planted a garden eastward in Eden and there she put the man whom she had formed'. For Christ sake, those woman-libbers are right about one thing. God is a woman — Mother Nature, from whom all blessings flow."

Gail was flushed — really angry. "Dan, you know you came to visit here and you've embarrassed me beyond belief. I can't believe it! You haven't joined us here, you've taken over. You're preaching some other religion. But we're here to learn our religion, no matter how foolish that seems to you."

"But what you're learning doesn't seem right. It doesn't make sense. The next thing you're going to tell me is that it was OK for all those holy people — those missionaries — to kill and enslave Indians in the southwest because the Indians believed something else. Indians didn't believe this bible so they were killed — even though the bible says not to kill. A few people here are as immoral as hell during the week and come here to learn morality from a god which ..."

"I've heard enough," declared Gail. "If you don't like what we do here, maybe you should leave."

"Aren't you even interested in finding the truth?" asked Dan excitedly. "You said, 'Seek ye the truth for the truth shall set you free'. That's it. You don't want to be free. You want to continue to believe something which may not be true just so you can have refreshments and approval from ... Aw, forget it ... I'm goin' to take off. Thanks for putting up with me — and remember — God is a woman — a process ..." and he walked out.

Sarah turned to Wally and said, "You tell them what happened then."

"We had come home for February vacation, we'd been at the farm less than a day when the phone rang. It was Dan and he was as excited as hell."

"Hey, Wally, can I come over to see you — right now. I want to talk with you."

Dan came over all bubbling with frustration. He explained what had happened at church. Ben had told him he might want to talk to me. Dan wanted to know if I thought God could be a woman — a process called Mother Nature.

I told him that I thought the concept of God was probably a conditioned feeling from helpless childhood dependence upon parents. Parents appear to be gods to a child. The unconscious conditioned childhood need for a life sustaining God plus a social environment which encourages and rewards belief in God will make God appear to be real — even if God doesn't exist.

"I've never heard 'Mother Nature is God' but I might believe it, I guess. It seems realistic. I never was one much for religion."

"OK, well, let me ask you this, Wally: Why does the bible say that man should subdue nature?"

I hesitated. I wasn't sure I wanted to get involved but my own teaching and explaining disease took over even though Dan was practically a stranger to me.

"I think that man is afraid of nature because he carries around deep fears of the discomfort of living in the natural world, people hate nature and fight nature, only because they're acting out their fears against *her*. People are afraid to experience the feelings of cold, wetness, suffocation, hunger, death or sex, whichever they carry around inside them. That's what I think.

That's why I live as close as I can to nature. I let myself experience the actual elements, the real thing. That way I'm constantly reminded not to be afraid for there is little to fear, especially today, where nature is no more than a sorrowful, beaten, helpless polluted shadow of her former self. Anyhow Dan, the Bible really doesn't say that God told us to subdue nature. God may have said that to Adam and Eve, but they and all their descendants were drowned in the flood. According to the Bible, Noah and his family created the rest of us, right?"

I took the Bible off the bookshelf. 'OK, at that point, what were God's instructions to Noah in Genesis 9:1? That's what counts. That's what affects us. God said to us: 'Be fruitful and multiply and replenish the earth.' In this section God does not say subdue the earth! It would seem that 'God' learned a lesson from the first experiment in the Garden of Eden. Man subduing the earth evidently didn't work out, if you believe all these Bible tales. They're nice mythology, but are they accurate?

"You know, Dan, I think you can find just about anything you want to hear in the Bible if you look for it. Read what God says to Him / Her self in Genesis 8:21 when Noah opened up the ark after the flood."

Dan picked up my Bible and read, "The Lord said in his heart, I will not again curse the ground any more for man's sake; for the imagination of man's heart is evil from his youth."

"Now there," I said, "that's my favorite part right there because it describes exactly what I was saying before about man carrying imaginary 'evil' feelings in him which came along with his mentally internalized symbols of nature. Genesis 6:5 states this also."

"Do you think the Bible is the word of God?" asked Dan.

"I guess I think most of the Bible is man-made, man-created, man-interpreted," I replied. "I doubt we hear heavenly words at all. I think the Bible and 'God' are man's attempt through the ages to deal with the 'evil' feelings, the painful feelings he has inadvertently, unconsciously placed in his head from nature. The only part of the Bible I believe to be realistic is Ecclesiastes 1:2 and Chapter 3, especially if God is Mother Nature.

Ecclesiastes 3:18 and 19 are especially interesting. Ecclesiastes 3:18 states, 'I said in mine heart concerning the estate of the sons of man, that God might manifest them, and that they might see that *they themselves are beasts.*' Ecclesiastes 3:19: 'For that which befalleth the sons of man befalleth beasts; even as the one dieth so dieth the other; yea, *they have all one breath;* so that man hath no pre-eminence above a beast: for all is vanity.'

"How we unconsciously hate nature and the thought that we are but beasts subject to her whims. How we avoid Ecclesiastes and instead are conditioned to repeat, 'God made man in his own image.'"

We both sat quietly lost in our thoughts. Dan finally broke the silence, "Wally, I want to ask you something very serious."

"Yes?"

"Listen, Wally, I don't think I want to live with people anymore — at least not the way things are going around here. I've got to do something to be more tolerant of people. But I can't do it here. I keep screwing up!" he exclaimed as tears began running down his cheek. "Wally, maybe I could learn to get along with people if they weren't so rotten — so hurtful — so impatient. I desperately need another place — one where people are not that way, a place to learn in. Can I go on your school? Wally, please? Anything is better than continuing to be the town jackass. Maybe I can learn something by seeing how the rest of the country works. Maybe I can find a happier situation for myself, or can build one here if I can learn how. Please, Wally. Otherwise, I've had it."

"Perhaps you have. Talk about it with your dad and mom. We can get together next time I'm home."

"I want to go now. I just can't stay here anymore. Nothing works out."

"Why do you think that happens?"

"Because I'm so different."

"What's so different about you?"

"I'm not sure. Nobody seems to know. Dad told me you thought it might have something to do with my not being able to be conditioned. That makes me different."

"I don't quite see how that's affecting you in the situations you've been talking about. You obviously have different outlooks and are a threat to other people, but you also have many things that you enjoy, such as nature."

"I don't have any friends."

"Yes, but why?"

"I'm obnoxious."

"Nonsense."

"To them I am!"

"Not always, as I understand the situation."

"Yes, but in the long run I turn people off."

"Perhaps that's due to your conditioning."

"What? I am really surprised to hear you, of all people, say that. You're the person who thinks I can't be conditioned. I'm really confused. How could you possibly think my conditioning is the problem?"

"Well, as you describe them, the situations strike me that way. I think you walk out of situations — out of the church group, out of the party — because they strike you as being stupid and you're disruptive in them. Perhaps certain situations are stupid, but I'm not sure they're unworthwhile unless you make them that way. They all involve people. If you want people as friends you'll either have to be very selective as to who you'll be friends with, or not let your conditioning overwhelm you when you're with people as they really are ... or both."

"There you go with conditioning again. Could you explain where my conditioning enters into these situations?"

"It seems to me that you were conditioned just like everyone else for the first 3½ years of your life. You were conditioned to wanting acceptance, warmth and love from people. People satisfied all your desires, provided you with everything you needed to survive. You became dependent upon people just as all of us have. You were toilet trained, that's conditioned. You learned to eat with utensils, that's conditioned. Your desire to have friends could be a result of conditioning. My guess would be that you would have little use for people friends if you had been raised by a wolf. You might crave for wolf friends instead."

"That's the problem," Dan sobbed, "people shun me.

Yes, perhaps the feeling of wanting friends is conditioned, but so what! I still feel that way, but I don't have friends. I'm too different from others."

"Do you want to know what I think, Dan?"

"What?"

"I don't think your desire to obtain friendship is much different than anybody else's. It's probably not as important to you as it is to others, because you don't appear to me to be nearly as dependent as some kids are for the good feelings of others. You have awareness and relationships within the natural environment that others can't even see due to *their* conditioning. Emotionally they don't even know that there is an environment.

"I may be very wrong but it seems to me that what's happening to you is that your conditioned desire for friends is, after a while, overwhelmed by your conditioned need for a sane, warm, supportive environment. You seem to be able to see the environment more clearly than others because you have not been as conditioned as far away from it as others have. You seem to know that in the long run it's your best friend; your real-life support *is* your environment. So when it comes to a conflict between people and a sane social and natural environment you simply choose the latter because you have no other choice."

"But at times it's upsetting, sometimes I'm really lonely," he paused thoughtfully, "and lots of times I'm not," he said, suddenly smiling.

"Perhaps, the upsetting feeling is the conditioned feeling of rejection being a punishment. Like your mom being upset with you if you did something wrong at age three. Her rejection of you then was a form of punishment. The source of your life — food, warmth, people was being taken away. That's a punishment, so is a spanking. Through conditioning, rejection can be felt as punishment."

"That rarely happens," said Dan, "but you're right. It could be happening now."

"Well," I continued, "I think the school might really help you. You could learn to feel comfortable by staying in conflict situations like the party or the church group and not let the stress or the people in them overwhelm you. With additional contact and communication I strongly feel that kids could learn to respect and like you. I know this is humanly possible because that's how I feel about you — so do your mom and dad.

"But you're all my immediate family, or practically."

"What does that really mean?" I asked.

"Well you *have* to like me — you really know me, you've become accustomed to me, I mean, I'm not evil."

"Dan, there's another way of saying that. We've become conditioned to you — and we experience our conditioning as both understanding of you and love for you. Perhaps if you put more effort into people situations which seem worthwhile to *you* maybe others will get to know you as we do. They'll be fond of you because your intentions are worthwhile and beneficial to both them and you. That's precisely the same conflict that each of us as individuals have to face — our conditioning. It shows up in different ways, but the process of relating to it and others is something I think we all have in common. To me that makes you the same as everybody else — not different. You've just not yet learned how to relate and deal with your own conditioning. How is that different from anybody else? I think you may be correct in assuming that the school will help you with that problem. It has to because without good relationships the expedition community can't exist. It practically demands them — that's one reason that students choose to come along. Why don't you read our book, *The Trailside Classroom*, and let me know if the school is something you really want to do. I think you'll be able to see that for you the school will actually start with the problem of leaving Ann's party out of disgust, or the church group out of frustration. You'll have to decide if you want to face those conditioned feelings along with others who are facing theirs. It's your choice."

"What was the outcome of your talk with Dan?" asked Dr. Gitman.

"He's coming on the school with us this year. So is his brother Arty," Wally answered. "I think that's why Dr. Sullivan is giving us so much flack."

"I'm inclined to agree," returned Dr. Gitman, "He's doing it through the Department of Education. I might be able to talk to some people I know there, especially about this truancy allegation. I'll have to know about your certification. What subjects do you teach, and how are the courses taught? Do you have classes scheduled or what?"

Sarah responded, "We only offer one course and I guess that would be called 'Human Ecology'. The expedition, its adventures, problems and mishaps are what we study. Our curriculum consists of studying ourselves trying to live sensibly with each other and varying environments and situations. We don't dissect the environment into isolated areas commonly known as 'subjects.' We find it's a great mistake to do so. Some of the 'subjects' often offered at a regular school don't even exist in the natural environment, like 'philosophy' or 'theology.'

"We've discovered that the environment is a completely integrated entity. To dissect it into courses is to deny its integrity. I find this dissection misleads and confuses the student. It forces him to see the world through his own special area of knowledge and he never comes into direct contact with the environment itself — an entity much more powerful and important than math, chemistry or history. All subject matter is merely a part of life. What we study is really ourselves and our lives in our environment, and that takes in everything. We don't become separate objects or little cubbyholes of knowledge which sometimes are not relevant.

"Well," acknowledged Dr. Gitman, "that certainly is different than the schools I've attended . . . but I can see where your approach is practical. You know, the thing that always got to me at school is that the academics seldom were useful, seldom affected behavior. Mostly intellectual, dry knowledge and facts were presented and these often overlooked the cultural and emotional forces controlling how you think and feel. And one never did get the impression that everything was all tied together. Some of my classmates right now are so into engineering that they're totally blind to the environmental impact of what they are creating. They're earning salaries for planning an oil refinery on America's last wild coast. That's their own, and everything else's demise. The same thing happened to me, too. I am practicing psychiatry, but have no training in many areas which directly affect mental health — like conditioning, nutrition, recreation . . . so I know what you're talking about."

"On the other hand," interjected Sarah, "the end product comes around to being that the same worthwhile and necessary information is put across. It's hung upon a different tree, an important tree, the individual. An archaeological dig, for example, is a group coordinated effort which 'coursewise' involves social studies, math, geology, history, anthropology, ecology, physical effort and education, group dynamics, reading, writing, critical thinking, research, communication, instruction ... But what fun, what excitement! Who can forget discovering an ancient burial or cooking area intact with tools, pots, firepits, grinding bins and the like? And then visiting the descendants of the ancient people who are today living in similar fashion. Subjects and courses come alive. You live them. They're your environment. Even traditional schools recognize the effectiveness of our environmental approach for we're fully accredited on a high school and college level."

"Have you ever done any studies to determine the school's effect on a student's S.A.T. scores?"

"It's probably impossible. Why do you ask?"

"Because nationally S.A.T. scores are steadily going down and no one really knows why. It's very surprising because school systems have made tremendous plant improvements and raised teacher salaries immensely."

"Low scores are no surprise to me! Money and material goods alone can't supply what young people need. Kids today are overwhelmed by the interpersonal vacuum into which they are born. They can't locate themselves or others. Technology caters to their every need. Their childhood conditioning leads them to a dead end by the time they reach adolescence. Modern kids are out of contact with nature. They have substituted drugs, alcohol, competition and depression for 'life.' Their limited interactions demand a limited use of the language. The language they do use is heavily slang. I'll bet if modern slang words appeared on the S.A.T.'s the scores would go right up."

"Why haven't you tested your students to measure their improvement?"

"There'd be no control. The few who have taken the S.A.T.'s the second time have gone up in English but it could be due to their familiarity with the test. We have, however, received markedly improved attitude and 'maturity' change feedback in a questionnaire we once had sent out."

"What happens to your students after they finish the expedition year with you?"

"That varies with each student. They are all stronger, more worldly, all able to cope with academic and social life more adequately. They are very environmentally aware. But they still carry around with them their childhood conditioning and its effects. When, at times, they can't find situations or build relationships which avoid discomforting or destructive stimuli, they are temporarily subject to the detrimental effects of these stimuli. It is no easy task for a young person to avoid or control such stimuli for they are pervasive in our society. We are immersed in stimuli which tell us to consume, be dependent, tranquilize feelings, compete, escape and exploit people as well as nature. It takes a long time to fully mature.

"How do your students do in traditional school settings?"

"Much better than they did before participating in the expedition. That we definitely have observed. But frankly, I'm not sure I'd want to subject myself, or anybody, to the environment of a typical college dormitory in order to obtain an education. I just might be doing myself more harm than good. I only wish there was some way to make our expedition environment available as a full secondary school and college program."

"Well, I think I've heard and seen enough at this point to produce a preliminary report. I'll get back to you if I need any further information."

It was early evening when the meeting finally ended. Wally and Sarah didn't hear a word from Charlie for three days. The telephone finally rang.

"Wally, I have some good news. The state has agreed to drop the whole thing, at least for the time being."

Wally was overjoyed. "That's great! How did you ever do it?"

"I went to see Dr. Sullivan, and I forced a few questions on him. I asked Sullivan specifically what diagnosis he thought you had made."

"He's told the family that Dan's problems are due to 'immunity to conditioning'," Sullivan answered.

"Have you any evidence whatsoever that this alleged diagnosis is incorrect? Is there any shred of evidence that Dan has been able to be conditioned?"

"No," admitted Dr. Sullivan. "We don't even have any tests for that situation, and Dan won't concentrate enough to let us try to condition him."

"Why are there no tests?"

"Because nobody has ever even heard of this disease for which the Bryce's are offering treatment. It's a product of their imagination. Believing it has led to Dan attending Mr. Bryce's expedition school. Dan will be deprived of qualified treatment for retardation and emotional disorders."

Charlie responded "Dr. Sullivan, this is all quite questionable to my way of thinking. I am going to ask the court for a stay on this matter. This is an infringement of my client's civil rights to pursue an occupation of his choice and design. You are going to have to prove beyond a reasonable doubt that: first, Dan can be conditioned and therefore the Millers are being misled, and secondly, that immunity to conditioning is actually a medical disorder. How can you accuse my client of illegally practicing medicine if he has not treated or diagnosed a recognized medical disorder, disease or symptom? Frankly, you may look rather strange if I bring this matter to the courts. I don't see how you can prove your case. I don't believe you can.

"I suggest that if there is any way you can get the Attorney General to rescind the subpoena you should take the initiative and do it within the next forty-eight hours. You may save my client some money and your reputation as well. Wally and Sarah may be operating in a fantasy. That's their legal privilege. But I don't see how you can legally justify entering their alleged fantasy world and declare part of it illegal. Unless you consider withdrawing your case, or present us with a documented piece of evidence that Dan can and has been conditioned, and that this is a legitimate medical problem, I am going to be forced to initiate a countersuit against you personally as well as against the state."

"I then went with Dr. Gitman to speak with several state legal advisors and even to the Attorney General. I guess that's what led to this postponement, permanent or not.

"There's one thing I must warn you about Wally. You should be very aware that this could be a medical issue. You should use *all* possible discretion when talking about Danny's disorder or counseling him. Be careful. This whole matter can easily be reactivated and another hearing scheduled! Got it?"

Thus the expedition started in mid-September free of any immediate legal entanglements; free, that is, until that fateful January day in the Everglades when Wally and Sarah were again subpoenaed to appear at a hearing.

XIII

The sea birds glided in and splashed down. They were but silhouettes in the sparkling sunlit water whose motion was a rhythmic display of energy. Energy was everywhere, I thought — in all forms and motion including my thoughts.

From a composition by Dan Miller, Age 16.

From *The Downeast Gazette,* October 4, 1976
The tanker's inflammable cargo contains as much energy as a two megaton hydrogen bomb. In Africa the Richton tanker spilled 16,000 tons of oil, causing a firestorm. Hurricane force winds whirled huge amounts of oil aloft which became a mist and rained down upon farmlands. A great deal of death and damage resulted.

Marshal Fredericks
FACTS ABOUT TANKERS

Although somewhat relieved by Charlie's temporary success in Augusta, Wally and Sarah were by no means at ease. They expected that somehow the worst was yet to come. Wally treated his journal entries as a matter of life and death. It was his journal which had really saved the day. It had been extremely influential, and practically acceptable as evidence for Charlie and Dr. Gitman. He and Sarah decided to maintain the journal together, checking each other's entries to be sure of accuracy. Both of them were fully aware that if the hearing was scheduled again their journals would undoubtedly be read by others.

The following are excerpts of their notes:

Journal Entry by Wally: September 8, 1976 Whitehorse, Maine Cloudy and cool.
(Start this page at the end of the first paragraph and read up)
.egassem a dna segami syevnoc llits ti ;elbisnes sa tsuj s'ti tub yaw siht tluciffid erom neve s'tI .training and books environment's regular your by conditioned been already have you which to skill a relearning are You .readaption a is it because difficult is process this Actually .adapt now must you which to environment reading normal your in change the by interrupted being is here written being is what of retention Your .with deal to hard be but strange feel only not would it backwards this read to had you If (START HERE AND READ UP)

Believe it or not, Dan could read and understand the preceding paragraph just as quickly and easily as he could read the words which make up what you are reading at this moment. A week before school started, we gave him the paragraph to read aloud each way. His response had us convinced that my original ideas as to what had happened to him with respect to conditioning-immunity were correct. It was something we thought we should check before school started. We figured his "immunity" was the seat of most of his difficulties in getting along with others. In addition, our legal fate, and that of the school's, now hung upon the test results and his well-being at school.

We had had a long, thorough interview with Arty during the summer. He seemed to have many personal problems. Interestingly enough, Dan's difficulties turned out to be the cause of many of Arty's conflicts. We discovered that many of Arty's anxieties and insecure feelings seemed to stem from his interactions with Dan, and with Carol and Ben, both of whom were very much emotionally tied up in Dan's problem. The extra attention paid to Danny gave Arty the unconscious feeling that he was second-rate. Being an identical twin of the high school screwball did not help Arty's popularity with his peers. They often thought he was Dan and acted accordingly. Arty seemed overly dependent upon the approval of others to maintain his self-esteem.

It was time for my weekly trip to the store for supplies. I put Dan's bike in the back of the car and drove him into town. He seemed kind of tired, and yawned excessively. When we stopped at the supermarket he trotted in behind me, for he wanted to use the pay phone by the cashier's window. He was very friendly and polite with all the people in the store, exchanged hellos with everyone. Then came the backbreaker.

As I was getting a shopping cart I saw Dan put a dime in the pay phone and start dialing the number he wanted. I knew what was going to happen next because that particular phone is what gave me the idea of buying stock in the telephone company. It makes "Ma Bell" a lot of unearned bucks. At every other pay phone in practically everywhere U.S.A., one puts his dime in and dials the number. Not this coin eater; with this phone you first dial your number and when the party answers you quickly put your dime in.

I've dropped many a dime into that trap only to get my party and discover that they can't hear a word I'm saying. Then I'll read the instructions carefully and will have to sacrifice another dime. Often it takes so much time to go through this procedure that the party has hung up. With much frustration, and preoccupation with my frustration, I will go through the whole exact routine again, losing still another dime! That's conditioning for you. I'm so used to putting dimes in first that I will often do it again, even though I know not to, and even though I've lost two dimes already. The stimulus-response syndrome takes right over. I've mentioned that supermarket phone as an excellent example of a conditioning agent on many an occasion.

Sure enough, Dan got his party, but he had to put in another dime. As expected, by the time he found a coin his party had evidently hung up. He read the instructions again, got some more change out of his pocket and, without thinking, put the dime in the slot. Again he lost it. That darn phone does it every — HOLY MOTHER OF GOD! Dan got taken by the phone a second time! The son of a gun *is* conditionable!! I figured that the first time he hadn't read the instructions, he had done it out of ignorance. But then he read them! I saw him! To have it happen a second time means that it was a conditioned response from all those other regular pay telephones he'd used all his life. I didn't know what to think! Twelve years of theorizing about this kid, changed just like that! I thought I'd like to die! I figured I had been objective about the whole thing but now I could see that I had been conditioned too. I only expected Dan to show non-conditioned behavior. I never thought that *this* would happen! All that discussion, all that arguing with Dr. Sullivan, all that observation! The state's allegations — was I wrong all along? This is the first time I've seen or heard anything like this from Dan. Maybe he's just been conditioned in certain areas. Maybe he's starting to pull out of the whole disorder, starting to outgrow it! Who knows?

I was aghast. How could I now challenge Dr. Sullivan? I had accepted Dan on the school under one premise and now had to readjust my thinking. I decided to say nothing for a while and keep an open mind. What a stupid expression, how can one really do that? Our outlook is always prejudicially conditioned by the environment. That's precisely how I got into this jam. Frustratingly, "watch and wait" continued to be the word.

Journal entry by Sarah: September 14, 1976, New York City. Exceedingly hot and sticky, noisy and smelly.

Today is the first day of school.

Once again we are starting our expedition in order for its staff and students to personally encounter both the environment and the conditioning process. We all learn to be confronted by these two forces and their effects. We question them and personally develop reasonable means of coping with them.

The only way that we've discovered that these important goals can be achieved is by having the school participants directly consider and live out the effects of their feelings, thoughts, and actions. Both Dan and Arty would now have this opportunity.

How is this process accomplished? We simply arrange the school's social structure so that it has no outside authority dictating what is to take place. All actions emanate from and are governed solely by group consideration. There is no "outsider" to blame if things become uncomfortable. In this manner, the school's social environment, and each individual's daily experience, completely results from the participants conditioning, feelings, thoughts, planning and actions. If the results are uncomfortable or unsatisfactory, then the expedition participants must discover what has gone wrong in these areas if the situation is to change for the better.

The answer to most problems which come up lie within the parameters of the expedition. Conditioning to the environment past and present must be discovered and modified if its discomfort is to be alleviated or avoided.

Journal entry by Wally: September 14, 1976, New York City. Warm, smoggy.

The first month of school is always an incredible eye-opener. Indeed, the first day is illuminating, for once you remove the lid of authority, things you can never quite predict will pop up. We especially wanted to see what would come out of Dan. Our curiosity after the telephone incident was almost getting the better of us.

The students and staff got together for the first time in a quiet, empty room at a school in New York City. Now here was an environmental mold and what a stimulus! Twenty-four of us sat in the classroom with the seats facing forward toward the teacher's desk. I sat in one of the seats in the back row. Through their conditioning the whole class was silently waiting for the teacher, the authority, to take his proper place in front. But there was no teacher. We were to learn from the environment and from each other. It was fascinating. Finally one student asked what was going on and who was the leader?

"I guess we all are," timidly suggested another.

"Well, what are we supposed to do now?"

"Hey Wally, what are we supposed to do now?"

"What do you think? What do you want? What seems sensible?" I replied.

Dan interjected, "Why ask Wally? I thought we were going to plan our own year." (That doesn't sound conditioned, I thought to myself. I was torn between trying to catch him in a conditioned response while desperately hoping I wouldn't.)

They started coming up with ideas about traveling up to Vermont where the camping and cooking equipment was stored. They asked me if they could do that.

"Does it sound reasonable? Is that what you feel like doing?"

"Oh, yes," blurted three of them and they started to rise, getting ready to leave.

"How do you know everybody wants to do that?" I asked. The three looked questioningly at each other, sat down and were quiet.

"What does everybody want to do?" queried Dan. Nobody answered. "How can we decide what to do if nobody is going to say anything?" asked Dan. (Asking questions is not necessarily conditioned, I thought to myself.)

"We can't decide anything," explained Nancy. "We can't talk 'cause we don't even know each other's names."

Arty added, "It's hard talking here because all the seats are facing forward. All I can see are people's backs."

"Maybe we should go somewhere else or sit on the desks in a circle," suggested Richard.

"Let's sit facing each other," added Holly, and without further adieu we did. It seemed to make common sense. The group began to face each other as well as the reality that it was up to them to decide what else was going to happen, what seemed rational. They had just taken their first action in that direction. They had sensibly modified their total environmental setting. They faced the way *they* decided, even though the desks were firmly bolted to the floor in a direction chosen by an authority they didn't even know. We are on our way.

"Let's learn each other's names," said Nancy.

"Perhaps I can help," I responded, "I have some tape and marking pencils. If you want, you can make up name tapes and wear them so you'll get to know each other."

"That's too organized," complained Nancy. "That's like being regimented or something. Let's just sit and learn names."

"Won't that take a long time?" asked Dan. "Are we in a rush? I'm not that good at names. It might take me all day to learn them."

"Yeah, me too," added Sue.

"Let's use the tapes," said Dan. "It will save time." (A reasoned suggestion is not necessarily conditioned, I thought to myself.)

"I object," proclaimed Nancy.

"How will we decide?" asked Richard.

"Let's vote on it," said Arty.

"I don't like voting," objected Nancy. "That's like regimentation too. The majority rules even if it's a dumb idea."

"Well, what do you want to do?" asked Dan. (Another unconditioned question, I thought.)

"I don't want to make this school year into college and high school USA," argued Nancy. "Once we start making rules, we're just going to be back where we came from, and that sucks as far as I'm concerned. Wally, are we really in a rush?"

"I don't know what our plans are for the day since they haven't been made," I replied. "But it seems to me that since all the equipment is in

Vermont, we should drive up there sooner or later. We have to get food too, don't we?"

"How long does it take to get to Vermont?" asked Holly.

"It took me six hours when I drove up for my interview with my parents," contributed Sue.

"How are we going to decide what to do?" Dan inquired. "I don't want to go by a majority decision vote because it could be stupid. For example, the majority of the town council up where I live voted to put in an oil refinery, and nothing could be dumber than that." (That's close, I thought, but it was based on reasoning and opinion, not emotionality alone. It's a conditioned craving for environmental support which goes way back before the age of three and one-half.)

Nancy smiled.

"But if our time is limited," continued Dan, "maybe we should use the name tapes for now because it makes sense in this situation. That's not regimentation, is it Nancy?" (Questioning, suggesting, figuring out is not conditioning.)

"Yes, it is. Here it is the first day and we're already making rules saying how we're going to do things. That limits my freedom and this is only the first fifteen minutes of school."

"Yeah," said Arty angrily, "we'll just end up being like a regular school with rules and punishment." (Now that sounds conditioned, I thought. The emotionality of conditioning is evident.)

"I just don't see how the using of name tapes is a rule," said Dan inquisitively. "It seems to me that it's an agreement as to something we're going to do to make things easier. If it doesn't work, we can change it." (Asking or explaining is not conditioned, I thought; nor is flexibility.)

"Look whose idea it was!" said Nancy accusingly. "Look who brought the tape and marking pens — the teacher." (There's conditioning again.)

"That's the craziest thing I ever heard," said Dan with frustration. "We can change the idea if it doesn't work, so it's not a rule. And just because a teacher suggests something doesn't mean it's a bad idea." (Flexible, reasoned opinion is not conditioned unless it comes from past unconscious experiences.")

"I just don't want to be ruled by teachers," retorted Arty. "It could end up just as dull and strict as school in Whitehorse."

I added, "It's fine with me if you don't use the name tapes. I brought them because they were helpful in this situation before. But it seems to me that it makes little sense not to follow a useful suggestion just because a teacher made it. I'm a person, too. It's certainly not a rule. I don't even care if you use the name tapes or not. I was just trying to be helpful. Do you really see that as being a rule?"

"I guess not," said Nancy sheepishly. "It just looks like it, but it's sensible and it is our decision."

"Who else doesn't want to use the tapes?" questioned Dan.

Nobody responded. Perhaps unwittingly, Dan had hit upon the guiding force of the American democratic process, namely: phrase questions so that your opposition has to act. Inertia due to conditioned fear or embarrassment, both caused by punishment will take over and you'll get your way most of the time. At this meeting, which had gone twenty minutes already, only six of the twenty-four people had spoken.

It was interesting to me to see the contrast between Dan's and Arty's outlooks with regard to the name tapes. Dan could see and feel the actual immediate effects of the suggestion with respect to getting things accomplished. He was unhampered by conditioned associations such as "rules are limiting", "teachers are authorities", "teachers are punishing and not to be trusted". To Arty and Nancy, conditioned feelings had transfered a seemingly harmless, perhaps helpful suggestion into an authoritarian ruling.

"Then I guess we'll use the name tapes," said Dan. "That's unanimous and we didn't even have to vote. Good deal!"

The tapes were handed around with the marking pencil. Some wrote large, some wrote small, some boys wrote nicknames which weren't very complimentary, like 'Ding-Dong' or 'Dum-Dum'. Thinking about the conditioning evidenced by those actions, I decided to have a little fun. I purposely marked my tape "No-No". Sure enough, there was some discussion about that. Most of the people thought that name appropriate because I was the person who would tell them what not to do.

Finally Nancy asked, "Is that why you have it there, Wally?"

"No," I replied, "that's my first name."

"I thought your name was Wally."

"Wally is my second name."

"I thought your second name was Bryce. What's going on?"

"When I was a kid my parents were forever saying to me, 'No, no, Wally, don't do this. No, no, Wally, don't do that' so I've figured my full name is No No Wally Bryce. No-No is my first name."

"You're kidding, right?"

"Yes, but I suspect the same conditioning has happened to others here who are using nicknames which are not so complimentary."

"We're wasting time," complained Richard. "Let's decide what we're going to do. We've all brought our lunches, but what are we going to do for supper?"

"I wasn't wasting time," I said casually. "It was a serious joke to give people a reaction. While we put on the name tapes, I asked Chuck where his name 'Ding-Dong' came from. He said that's what his friends call him because he's so foolish sometimes. If he chooses that name now, it sounds to me like he believes it, so I just fooled around a little bit to get the point across. But it's important because if one actually believes they're a Ding-Dong, they will be one. People are rarely able to accomplish more than they think they are capable of doing. One way or another, I think it's important that people here get some kind of feedback to their feelings or thoughts, just to think about."

"Why?" questioned Nancy. "Did we do something wrong? Did I miss something?"

"Well," I responded, "do people here think a real group decision was made about the tapes?"

No response.

"I'm not so sure we did, because there were only six people who said anything. Maybe there are others who felt like Nancy did and yet were not confronted by the effects of their own feelings on others. They never even heard other points of view because they never said anything. Right now, they may still have uncomfortable feelings that the 'teacher' is making rules. They're hiding. I don't feel comfortable with becoming a 'rule maker' all year long in their eyes. I'm not one, I don't want to be one, and I do not want to be the whipping boy for peoples' prejudices and / or conditioning. I'm uncomfortable with that and I'm letting you know here and now so that people can react or think about me as a regular person with feelings rather than being a rulemaker or a stereotype of some other ingrained fantasy. It would be helpful for other people to speak up about how they feel, too. That would be an open, honest, and friendly thing to do. In that way we'll get to know each other better and not be tongue-tied because we're afraid of what the other person might think or feel. We can't determine the sense of any of our outlooks or actions if we're not brave enough to express them. There is nothing to fear. There is no punishment here. But we can't look at something and consider it if we can't see it.

"Yeah," interjected Nancy. "If we all know where everybody is 'at', then we can together determine what seems reasonable in everybody's mind. Then we won't have to vote but will still have everybody's opinion. In addition, we all might learn something, which is why we're here."

"That's just what happened with the name tapes," I continued, "but it actually only involved six people. It was like everybody else was watching a movie. I really appreciate Nancy and Arty's honesty and forthrightness. I don't fully agree with them, but at least I know they're involved. It's easier for me to relate to them than to John or Cindy because they've shared part of themselves with all of us. So have Dan, Holly, Richy, and Sue. I think you might all agree at this point that you know them better and feel more comfortable with them than you do with 14 other people here who have not said anything."

"I think it's too soon to expect people to talk if they don't know each other," suggested Cindy.

"Obviously we each have our threshold where we can overcome our conditioned concern about saying the wrong thing. But if you really think or feel something, how can it be wrong? It's the real you, and the best thing you can do is say what you feel and get reactions. The reason that's difficult is because we've all been conditioned to being put down or punished for saying what was on our minds to parents, teachers, or people who could hurt us. Who do you think is going to hurt you here? Is that person real or imagined? What is more important: expressing your ideas, or protecting people from hearing how you feel?"

"But Wally, we've only been together for an hour," said Cindy.

"That's true, but there have been pauses where people who had things on their mind could have spoken out. I've seen school go on for months where only a third of the students actually talk at meetings. The sooner we avoid that from happening, the better."

"Why is it so important?" complained Nancy. "It's beginning to sound like rule No. 1: you must say something in meetings."

"I don't think it's a rule," I replied. "But in a school like this, where we have no rules to guide our actions, it's very important that people let others know where they're at, otherwise they'll be unintentionally ignored or walked over, and feel put down. We are replacing rulemakers with open communication and meetings so we can work together. If we can't make that work, then the *expedition* won't work. I think that although it's not a rule, people should be very aware of the effects of not sharing what's on their mind. Remember, there are no guarantees that this expedition won't come to a screeching halt — will just not work this year. That entirely depends upon all of us contributing to its success. A major part of that contribution is letting others know how we think and feel. That's what Arty and Nancy have done, and in doing so, we've perhaps located some problems which we can work on before they undermine us. For example, Nancy, do you still think my suggestion that we use name tapes is a rule?"

"No, I can honestly say that I was reading into that situation from other teachers I've had. I can see now where that idea could have caused you to feel bad, and there's no reason for that to happen 'cause it wasn't a rule. I can see where it could have caused trouble if I didn't say anything. Now I wonder what would have happened if I'd said something to some of my teachers back home. Some of them seemed nice; other kids liked them, but I knew they were teachers so I avoided them whenever possible. Maybe we'd have gotten along better. But it's not only my fault, they never asked me what I thought."

Sarah interrupted, "Maybe we should continue to talk about this later, we still have a lot of immediate things to do."

"I agree with that," blurted John. "See, I said something."

"And your input was helpful in making a decision at this point," said Sarah. "It would have been just as helpful if you had disagreed and said why. You see, all you have to do is express what you really think or feel and it makes an important contribution."

"That sure is different than school at home," said Arty thoughtfully.

XIV

The locust tree became more than a piling for a pier. It became a tourist home for luxurious growths of algae, barnacles, hydroids, sponges, bryozoans, and tunicates who clung to it for support. They were all like friends living together. I wondered if they actually knew each other. Along with the colonies came shipworms, which bored into the piling and weakened it. There were times when I've listened to their little monster relatives crunching and grinding away while eating out the underside of a wooden boat not treated with antifoulant or protective coatings.

From a composition by Dan Miller, age 16.

From *The Downeast Gazette,* April 9, 1975

Proponents of the refinery believe it will bring new jobs, new people, economic growth, a broader tax base with lower taxes. That's all propoganda. New technocratic people bring with them the demand for modern technologic living to which they are practically addicted. They'll impose it on the land here: modern roads, sewer systems, homes, schools, utilities, and law enforcement. Taxes will go up, way up. Look at the record in other factory towns. Taxes tripled ten years after the refinery moved into Petersburg. The natives remained unemployed because they were untrained and unaccustomed to refinery work. The rich were the ones who got richer.

Dr. Alan Rogers
Economic Consultant

Eight months had now passed since that first day of school in September. May 18, 1977 began as any normal day would begin for any normal person. To Wally and Sarah it felt strange to be living in the realm of "normalacy." Three days earlier the expedition had completed its school year. No longer were the Bryce's living out of a school bus, crowded with students and camping equipment. The continuous travel and variety of environmental encounters was over until next September. Interviewing new students was the immediate order of the day.

This year's school had been a true success. The only irritating carry-over was the continuing threat of the Attorney General's hearing, now set for June 11th, less than a month away.

Sarah was unable to relax. Three weeks of sitting still would be out of the question. "Wally, why don't we write Dr. Sullivan a letter?" she suggested. "Let's present to Dr. Sullivan our observations of Danny this year. Perhaps when he's digested them he'll have a change of heart about the necessity of this hearing. How can he possibly deny documented occurences?"

"I don't know. It might work. Let's call Charlie and ask him."

Charlie thought the letter to be a worthwhile idea. He offered to read it over first. If it sounded as if it might help, he'd not only send it to Dr. Sullivan, but to everybody else involved with the hearing. "Write it," he urged. "Give 'em hell, but be polite."

With a mixture of apprehension and annoyance, Wally and Sarah dedicated themselves to the task. They began to search through the past year's journal entries, picking out those that pertained to Dan Miller. With the exception of the perplexing telephone incident, each entry strongly supported Wally's hypothesis about Danny's conditioning immunity. Out of the many diverse entries, Wally and Sarah selected representative samples and constructed a letter with which to present them.

>Bryce
>R.D. #3
>Whitehorse, Maine
>May 18, 1977

Dr. Richard Sullivan, Director
Psychiatric Division
State Department of Public Health
Augusta, Maine

Dear Dr. Sullivan:

We are writing to you because we are aware of your concern for the well being of the Miller family and the health of Dan Miller. Unfortunately, we are also all too well aware of your lack of concern about the welfare of our school.

As you know, Dan has been a member of our environmental expedition for the past year. He has done extraordinarily well in our group situation. His evaluations in all areas of endeavor and interpersonal relationships have been excellent. Dan has grown a great deal.

Obviously you do not agree with Wally's hypothesis of twelve years ago: specifically that Dan Miller is immune to conditioning. To the contrary, we do find him to be immune, at least, as of his fourth birthday.

You do not seem to believe our environmental expedition is an appropriate nor legal form of education. Much to the contrary we, and many others, have found it to be extremely rewarding for Dan and his classmates.

To sensibly resolve these conflicts it is urgent that we bring to your attention some very revealing incidents which occurred during this past school year. They will provide some help in your consideration and understanding of the true nature of Dan's disorder as well as the validity of our educational approach. We hope they will provide enough information to make the forthcoming hearing completely unnecessary!

In our culture a person who is neat and organized is considered to have "good conditioning". This year on the school we had a set of identical twins, Arty and Dan. Arty was neat, Dan was not. Yet they have both been brought up in the same household and have an identical heredity.

Dan obviously has "bad" conditioning or *no* conditioning when it comes to "neatness" for he is anything but "neat."

Dan Miller clearly demonstrates a lack of conditioning in the typical situations described herein. They are representative of his behavior in general. The situations have been transcribed word for word from our journal. They were entries which were made by us on a daily basis. If you have any doubts as to their accuracy please note that our entire student body and faculty were witness to most of them. Our expedition members have consented to testify to the accuracy of these observations if necessary. In addition many expedition participants have kept personal journals which will confirm the accuracy of the enclosed materials.

We understand that your complaint about our school initiated the forthcoming hearings. We therefore demand that you, as a professional and responsible public servant, be fully cognizant of the information contained in the following journal entries:

Journal entry by Sarah: Sept. 27, 1976. Acadia National Park. Sunny but cold. A.M.: visited bog (seminar on bog ecology); P.M.: visited Indian museum; Eve.: astronomy seminar, meeting.

Kitty began making suggestions about what we were eating. She was sure that foods with sugar and chemicals in them were not healthy and could cause cancer. She discussed it because she was very upset that the government did not take saccharin off the market immediately when it was discovered to be a possible carcinogen. She felt we were being used as guinea pigs. She said foods which were suspect should not be allowed until they were proven OK. Arty would eat everything that tasted good, no matter what it contained. He just liked to eat. Dan, on the other hand, began to read up on wild foods, organic gardening, and the effects of chemicals in the food we eat. He experimented with eating weeds, insects, fish eyes, raw fish, and seaweed, much to the disgust of some. It was way too much for me. I wouldn't go near some of that stuff due to my own conditioning. Grubs! He'd eat grubs! I wouldn't even eat discolored blackberries! Dan concluded that people should only eat uncooked wild foods for nourishment because that's how nature had designed us to live. "We evolved on these foods," he said, while blithely swallowing a live minnow, displaying what must have been the height of unconditioned food behavior in our culture.

Dr. Sullivan, this and other differences between Arty and Dan raise some important educational questions. The constitution may guarantee us freedom, the right to life, liberty and the pursuit of happiness, but what does that actually mean in our culture? As children we're conditioned into immobile behavior patterns, feelings and thoughts which fit into a pre-set socio-economic way of life. Where is the freedom? Is a dog which has been conditioned to eat only chicken really free to eat dog food?

Why do we knowledgeably continue to eat foods with detrimental chemicals in them, chemicals which are banned in other nations? Are we conditioned to the kinds of food we eat? Does our economy feed from and cater to our nutritional conditioning thereby reinforcing it? Is our conditioning causing fatal diseases?

Students should be made aware of the effects of conditioning. Encounters with the conditioning process should be part of the environment in all traditional schools. Does it make sense to prosecute our environmental school because we have been innovators in this area?

Journal entry by Wally: Oct. 3, 1976, Cape Cod, Mass. Raining. A.M.: Bought food and did laundry; P.M.: Wrote papers; Eve.: Meeting.

We have now been together for seventeen exciting and challenging days. Students are having a difficult time finding each other. They seem afraid to react to each other and to share their real thoughts and feelings. They often experience each other as if in a vacuum. This has caused some mistrust and irritating problems for each of us.

Today the group decided to write papers to practice and improve written communication skills. Perhaps papers would bridge the communication gap. After lengthy discussion they decided each student would write a paper on a topic of his choice which was personally important and of interest to the rest of the students and faculty. Everybody would read them and would give their reactions to the writer. From such a multitude of reactions a person could learn a great deal about their writing ability.

Dan's paper was a poem about a dream he had concerning his feelings while being with the rest of the kids on the school and certain students in particular.

Arty and fourteen other students wrote dry, factual reports on specific topics which they selected from the encyclopedia or from their travels. Reactions by others were that these papers were uninvolving and difficult to read: they were inappropriate shields behind which people were hiding from each other.

Two students did not write because they couldn't think of a topic.

Only two students besides Dan wrote about their reactions to the expedition and things they had done in common. Their papers were warmly received and encouraged by all. We all wondered why so many students had selected to write cold, detached reports especially in light of our present problems in relating to each other.

> Dr. Sullivan, does the traditional school system condition students to be distant from each other? Are our schools actually factories turning out cold, technocratic businessmen and consumers? Is that why we have become a crowded nation of alienated people? Is that what schools should teach? You are participating in an investigation designed to thwart a school which helps people learn how to find each other and establish supportive relationships. Why the investigation?

Journal entry by Wally: Oct. 20, 1976. N.Y. State. Clear and crisp. Visited noted enthnomusicologist Alan Sebert: saw films he made about traditional musicians, sang and played old time music with his family.

Arty, as well as others, is not accustomed to being without "canned" entertainment like TV, hi-fi, movies and radio. He is having difficulty feeling comfortable with traditional or homemade music produced within the group. He bombastically declares that singing or playing a fiddle, pennywhistle or dulcimer has no meaning to him. "I can't even hear it," he would complain frequently. "There's no beat or words that I can relate to like with rock," ... "big name musicians don't sing or play this junk!!" ... "I don't like to sing or play instruments or do country dancing — only dips in music classes at home do that." ... "Who can relate to this stuff? Traditional music comes from places I've never even heard of. It's the music of people who are dead and gone. Who cares about unknown Blacks, Indians, fishermen, cowboys, Cajuns, sailors, whalermen, farmers?"

Traditional music is new to Dan but he's already deeply involved with it. He's making efforts to sing and play it — to keep this music alive in the non-technologic atmosphere of the school so it becomes a comfortable and familiar part of all of us here. He says the songs really help him hear and understand the feelings and viewpoints of others — no matter who they are. It makes extinct cultures and people come alive again. He experiences it as enhancing a group spirit of fun — a simple form of music which is not under the influence of mass media, money, economics, or subliminal stimuli. "Traditional music is a product of people — easy, fun and beautiful — a statement that the individual, his personal experiences and his ways of life are important. Dan enjoys all kinds of rhythmic music. He says that the "beat" is reminiscent of a human's earliest conditioning. It is the conditioning of the secure embryo in the womb to the beat of the heart of the mother.

Interestingly enough, Arty agrees with Dan intellectually but on a feeling level he is not comfortable with homemade or traditional music.

> Dr. Sullivan, doesn't conditioning unconsciously addict us to the music of our culture? Doesn't the music made for money purposely contain subliminal stimuli which bind the listener to its sexual, drug laden message? Isn't it a paradox that young people who may disagree with many aspects of our culture are unconsciously tied to it by conditioning to rock music. Our expedition is one of the few opportunities for students to become familiar with traditional music on a cultural level of learning. Haven't you found that people feel and act differently depending upon what kind of music they are listening to? Why deprive students of the chance to be exposed to music which is not so destructive?

Journal entry by Sarah: Nov. 3, 1976. Amish Farm, Lancaster, Penn. Sunny, warm. A.M. Collected eggs from 10,000 chickens, worked on fixing barn roof; P.M. Discussion with Old Order farmer, visited market; Eve.: Astronomy seminar.

We had an astronomy seminar for the purpose of gaining an understanding of the motion of the stars through the heavens and how that motion could be used for navigation or to tell time. Each student learned to be able to tell what time it was by the position of certain star formations. Just as we were finishing Arty said, "I left my watch back at the tent. Dan, what time is it?" Dan thought that to be very funny for Arty had just finished reading the time from the stars. Now, when he wanted to know the time for his own information, his conditioning demanded he obtain it from a watch. Conditioning had blinded him to his natural environment. Dan pointed this out to Arty and they both had a good laugh over it.

Journal entry by Sarah: April 20, 1977, Grand Canyon National Park, Arizona. Cold, snow on the ground, clear, A.M.: Visited Flagstaff Museum (a museum of ideas, not things); P.M.: travel to canyon; Eve.: Naturalist talk on park management.

When we first reached the edge of the Grand Canyon, we took a half hour to just watch as the sun was setting. Dan came back from the canyon's edge very critical of Arty and some of the others. "All you did was sit there and talk for thirty minutes about Evel Knievel jumping across the canyon on his motorcycle and how they put a Chevrolet on one of the buttes for a TV commercial. That's disgusting. You've traveled 3,000 miles to be exposed to this canyon, this fantastic beauty, space, geology, raw action of nature and the elements and all that you can talk about is TV, advertising and motorcycles. The canyon is sitting right in front of you and you still can't reach it. Last time, after we had arrived in and seen Zion Canyon all that came to your mind was "Are there flush toilets at the campsite? Do they have showers and hot water? Your heads are full of home — maybe you should have stayed there. You're much more excited by going to get the mail than any place we've been so far. What a waste." (Is Dan acting out of the past or present here? The present is unconditioned.)

Journal entry by Wally: April 3, 1977, Barstow, Calif. A.M.: Cloudy, warm; P.M.: Windy. Visited Calico site; discussed archaeology, travel to Death Valley; Eve.: meeting.

One of the most fascinating events of the school year has been our visit to the Leakey prehistoric site in Calico, California. Here were the remains of stone axes chipped by stone age men more than 50,000 years ago. The archaeologist showed us how to make stone axes using rocks as hammers to cut the stone. The students used rock hammers all morning and made some axes. We then proceeded to Death Valley, arriving in a blinding dust storm. We immediately proceeded to set up our tents. I was surprised to find all the students standing in line, coughing with eyes tearing, waiting to use the single hammer in the tool kit to hammer in their tent stakes. Dan was not in line. He had already hammered in his stakes using one of the numerous rocks lying around us as a hammer. The inconceivable had happened. Nineteen students, who had been told and taught to use rocks for hammers just three hours before, had somehow forgotten that rocks could be used as hammers. Choking and with stinging faces, they waited on line for their turn to use the metal hammer to which they had been culturally conditioned. Only one student had turned directly to the rocks in his environment in this time of need. It was Dan, for he was seemingly immune to cultural conditioning in this situation.

> Dr. Sullivan, hasn't conditioning to technologic assistance and mass media made us become so dependent upon technology that we can no longer recognize or respect the world of nature or our own rationality? Has conditioning unconsciously made us slaves to the economy and to technology? Our school teaches its participants how to become more self reliant, independent and confident. Why shouldn't our school be permitted to exist?

Journal entry by Sarah: Jan. 11, 1977, Everglades National Park. Clear and cold. A.M.: Ranger guided walk into sawgrass prairie; P.M.: Snake demonstration and seminar; Eve.: talk by naturalist on Everglades ecology.

One amazing aspect of the meeting about stealing the doughnut was that Arty point blank accused me of stealing the food. He was quite sure I had done it.

"If I did, Arty, why haven't I admitted it?" I asked. "What am I hiding?"

"You want us to have all these meetings so we'll understand that we shouldn't steal," he said accusingly.

I was shocked. "Arty," I said with some emotion, "you are dreaming, Wake up! You are not really talking to me. I may be standing here in front of you and you may think you're looking at me, but you are talking to somebody else. Although you are right now sitting in this room, your mind is elsewhere. You are accusing somebody who is not me. I don't know who it is or where in God's name you have gotten this crazy idea that I stole the doughnut. However, I'll guarantee you this: no matter where your fantasy world has taken you, you're physically here speaking to me and I resent your accusation that I stole the doughnut in order to manipulate this group! Just who is your past life are you talking to anyhow?"

Arty looked a little dazed and had nothing to say.

Journal entry by Sarah: Jan. 14, 1977, Everglades National Park. Warm (finally) and sunny. A.M.: hike pinewoods hammock (seminar on effects of fire); P.M.: Naturalist led walk to observe wading birds; Eve. Naturalist talk on sensitivity to nature, meeting.

Arty came up and said, with tears, that I was absolutely right. This morning, just as he was waking up, he remembered that, when he was much younger, Ben and Carol had bought him a bicycle. He was told never to leave it outside in front of the house because it would be stolen. He would occasionally forget and leave the bike out, and sure enough, one day it was stolen. Carol was very upset and very angry with him. He felt miserable for weeks as she scolded and punished him.

Almost a month later, Carol gave Arty the bike back. *She* had purposely taken the bike and hidden it in the garage just to teach him a lesson. Arty was sure that that was why he accused me of stealing the food and not telling. I was right for he was surely talking to his mother when he made the accusation of me. That experience (and perhaps others) had conditioned his feelings about adults when similar situations arose. Dan, on the other hand, had lived in the same exact household but did not have this attitude. It was a clear demonstration to me as to how conditioning leads us to emotionally live in the environmental settings which have originally conditioned us. Certain feelings and prejudices return us to certain environments and vice versa.

> Dr. Sullivan, does conditioning make us project the hurt or disapproval we may feel from childhood onto others who don't deserve it? Is conditioning the real source of the prejudice which infiltrates every aspect of American life? Are we conditioned into holding the attitudes and biases of parents and friends in order to gain their approval or avoid their rejection or punishment? Why are you protesting the existence of a school which confronts prejudice and teaches people to overcome it?

Journal entry by Sarah: Jan. 15, 1977. Everglades National Park. Warm, cloudy. A.M.: visited Eva Sheering; seminar on science of bird banding; P.M.: Discussion with animal behaviorist at Seaquarium (cetacean conditioning); Eve.: traditional music seminar, meeting.

It was finally considered by some that maybe the person who took the doughnut had done so unconsciously and didn't realize he or she had done it. A similar event had happened in the Adirondacks in September when people were selected for committees and didn't even remember which committee they were on, or that they had even been at the meeting. They had been daydreaming much of the time. The emotionality of the meeting a few days ago about stealing and trust really cut through. It was decided that everyone would have to talk about how they felt about the theft and things in general. They did — some for the first time. In past years when this type of meeting has occurred the atmosphere has been better, people have been more open. Theft has never recurred. From the intensity of this meeting I expect the results will be the same.

> Dr. Sullivan, hasn't conditioning caused us to be so preoccupied with anxiety or fear of authority that we spend many of our conscious hours fantasizing or daydreaming escapes? Does it interfere with our effectiveness as human beings? Doesn't our school bring this problem to light and teach students how to do something about it? Doesn't the expedition help people become aware of the feelings of others to the point where theft is eliminated because it is hurtful to others? How many other schools encourage, let alone achieve, total honesty?

Journal entry by Wally: Jan. 22, 1977. Virgin Island National Park, St. John, U.S. Virgin Islands. Hot, occasional showers. A.M. tropical ecology walk; P.M. reef ecology, skin diving; Eve. naturalist talk on history of island.

Last night Dan and I were walking across a field near our campsite when we stumbled across Arty and Barbara lying together, "looking at the stars," said Arty. Since it was a cloudy night, we doubted it. Barbara seemed to be embarrassed, hiding behind Arty, saying nothing. Dan and I were quite uncomfortable with the incident. It was a transgression of an agreement made by students at their interview that they would not pair off, form cliques, or become involved in relationships which might hurt the school itself or others on the expedition. A mobile, closely knit co-ed community would have a difficult time existing in our culture if it allowed sexual relationships to develop among its participants. My book goes into details which I'll spare the reader here. Basically, it becomes a hurtful, destructive, emotionally charged explosion when such exclusive relationships occur; they pull the school apart at its seams. One just cannot severely kick the conditioned taboos of parents, campsite owners, boards of education, fellow students, teachers, law officers and businessmen without violent repercussions.

Since Barbara and Arty both seemed uncomfortable with what had taken place, I thought they would bring it up at a meeting. When that didn't happen, I was going to talk about it, but Dan did it completely on his own. (I thought that was uninhibited and unconditioned.)

"I'm not comfortable here," he said, "because I think that Arty and Barbara are not keeping their agreements. There are girls here I would like to pair off with but I know this is not the time or place, for there could be detrimental effects on others, and it breaks our trust. But Arty and Barbara don't seem to be acting that way," and he explained the situation to the group. The relationship turned out to be completely "innocent", but it brought up a question which everybody had pondered but only Dan had asked:

"Why is sex such a taboo in our society?"

Several students excitedly volunteered to research the question at the library of the University of Miami.

Journal entry by Wally: Feb. 7, 1977, Chesapeake Bay. Sunny, freezing: A.M.: estuarine ecology; P.M.: Miocene fossil collection.

Interestingly enough, the students discovered no single answer as to why sex is a taboo in our society. In general, it was concluded that man's withdrawal from nature bottled up many natural feelings which then sought release through the sex drive. In addition, the incest taboo in primitive hunting and gathering cultures was a vital necessity for survival. The incest taboo urged marriage relationships between different families in order to establish familiarity between small groups which otherwise might be hostile. Marry out our die was a reality. The incest taboo fostered intertribal trust and was therefore encouraged.

The marriage alliance was carried out to the point where if one of the partners dies, the brother of the deceased would have to marry the widow in order to sustain the family and intertribal trust. This became law in more complex societies and is found in the Bible where God kills Onan for "spilling his seed on the ground" instead of marrying his brother's wife. Onanism, or masturbation, became and is a conditioned taboo in our heritage today. The conditioning rejection of childhood masturbation as well as social reinforcement for sexual restraint have produced our present-day sexual taboos and repression. Sue and Cindy used Peter Farb's *Man's Rise to Civilization*, Chapter 2, for the most complete resume of the subject. I must remember to recommend it to all interested in the topic. Looks like a good book for our reading list.

> Dr. Sullivan, isn't it true that our sexual fears and shame are conditioned at a very early age? Is it healthy for people to carry around sexual anxiety and stress? Our school gives students the opportunity to live together and discover each other as people rather than sex objects or symbols. Our students learn to maturely regulate and direct their sexual feelings as part of their total relationships with others. Where else can young people obtain this opportunity?

Journal entry by Wally: Feb. 1, 1977. Okefenokee Swamp State Park, Georgia. Cold, sunny. Canoed to Billy's Island all day. Eve.: Meeting.

Several days ago Dan had overheard Arty talking with some kid in the next campsite. The kid told Arty that they were going to "party" that night, they had some real good grass to smoke and he should come over. Arty had said that maybe he would after everybody went to bed. Dan told Arty he was really uncomfortable about the conversation and that Arty should tell everybody what happened. Arty replied he would, but didn't. He had been very uncomfortable with Dan that day and referred to him as a 'freak' while talking with others. Dan heard about it and he called a meeting to discuss what was going on. Arty confessed he never intended to go party, he was just trying to put the kid off. He was really uncomfortable with Dan because Dan thought he would go and smoke pot even though he agreed not to. He stated Dan didn't trust him. Dan responded that maybe Arty had misled him while he was misleading the kid; why couldn't Arty have just declared he wasn't going to go and be done with it? Arty felt the kid would think he was a dip if he didn't smoke. Others wanted to know why the impressions of somebody Arty didn't even know meant so much to Arty that it made him lie. He really seemed to be controlled by the kid, and that was part of the problem. Why didn't he bring it up after he had promised Dan that he would? Why did he call Dan a freak? What did he really feel about himself that could make him get into such a situation?

Once confronted, Arty had to think about what was being discussed and said he'd talk about it later.

Dan was still concerned. He said Arty had referred to him as a freak and other people not only let him get away with it, but agreed and had insinuated the same thing. This was exactly what had happened in high school and Dan hated it; he did not want it to happen here now.

"Why do people think I'm a freak?" he cried. "I try so hard to think things out, to get along with everybody, and it ends up that people still think I'm a freak. I can't live here, I've got to leave. I've got to find someplace where I can be me. Out in a forest someplace, maybe in an insane asylum."

The students were very concerned about how Dan felt. They explained that he came across as a freak because he thought so differently and acted so differently. Why was he so different? Dan again explained that he had a problem: he was just never able to be conditioned since he was three and one-half years old.

Dr. Sullivan, please note that a week before school started Wally observed Dan Miller act in a manner which

> indicated Dan *could* and indeed *had* been conditioned. On September 8, 1976 Wally observed Dan place dimes into a pay telephone contrary to the instructions on the phone. With full awareness of his mistake Dan repeated this inappropriate action much to Wally's amazement.

I could contain myself no longer. "Dan, perhaps that's not entirely true, I confessed. I guess you should know this before we go any further. I've seen you act in a manner which appeared to be conditioned."

"You did?" said Dan increduously. "When? Where? Oh, goody, goody maybe I'm normal after all," he joked. "No, really, what happened?"

So I told Dan what I had observed with the telephone call at the beginning of the year in Whitehorse. He grinned sheepishly and said, "Gee Wally, I figured that if you had seen that happen you would have brought it up with me and talked about it long ago. I've got to tell you something: I guess I didn't trust you then. I was afraid that pressure from Dr. Sullivan was changing your mind about letting me go on the school and that's why you had invited me over to read that paragraph. Despite Dr. Sullivan's wishes I desperately wanted to come on the school. I figured that if you thought I was more normal, then you would have no reason to change your mind and exclude me, Dan "the freak" from school. With this in mind I took the opportunity, whenever I could, to act in a conditioned fashion in order for you to accept me. I'd heard you talk about that strange telephone before, so I acted as if I was conditioned by putting in the dime first both times. I did it purposely to mislead you! As a matter of fact the thought first came to me when I was reading that paragraph backwards: 'Maybe I should stumble and do it slow so you'd think I was normal.' By the time I got to town in the car with you I started to act like I had been conditioned. You missed a good part of it. I yawned and I covered my mouth three times on the ride into town. I said 'thank you' and 'excuse me' or 'pardon me' whenever I could. I combed my hair. I smiled continually. I waved hello to people from the car, and I shook hands with acquaintances when I got to the market. Then I realized the phone was there and you know the rest. Don't worry Wally, I've not changed. I'm still the fabulous, friendly fuck-up you know and love."

I couldn't believe my ears! The kids roared with laughter. So did I, but it took a little while. "Sherlock Bryce" had been dealt an incredible left hook to the ego. Wally Bryce had not followed his own advice. He had neglected to fully question and discuss what was on his mind. I had fallen into my own trap. It happens to us all once in a while, doesn't it? The old conditioned, pre-set idea teamed up with non-communication takes its toll no matter how hard you try not to let it happen.

I explained the whole story to everyone at the school meeting including what I thought had happened to Dan when he took the overdose of mescaline — that he could no longer be conditioned. I told the students I thought that when Dan seemed to be acting strange or making them uncomfortable they were actually reacting to the anxieties or insecurities Dan had aroused in them. Dan's thoughts and actions were activating — hooking — aggravating their own conditioned feelings. Many of them admitted that was true. They had been punished or rejected in their own lives for some of the things Dan talked about, or were copping out in those areas, and that's what made them feel uncomfortable when he was around. Dan's presence made them see how foolishly conditioned they were and they felt badly about it. Most of the students were turned off by any person who was making them feel that way, and got back at him, by calling him a freak. They now felt really badly they had done that. Some of them were crying.

At no time did any of them think that Dan was intentionally trying to hurt them or purposely make them unhappy.

Dan honestly asked everybody what they thought he should do about his situation on the expedition and at home. After much discussion, people suggested that:

(1) Dan should decide which people he wanted to be friends with and tell them about his problem so that they could understand as well and maybe not hold things against him or call him "freak."

(2) He should make sure that he was being understood whenever he spoke, or in whatever he did. He also should find out how people felt about what he said so there would be no more hard feelings if they misunderstood him; that way he could clear up any problems that arose on an immediate basis.

(3) He should make efforts to speak and write distinctly, as powerfully as possible, to be sure that people would listen. He should check to see if they were listening.

(4) He should try to make what he said very attractive so people would want to hear it and appreciate his ideas instead of laughing at him or calling him "freak."

(5) He should have some place he could go to when he didn't want to be with people.

(6) He should decide which of his unconditioned actions were intolerably detrimental. With medical assistance and of his own choice he should experiment with doing something "wrong" and receiving excruciating pain as a punishment. Intense pain, or the promise of it,

might help him overcome his threshold to immunity from conditioning. It might inhibit that particular action on a conscious, but immediate basis. Bed wetting and not buttoning his fly were two suggested areas.

(7) When he was with strangers, he should try not to be outspoken but should try as much as possible to imitate their manners and customs like he did to impress me with the telephone and the dime. He should try to get strangers to talk about their feelings.

(8) He should not leave school but should use the expedition to practice these suggestions. (Everybody was very enthusiastic about this. Dan had temporarily become a hero, only because at the moment he was not being confronting.)

It was quite late when the discussion with Dan finished, but Arty said he had something else to say. It had to do with Dan's situation and the effect of Dan bringing this whole thing up. He could see that he was very controlled by the idea that he should "share" with people no matter what kind of trouble it might get him into. It was a "loving your neighbor" kind of image.

He hadn't really planned on going to the party, but there was a strong inclination in him to go just because the kid invited him. Had the kid come again he might have gone. Actually, the idea of "loving your neighbor" made it easier to go because he was really relating to a *concept* rather than a real person. He had a hard time "sharing" with the real *people* he had been living with on the school for four months, due to his conditioned fear of exposure. But the *concept* of "sharing" was an "in" thing and, because of Dan, he had a great need to be "in" no matter what. So he did consider going to the party even though it was senseless in the school situation.

The other thing Arty brought up, with trepidation, was that his girlfriend had mailed him some marijuana leaves as a present. She had grown them in her garden which they had worked on together all summer. He had liked the gift, but didn't smoke it. He had planned to save it for home. It was all in his pack and had been there for a month. He was beginning to see that possession of a match-box full of marijuana was a tremendous threat to the school, but he didn't know what to do about it. It was completely controlling him.

Believe me, the news was like somebody had thrown a bomb. People couldn't believe it — especially after all the talk about trust and being concerned about each other and the welfare of all. It was just too much. Arty ran out of the meeting crying hysterically. People were afraid he might commit suicide or get lost or hurt in the Okefenokee Swamp. The meeting broke up and everyone dispersed to try to find him, to no avail.

Sarah and I were terrified.

Finally, hours later, Dan discovered him in a phone booth a mile away. He was calling Ben and Carol about coming home. Dan and others urged him to stay, which he decided to do. The confrontation made him aware of just how conditioned he was to dependency on marijuana as part of his life and relationships. He worked very hard to discover the uncomfortable feelings which were being tranquilized by it. Many of them came from having a twin brother who was a freak.

Arty said it was difficult being the twin replica of a freak and trying to gain acceptance amongst peers at any age. So Arty took the road of least resistance, perhaps the only road which is open to a young person in his situation. He gained acceptance by using and doing anything and everything which was acceptable to the "in" crowd. His insecurity led him to grasp for every straw in the wind which might make him feel "cool." But this incident was the *last* straw. It brought him full circle to see where grasping had led him.

Arty was also learning new ways of relating which were satisfying and didn't necessarily lead to demise. He had begun to find that he was Arty; he had some worthwhile fulfilling interests, feelings and standards of his own. He began to no longer be as dependent upon others and their demands. He was beginning to respond to his own ability to figure things out and discover rewarding environmental settings which did not sell him short. They let him be Arty 100%. He did not have to pay dues to be Arty, nor did he have to use crutches. He was starting to gain good feelings and acceptance from others just by being himself, by letting others get to know his real thoughts and feelings — no matter what they were. His ideas and feelings were most important, more than anything else because they belonged to him. He was beginning to break his conditioning.

Journal entry by Sarah: March 5, 1977. Travel to Big Bend, Texas. Warm, overcast.

Arty announced today that when he had been home during the February vacation he found out from his girlfriend that the "match box of marijuana" he had scattered in the woods was actually full of mint tea leaves that had also been part of their garden.

> Dr. Sullivan, is "blowing our minds" a reasonable way to relate to the personal problems and feelings caused by our conditioning? Aren't we becoming conditioned to tranquilization of problems through drugs and alcohol? Do we tend to avoid the irrationality, dependency, and

pitfalls of the drug solution by tranquilizing our problems while becoming dependent upon the escape? Are drugs and alcohol actually authoritarian conditioning agents which control our feelings, thoughts and actions? Our school teaches young people to substitute self-reliant action for drugs. Isn't that precisely what is needed today?

Journal entry by Wally: Feb. 4, 1977 Rabun Gap, Georgia Cold, Clear. A.M.: Toured Foxfire, oral history seminar; Eve.: drove to Smokies.

Students seem to be conditioned to stand in line or follow their peers. We could arrive at a corner with four gas stations, and students would line up at one to use the bathroom. I would just walk across the street and use another facility. I would not be lonely. Dan was usually there too.

Journal entry by Wally: March 10, 1977, Tucson, Arizona. Warm, partly cloudly. A.M.: question seminar concerning Sonoran desert. Visited Sonoran Desert Museum; Eve.: Lecture by Jim Shire on Folk Catholicism on Papago Indian Reservation.

At the Sonoran Desert Museum, a group of Cub Scouts were shouting and screaming at the jaguar in the cage. They were really disturbing the animal. Dan told the group of strangers loud and clear to "simmer down, can't you see you're disturbing the animal." (Would I have said something?) Arty and others said nothing. (Probably due to conditioning.) The Cub Scouts did not quiet down until their Scoutmaster in charge said, "Be quiet, can't you hear what that man just said? Now stop it." Suddenly it was so quiet you could hear the jaguar breathing.

Journal entry by Sarah: April 13, 1977, Yosemite National Park, Calif. Cold, clear. A.M.: Rock climbing school.

We went to a rock climbing school which at the end of the day of training gave you a grade on how well you climbed. The grade meant nothing, absolutely nothing to the students. It was part of a study by the climbing school as to how well they taught and which students might be eligible for advanced classes, which we were not going to take. Some students were practically in tears when they got a low grade. All were anxious. Dan's grade was low, but it didn't even faze him. It was like it never happened. The discussion which followed revealed that getting grades was the stimulus for punishment from parents — even if the grades meant nothing. (I thought Dan's lack of fears or anxiousness about grades demonstrated a lack of conditioning where others were conditioned.)

> Dr. Sullivan, has conditioning to institutions, peer groups and authority made us oblivious to non-authoritarian rationality? Have we become conditioned into insensitivity to other living things? Have institutional taboos conditioned us into unquestioning obedience? Isn't conditioning the real explanation of Watergate? Our school reverses these harmful and destructive processes. Why shouldn't we be permitted to exist?

Journal entry by Sarah: March 25, 1977. Santa Fe, New Mexico. Cold, Cloudy. A.M.: Los Alamos Atomic Energy Museum. P.M.: Indian ruins.

A ranger anthropologist at the pueblo ruins we are visiting was intrigued with our school and decided to take a hike with us in order to get to know the kids better. We were kind of spread out and the ranger was a bit tongue-tied so conversations were not developing. Arty and Dan walked by. Arty's shoelace had broken. He said it was due to all the sharp arrowheads and flint chips left on the ground by the dog-gone primitives. The ranger saw his opening and jumped in.

"What do you mean when you say primitives? What is a primitive?"

Arty started thinking about it but Dan said immediately, "A primitive is a person who does not shit in his own water supply."

The ranger was so startled he clammed up and the two boys walked on ahead. (Was Dan's reply unconditioned in comparison to Arty's? I think so.)

> Dr. Sullivan, isn't conditioning responsible for the order and sterile atmosphere which we so often desire; the square corner, the "unsoiled" home or "clean" word, the mowed lawn? Is efficiency and cleanliness our most important product? How does it affect the natural environment? Has it become a liability rather than an asset? Our expedition school reverses this process by confronting foolish fears of dirt and nature.

Journal entry by Sarah: April 4, 1977, Death Valley, California. Hot, sunny. A.M.: hiked through Zabriskie Badlands; P.M.: Ranger walk to desert Pond (pupfish ecology); Eve.: Ranger talk on Shoshone Culture.

When it came to clothing, Arty would not only be neat but would wear and buy all the latest fashions in camping jackets and equipment. Dan never cared much what he wore, including wearing nothing at times. (In this culture that's a real lack of conditioning.) There was a large protest to this as it affected the group as a whole. Some girls thought it was obscene. They not only feared that we could get into trouble with local authorities, but that walking around with bare feet was dangerous (Dan did cut his foot on glass). The total effect was negative, and Dan made a conscious effort to remember to dress. In discussion today, he said he was trying to learn to depend on as little clothing as possible and become acclimated to cold weather. He had heard of people who wore nothing all winter long near the South Pole and did fine because they got used to it. Then the missionaries brought them clothes and these people died off because they caught pneumonia from wearing wet garments. Dan was able to walk around in his shirt sleeves during most of the winter and never caught cold during the year.

> Dr. Sullivan, has our distance from nature led us to being conditioned into feeling comfortable only when we look acceptable to other people? Are we addicted to getting good feelings from others because in our present state we can't get them from the natural environment or ourselves? Does our fashion and deodorant industry feed off and cater to our conditioned discomfort thereby reinforcing it? Wouldn't we be more secure and closer to each other if we didn't feel unacceptable because of what we were wearing or how we thought we might smell? Why are you helping close down a school which gives people good feelings and self confidence for naturally being what we really are?

Journal entry by Sarah: May 13, 1977, Cutler, Maine. Sunny and cool.

Our long discussion in Boulder, Utah ten days ago had ended in consensus that the school should finish with a six day pack trip along a wild, rocky-cliff portion of the Maine coast. It was perhaps the only remaining wilderness coast in New England, the rest was megalopolis. The school had the opportunity to experience a wilderness which could be developed at any time by the paper company which owned it, or contaminated by an oil spill.

Dan was delighted. It was a part of his own back yard which he had never explored. He would be reunited with his old friends: whales, seals, clams, barnacles, etc.

For five days all kinds of questions and problems have arisen. We climbed across geologic formations, waded through tidepools, crawled under fragrant spruce and balsam brush, hiked spectacular headlands, pounding surf, and magnificent coastal scenes. We drank from small springs, lived directly in nature's energies, watched the osprey nest, the eagle soar. We crossed the running tide — held productive meetings amid the splendor of a most striking wilderness — came in contact with wildness as well as ourselves — found equal meaning and sense in both.

On the evening of the fifth day, a freak snowstorm with gale winds struck New England. It tore into the rocky cliffs of the Fundy shore where the school was camped. We stayed holed up for the day with only summer tarps for protection from the eleven inches of snow. Temperatures were below freezing. Wetness led to danger from overexposure. Every possible precaution was taken.

Many students including Arty were somewhat disappointed by the blizzard. They felt it was unfair that they had been snowed-out two days early and gotten cold and wet. Dan enjoyed every minute of the hike. He said that if you are to visit with nature you shouldn't expect her to change her ways just because you dropped by; one should appreciate her for what she was. (Was this a conditioned attitude or were the remaining students "spoiled" by overprotective technologic conditioning. In retrospect everybody enjoyed the hike, learned from it and wanted to do it again.

> Dr. Sullivan, isn't it a duty of education to expose the student to the world he lives in and prepare him for it? Isn't nature part of our world? Why are you questioning our school when we are one of the few which responsibly fulfill this obligation?
>
> Thank you for your kind attention and consideration of this letter. Be aware that this letter contains less than half of many similar journal entries concerning Dan Miller. We hope it clears up any misunderstandings which have led to the necessity of a hearing and possible prosecution. It is obvious that each of us in his own way is making an important contribution to the welfare of the Millers and to young people everywhere.
>
> > Very truly yours,
> > Sarah and Wally Bryce
>
> cc:
> Mr. Charles French
> Dr. Steven Gitman
> Office of the Attorney General
> State Department of Education

With mixed feelings of anger and relief Wally read the letter a second time and then yelled, "Hey, Sarah, look at this. Dr. Sullivan must have fallen off his desk and on to his couch. His response to our letter seems damned close to being rational!"

                                  Psychiatry Division
                                  State Dept. of Public Health
                                  Augusta, Maine
                                  August 23, 1977

Wally and Sarah Bryce
RD #3
Whitehorse, Maine
Dear Mr. and Mrs. Bryce,

    Thank you for your thoughtful provocative letter of May 18, 1977. Although I believe I understand most of the points you have made, several questions still remain unanswered to the Attorney General and other commissioners.

    Please be advised that the status of the forthcoming hearing is now entirely in the hands of the Attorney General.

    I have heard nothing but glowing reports about your school from the Millers. It sounds like you had a great year.

                                    Cordially,
                                  Dr. Richard Sullivan

XV

I'd grown to know and love all these plants and creatures. I think my favorite was the sculpin, a harmless bottom feeding fish. The feller looked like a midget monster just emerged from either the age of dinosaurs or Sesame Street—bulging eyes and sharp spines coming out of its head and fins. Its bottom fins almost looked like legs. Maybe it walked on them across the ocean floor.

I felt sorry for it. Everybody who caught one was greatly alarmed one way or another. It was a bad dream come true. People on the dock would scream, curse it, stamp on it, stab it, throw it violently on the ground, torture it, call it "baitstealer", "disgusting," "horrible," "ugly fish," refuse to touch it, swing it around hitting it against objects, beat in its head, mangle it, crush it, kick it, burn it, or leave it to suffocate on the dock. But I thought it really mysterious and different; perhaps the sculpin is a visitor from the geologic past. The small ones were quite cute.

From a composition by Dan Miller, age 16.

From *The Downeast Gazette,* August 19, 1976
The Northpoint City Council sold the land to the Richton Corporation despite four higher bids. Our bid was twice as high as theirs. At the very least the council could be half honest and just sell the city and its people outright to the corporation for a profit. At least then we'd get something out of it besides pollution, higher taxes and industrialization.

Marie Wensell, President
Northpoint Conservation Society

Dr. S. Gitman
907 Central Avenue
Augusta, Maine
May 25, 1977

Wally & Sarah Bryce
RD #3
Whitehorse, Maine

Dear Wally & Sarah,

Thank you for sending me a copy of your May 18th letter to Dr. Richard Sullivan. It was most enlightening and will be a great help in my advice to the Attorney General with regard to your hearing.

I have in my possession a copy of an article written by Dan Miller entitled "The Party." You told me he was ashamed of it, or afraid to let others see it. He never showed it to anyone. You gave me a copy of it last September when we met at your attorney's office here in Augusta. In the letter you just sent me your journal entry of Feb. 1, 1977 states that "Dan was encouraged to powerfully communicate his thoughts and feelings in every possible way." Did he ever learn to do this? If so, do you have any sample(s) of his writing after that meeting? I would appreciate your forwarding one or two compositions by Dan to help me further determine the school's effects upon him. I would also be interested in hearing any further examples of Dan's immunity to conditioning if they are different than material already covered in your letter or in our previous get-together.

I've recently discovered that Nancy Baker, the daughter of an old classmate of mine, was on your school this year and enjoyed it immensely. Her parents are very enthusiastic about the changes which have taken place in her. They tell me she is a much happier, involved individual. Congratulations!

                Sincerely,
                Steve Gitman, M.D.

                Bryce
                RD #3
                Whitehorse, Maine
                May 27, 1977

Dr. Steve Gitman
907 Central Avenue
Augusta, Maine
Dear Dr. Gitman,

It was nice hearing from you and discovering your familiarity with Nancy's parents. It's a small world, isn't it?

Enclosed, with his permission, are the compositions by Dan Miller which you requested. We're glad you asked for further comments about Dan for we inadvertently omitted the following observations: "During the year it has been both obvious and refreshing to us to note how Dan relates to all people as people. He experiences and treats girls in the same way that he treats boys. Girls are not considered different, inept, weak sex objects who are only allowed to play certain roles or do certain kinds of work. In his eyes girls are equals in every sense of the word.

It was not until March that Arty and many of the other boys began to realize the equality of people and act accordingly. Until then many of the boys would occasionally give back rubs, but only to girls. They would tend to have girls do the cooking and shopping while they did equipment repair and bus maintenance. They would often disregard what a girl said just because she was a girl. They would not use foul language when girls were present.

Most of this prejudice disappeared by the end of the school year but we consider it to have been the unconscious result of cultural conditioning. At no time did any of the boys say they ideologically believed girls were inferior or different. They just acted that way — with the exception of Dan Miller."

Due to continuous close contact with Dan this year it was hard to determine if and when changes were taking place in him. However, one thing was quite noticeable.

Dan was no longer backing off from people or issues. He was not drowning in bad feelings while he was with others of any age. By mid-January he was writing papers which dealt with his reactions to his classmates. He was hiding neither his feelings nor his papers. They were becoming an important tool with which he could affect his immediate environment constructively.

Dan was quite distressed about Arty's self-image crisis at the Okefenokee Swamp campsite. He was also very concerned about the effects of his own communication problems with others and attempted to follow some of the group's suggestions made at the Okefenokee meeting. He wrote the following paper about Arty being ready to sell out his better interests in order to please a "neighbor." It was Dan's first attempt on the school to write about people's actions and communicate his viewpoint to them in writing. He tried to make the paper interesting in order to catch and keep the attention of the reader. It was read by all the students and staff (as are everybody's papers at school). He received favorable comments from everyone. The paper not only got his point across, but it was fun to read.

Feb. 5, 1977

A Little Known Discussion Which Took Place Awhile Back
by Dan Miller

God: Moses, I have here several tablets which I think will be of interest to you.

Moses: Jesus, that's great! I've been a little under the weather lately. I'll take two.

God: No, No, these are written tablets. I'll read some to you. You might want to take notes. (God commences reading)

Moses: I must say, these have certainly been interesting commandments you have been dictating to me, God. It's amazing that you could figure them out.

God: Oh, it's nothing really. I had a few spare moments and jotted them down. I was really dying to try out my new ball point pen anyhow.

Moses: You certainly are humble. Why, these are wonderful. Are they copyrighted? Can I use them to tell my people? I can keep my job as leader for another couple of terms by trying to push these.

God: Sure, go ahead, have a good time, make a buck.

Moses: Do you get a commission on them — do you have an agent?

God: No, go ahead and use them with my compliments.

Moses: You mean they're free?

God: Yep!

Moses: Terrific, you got any more?

God: What do you have so far?

Moses: Let's see — "Thou shalt not kill" — that's a winner for sure. "Thou shalt not steal" — really — it's so true — "Thou shall not commit adultery" — terrific, but it will be hard to sell — I'll use pictures — that'll do it.

God: For sure!

Moses: Anything else?

God: How many you got so far?

Moses: Three.

God: We should have some more here somewhere.

Moses: You got anything which will make all of them hot sellers — you know something with a punch to it. Maybe it could rhyme — not too long though — I think I could print them on the bottom of ash trays and clean up.

God: How about "You should have only one God, mainly me."

Moses: Re-worded that could be a winning item — a beauty.

God: Let's see, how about "Thou shalt not chew gum?"

Moses: No good, no good — the gum industry is the economically stabilizing force — millions of sheckels are spent in advertising alone.

God: But it gives you cavities.

Moses: No good. Stick to philosophy or morality. Don't be authoritarian.

God: What's authoritarian?

Moses: God-almighty — look who's asking what authoritarian is. Mr. "A" himself. How about one more?

God: How many do you need?

Moses: Ten is a good number — five for each hand so those people who wear shoes won't have to take them off.

God: Let's see — nothing else in my notebook — I thought I'd remember the rest, but I've forgotten. How about "Thou shalt take complete and explicit notes" — that's helpful.

Moses: No good — we're still using parchment — some can't write.

God: Let me think — hmmm — How about — "Thou shalt love thy neighbor." OK? Everybody has a neighbor unless they don't wash.

Moses: Wash?

God: Oh, hasn't that come in yet? It's like anoint but more thorough and all over.

Moses: "Love Thy Neighbor" — I like it. It's confusing, but sell it along with the adultery pictures and it'll move.

God: In my infinte wisdom I think maybe you shouldn't use that one.

Moses: Why not?

God: People might believe it!

Moses: So?

God: They'll get very confused.

Moses: You must be one smart feller — What's confusing? I can't see it confusing.

God: The reason it's confusing is that people — when they're not making sense — do rotten things. They disobey other commandments — they should be avoided when they act that way — when they act like trash. How can you tell other people they should love trash? Do you kiss your garbage? Are you a dung hugger? You tell them they should love their neighbor, and instead of running when the pusher comes, they'll stick around and get smeared. A feller comes by who's going to rape you or mug you or put LSD in your beer and a commandment says "love thy neighbor." Hell, that's downright dangerous — it's misleading — a person could die.

Moses: Oh, I get it. If your neighbor is a jerk should you really love a jerk? Of course you shouldn't — but then If you don't who will?

God: Who will? His wife or his mother or a professional jerk lover will.

Moses: Love him even if he is a jerk — boy that's thoughtful — even deep. I think the public will go for it.

God: You should amend it!

Moses: Amend it?

God: Amend it and I'll be your best friend.

Moses: What should it say?

God: How about: "Love your neighbor if he's nice."

Moses: No good — A lot of the time he's drunk or high and so out of his head he's not really nice. He could even run over you or your kid with a car and at best say *nicely*, "I'm sorry." Why love him? Even though he thinks he's nice.

God: How about, "Love your neighbor like your father and mother."

Moses: Listen God, I thought you were smart. Now I'm not so sure. Why love your father and mother if they don't treat you right. When I was a kid I painted my teeth green 'cause it was interesting and I got such a crack — boy — I wouldn't have loved my mother then even if she was my neighbor.

God: B'gosh, you're right — I just remembered one commandment I didn't write down. "Honor thy father and mother" — for they still put up with you and maybe even liked you when your teeth were green. Honor — not necessarily love.

Moses: On some people green teeth is an improvement.

God: How about this one — ready?

Moses: Hit me baby.

God: "Love thy neighbor by telling him what you think or feel" — good, bad or indifferent — and tell your neighbor that any form of honest communication is really love — confuse the son of a bitch!

Moses: Terrific, but who'd believe you?

God: I give up. Are you going to use "Love thy neighbor"?

Moses: I don't know. I'll think about it during my vacation.

God: Where are you going for vacation?

Moses: I think I'll dig some clams. Do you know a good location?

God: The red sea at low tide — terrific!

Moses: Have you got a tide table — let me see it — say — a really low-low-spring tide right in the middle of Passover — I think I'll go and bring some friends with me.

God: Have a good time, and remember what I've been saying.

Moses: What?

God: "Love Thy Neighbor CAREFULLY." Don't let him do a number on you.

Moses: Are you telling me what to do? Now I feel badly 'cause you don't trust me. Is that love?

Dan's final paper of the year laid it all on the line.

Going Home
by Dan Miller

May 11, 1977

"We simply need that wild country available to us, even if we never do more than drive to its edge and look in. For it can be a means of reassuring ourselves of our sanity as creatures, a part of the geography of hope." Thus states Loren Eiseley, as quoted in

Time Magazine. I have heard similar statements by Ashley Montague.

Statements are words, not music. They fly by, activate images in your head, and keep on flying, taking the images with them. They are replaced by new words, new images.

I wish I could hypnotize you with my writing; reach inside you with my message so you'd fully understand what I'm going to say.

Will you let me in? Will you put aside disrupting intruders for just a few moments?

Why not test if you are actually going to listen to me? The test question is: "Am I going to try to understand Dan Miller's Paper — Do I want to? . . . . . Yes. . . . . . No. I hope you checked "yes". It's important. Written words are so weak yet can say so much.

I am frightened. Scared shit is more descriptive of how I feel. I'm leaving an environment of people who have meant more to me than anyone I have ever met. We know each other better than we know our families. It's happened because we wanted it to happen. Tearfully, joyfully, we ripped down the curtains which have kept us apart — now we can see and feel each other — know we know each other.

Words are so deceiving. We "know" each other. I also "know" my seventh grade teacher in school. My God, it's the same word: "know". But my teacher was a complete stranger compared to how I know you. We live in the words and the images they bring. Pictures do the same thing. They reach into us and turn our heads away from where they would otherwise be. We grow up with so many words — they draw us away from each other so that it can be truly said the curtains we tore down were woven of the warp of the word and the weft of the image. Words can be hypnotic.

That's why I'm so scared. Going home for me is going into a world which sees me as being fuel to burn for its economy. I know you. I also know me. We are not kindling. I'm a person. So are you. Once we leave here, the mass media images are going to grab us and unconsciously continue to condition us to forget about the importance of our own lives to us. The mass media will have us make "ashes" of ourselves. They are going to try to steamroller over the wonderful beauty which is you and me. They won't get me because I can't be conditioned. But they're after you and you're susceptible. You are very susceptible to such images and that's why I'm scared. I'm frightened because those images are insane just like Eiseley says. Capitalistic images don't really care about any effects except one: Does it make money? That's insanity, there's more to the world than money, but that's our conditioning.

Look at the rest of that Time Magazine, or any form of media. What the hell is it saying other than "join our madness or die of isolation and poverty." What am I going back to? Whatever "it" is, I don't want it. I don't need it. I won't have it. But you will be forced to live it, unless you can see how it grabs you. Only then will you be able to avoid its greedy arms. The American mass media environment will take you and shape you and make you into what it is: an escape from discomfort, discomfort due to a lack of direct contact with the essence of real life which is nature. I've seen this happen to Arty over the years. Now he can see it, too. Will he be able to remain a person or will he fall victim to the hypnotic trance and lure of the escape world? Must I stand by and watch my own twin and all of you become the robots of escape: beer drinking, power hungry, money grabbing, chemical eating, cigarette smoking, mind blowing, pinball playing, cigar puffing, fashion centered, pimping, sexually repressed, electrically dependent, peeping tomish, anti-homosexual, God-fearing, politically deceitful, competitive, stupid-law abiding, swindling, cancer infested, motorcycle racing, deceitful, murdering and raping, welfare cheating, con-artistic, charity receiving, war producing, religiously hypocritical, people manipulating, exploitive, anti-communist, new car buying, munitions producing, technology dependent, security seeking, ritual following, dictator controlled, oil importing, parachute jumping, water skiing, polluting, fast food eating, TV watching, rock music listening, roller coaster riding, overcrowded, girl watching, thrill seeking, wife cheating, sports fan, Hollywood idolizing, terrorizing, tax evading, lobbying, marketing, raunch producing, CB addicted, conditioned machines, Inc. That's a small part of what is known as culture — our culture — our way of placating our discomfort, our way of avoiding nature. That's what we're being conditioned to buy.

How can I say this? What special words can I use? None. They'll all come out meaning the same thing. So why be choosy. There's no escape from feelings. So here goes: I think it's a moral and ethical sin to grind up nature to produce the horseshit that we call our culture. Why, you might ask, why am I hesitant to say this? I'll tell you why: to do so, to feel so, to think so, to be so, makes me a freak in society's eyes, just like I was once in your eyes. But I don't like being a "freak". I hate it. Do you understand? I hate it! I hate it because it really hurts. But the economy hates self-reliance. It hates me. I can see through its exploitive, conditioned stupidity like it was naked. The economy does not want to be exposed. Exposure leads to awareness by others. Awareness could conceivably bring about more rational behavior. What would happen to the tobacco industry? The chemical food and liquor industries, the pushers, big business? They'd be dead from lack of interest. Consider: those bastards exist by finding every self-putdown we carry around (which they help give us) in ourselves and then sell us their poison and escapes on the pretense that these will build us up — will make us feel better. They could build and sell us something beneficial like a wildlife sanctuary or mental health if they so desired.

Lord, there's nothing much lower than giving poison to unsuspecting babies. Due to conditioning, that's exactly what we are — babies — living out our conditioned childhood rewards and punishments, even me. I can feel the results of the first three years of my conditioning. I'm not completely self-reliant. I'm addicted to warmth from people. I desire security of some kind. I feel bad if I wet my bed.

This year has taught me an amazing number of things. One of them is that it makes sense for me to clearly speak my mind effectively, controllingly, passionately.

The second is that I must do something to help people discover, understand and do something about their foolishly conditioned feelings and actions. My altered state of being could make a vital contribution in this area.

The third is that somehow I've got to get powerfully involved in the mainstream of our economy and take the profits from the big, successful conglomerates I will own and use them to promote both environmental awareness and wild habitats. I want to use the economy and beat it at its own game. I want to have its environmentally degrading aspects swallowed up by its own success.

As people become environmentally aware and concerned, they would make efforts to buy only from the Danny Miller food market, the Danny Miller clothing store, the Danny Miller college, and Danny Miller non-polluting cars. They would do so because the profits would go into the environment which is, in the long run, their own cause. They'd also be buying the most environmentally sound products which technology could produce, at prices a little lower than elsewhere. I would make the Danny Miller conglomerates non-profit, tax exempt, but donate money directly to environmentally sound government projects such as wilderness protection, the youth conservation corps, environmental education, etc. At this point I'm convinced it's the only way the environment can be saved. I only hope you can hear me, feel the same way, and at least respect me, if not help.

You may have a choice in life as to which way you will go. I have no choice. It is physically impossible for me to join the insanity of today without becoming terminally insane. That is obviously not true for you. You are already insane, feeling and operating accordingly. Your advantage over others is that perhaps you know you're insane and can do something about it. And if you don't know it now, please remember I've tried to tell you. I've tried to be as honest as possible even though I now realize that I've been hurting you right where you've been conditioned.

There's just one other thing I want you to know. I've often thought that if I took an overdose of drugs today, it might kill me — or make me a vegetable — or it might just possibly cure me. Perhaps I'd come out of it "normal", "conditionable," like everybody else. I used to think about overdosing and taking the chance. This year, your caring friendship, honesty and genuine concern for me has convinced me of my self-worth as I am in my present state. I'm different, but I'm OK. When I first came on the expedition, I did not like people very much. Now, I love all of you for just being you, for just being yourselves. Now, no matter how much it may hurt me at times, I want to stay as I am. Perhaps this way, through the environment, I can most effectively return to you what you have so lovingly given to me. I can't begin to thank you.
Dan Miller.

> Dr. Gitman, we hope these compositions are of some assistance to you. Thanks for your interest in us.
> Sincerely,
> Wally & Sarah Bryce

XVI

Without the clock I became aware of the natural rhythm of the tides. I was disciplined by their universal law rather than the arbitrary rules at school. I felt secure in the order that governed the rest of the world around me — the run of the smelt in the spring, the fall migration of birds, the regularity of the moon, stars, sun and tide. Only that rhythm would call or direct me. It would feel right to be in harmony with the celestial clock which would call you home at darkness and awaken you with the soft color of the rising sun.

From a composition by Dan Miller, age 16.

From *The Downeast Gazette,* July 23, 1975

Clammers, fishermen, lobstermen are forced to have their occupations jeopardized. They scream at the injustice of it all while the awestruck would-be-millionaires of the refinery may be destroying their livelihoods with an oil spill. Taking an individual's occupation from him knowingly, without consent, is just plain thievery. The job situation being what it is up here, it's close to being murder.

Jim Morris, Director
Downeast Fisherman's Cooperative

Journal entry by Wally: July 4, 1977, Cell block C, Windsor State Prison, Augusta, Maine. Cold and damp. Dreary forecast.

I suppose many the reader is not surprised by the date and place of this entry. Perhaps some of you expected it. I suspect that some of you out there thought this was where I belonged quite some time ago. Others might have figured this is where I'd end up. For many, it was a toss-up between jail and the state asylum in Bangor. After all, can the government — the "businessmen's representative" — afford to let someone with my inclinations roam around loose and not be convicted? Can "the people" have their children or their children's friends exposed to the unusual thinking, school and outlook of Wally Bryce? Not on your life, right? Justice will be, and was done.

By school's end some very mature young people were met by some very enthusiastic parents who were downright amazed by their youngster's increased awareness and general overall well-being. To say that Ben and Carol were anything less than thrilled would have to be an understatement. When Dan went away with us, he was anti-people. He came back ready, nay eager, to relate — enthusiastic about continuing his education, hopeful that there was a place in the world for him and his ideas. He was ready to try and constructively do something about his avoidance of people; he was eager to help the natural environment which he so loved.

Arty was a much stronger person, too. He had learned who he was, that his basic unconditioned feelings were indeed worthwhile. He was no longer dependent upon the approval of others alone. Self approval from the conscious, rational, aware aspect of his personality had become a strong, important part of his thinking. It was close to impossible to make him feel that he had to do something he felt was stupid, just to obtain the friendship or admiration of others. Now, he felt "cool" most of the time. He had no need to join activities which would prove his "coolness" to himself or others. When he felt the pain from a "bomb" of emotional discomfort, he would make efforts to de-fuse the bomb rather than tranquilize the pain. The bomb could be teachers, parents, friends, enemies, or Dan. He would avoid "parties," but if he did go would enjoy himself without the crutches of beer and drugs. He had become interested in psychology on the school, and was planning to major in it at the state university. School no longer seemed like a stupid prison; rather, it became a hardware store where he could obtain useful, interesting tools for his own projects. We had given him a conscious choice of relationships and directions. He could make decisions based upon their effects on himself and the environment. He was no longer a helpless pawn of the social or biological world for he had gained a new freedom which was previously beyond his reach.

But Carol had unwittingly lit a timebomb back in December. It resulted in the second subpoena and the hearing. The Millers had applied for state aid — financial assistance — for Dan and Arty to participate on the expedition. The State refused, saying the boys were not attending an approved school; they were, in fact, truant.

Carol thought that to be unfair. She checked with former parents and students; their enthusiasm convinced her that more people should know about our school and utilize its services. Carol felt it should be part of the federal and state government — they should provide grant money for scholarships and a college institute to teach others how to operate expeditions out of public schools, private schools, camps, youth centers and the like. She thought it should be incorporated in government youth programs and services in national parks. So last December Carol wrote letters expressing her views to various government officials, including the President of the United States. His offices evidently duplicated the letter, and sent it around to several departments. That was the problem. It aggravated our already explosive situation by giving us exposure to those who were threatened by something socially different. Pretty soon our congressman from Maine wanted to have more information. Then the Interstate Commerce Commission wanted to know if we had a federal license. Health, Education and Welfare wanted to know if we were authorized or approved by the State. The Surgeon General's office wanted my credentials. Inquiries literally came pouring into our office at the house as well as to the State Education Department. Then the State Public Health Department got wind of the investigation, none other than Dr. Richard Sullivan (my ol' buddy, right?) is the director of the department. He got the promotion. Now he could use publicity to go further up the ladder. Run for political office maybe.

Yes sir, that was a darling letter Carol wrote — all about how we cured the symptoms of this personality disorder and that neurotic trend — how we cleared up social problems like crime, how we cured cancer and heart disease by getting kids to stop smoking, how we cured liver ailments for the kids were no longer as dependent upon alcohol.

As it was, many people were already familiar with the school on account of the publicity it received from my book and articles and interviews I'd done. Then the co-ed stigma drifted into view through a TV interview with Dr. Sullivan. Was it mentally healthy that high school and college boys and girls be allowed to live together for a year on an expedition? That got him some publicity right there — even *I* knew something was going to happen when the sex bug-a-boo was dragged into the picture. Health, welfare, personality, commerce — all were dull — very dull. But sex, oh boy, sex even beat money.

The outcome of all this hysteria was that in January the Attorney General's office, tracked down and subpoened Sarah and I to appear on June 11th to answer to all the original charges. It really burned my ass to hear about that crock of shit. I was coming into these god-damned hearings fighting mad, ready to tear them apart. Hopefully I wouldn't take a swing at one of those officious bastards. Charlie, Ben, Carol, Dan and Arty came along.

The hearing was chaired by the old Attorney General himself. Seated on his right was Dr. Richard Sullivan. On A.G.'s left (I won't bore you with the Attorney General's full name, "A.G." is already a waste of two ordinarily respectable letters). On his left sat a representative from the Department of Motor Vehicles. I'll call him Transportation Boy — T.B. for short — that's perfect: "T.B." a disease that sticks in your throat. And to his left, weighing in at 285 pounds of educated blubber, was my favorite candidate for "target" in the "pin the tail on the donkey" game — Wallowing Eddy Fotch — the Commissioner of Education for private and other nonconforming schools.

"Hi, piggy," I thought to myself. "You still around? How about we'll have lunch together — I'll meet you down at the trough when the twelve o'clock whistle blows sooooooweeeee and they slop the department."

It's a good thing I don't have any problems with authority figures, right? Believe me, if I did, I would have just moved the school into a different state rather than put up with this gang.

A.G., T.B., Richard and Piggy, the formidable, fearsome foursome, are nothing more than the top of the hierarchy of their powerful, controlling institutions. I'm sure they each have a family, they love their children and dog. But I don't know them personally. I'm just an entity to them, an image, an aspect of the system which we all invented and which they enforce. If they knew me personally, or were involved with me financially I would have "pull" and somehow not be the subject of a hearing. The foursome are the ultimate personification of mankind's great mistake: leaving nature and living in ignorant man-made images and letting themselves be conditioned by them. The foursome represent the images, the institutions, and the rules that can condition our lives. Nowadays people do not direct the system, *the rules alone* do. We can't relate to rules, we merely obey them or disobey them. They are inhuman, imaginary stimuli to which we are conditioned from birth and before. We, on the other hand, are human. We are living things which have lost the ability to relate to nature and are now stuck only with each other and the rules. The rules, the system, is never right for any *individual*. It never quite pertains to any single person's particular situation. The system is just a degrading but accurate statement that we are so out of contact with the environment and each other that we must be directed and protected if we are to personally survive. The first man that drove through an intersection carelessly was the reason for the first stop sign. We now obey stop signs blindly, even if we're not careless. By now we're incredibly dependent upon the signs, and punished if we don't obey them. We're conditioned to them. Hell, I'd rather be conditioned to a tree, a rabbit or the wind.

Fortunately, A.G. starts off the hearing with Piggy. I say fortunately because I think I might have burst if I had to put up with another second of the idiocy of the State Department of Education. The proceedings went something like this:

A.G.: Mr. Bryce, is your school approved by the State Department of Education as described in Statute 1094?

Me: We have applied for such approval on several occasions but have never obtained it.

Piggy: A.G., sir, the school has failed to meet the standards set up by the legislature. It refuses to meet them.

Me: We don't refuse. We physically can't. The state code requires a physical plant which is to be inspected by the public health officer, the fire marshal, the plumbing inspector, the electrical inspector, the commissioner of education's office. Our school operates out of a school bus. That's our "plant". We don't have any blackboards, washrooms, plumbing, audio-visual department, fire escapes, nurse, instruction rooms, officers, etc. We camp out rain or shine. We study and examine the environment directly, not through images alone. We operate as a coordinated team, without attendance officers, deans, principals, schedules, and the like. The education commissioner has been fully informed of this on many occasions. We even offered to drive the "plant" up to his office for inspection.

Piggy: The regulations specifically state that all these requirements must be met if we are to give approval to a school. The legislature makes the regulations, we make sure their wishes are legally fulfilled before offering approval.

Me: For five years I have been informing the Education Commissioner that his department is not prepared to even begin to deal with a school like ours. He should continue to ignore us, until he is able to appreciate this program.

Piggy: The law specifically states that all schools operating within the state be approved. Your mailing address is within the state. You are a school, an accredited school. Therefore, you must be approved.

Me: Would it be helpful if I built a miniature schoolhouse which fulfilled all state regulations and put it into our post office box? You could inspect it with a magnifying glass. Maybe that's the answer. We don't spend more than a week or two in this state otherwise.

A.G.: Mr. Bryce, this is a serious matter which is not to be taken lightly.

Me: I was serious. What's your solution other than that we cease to operate? That's basically all I've been told to do by the state for the past eighteen years since the school opened. Shape up or ship out. That's all the assistance I've received from the state: harassment! To my way of thinking this kind of behavior is unbecoming to an educational community, and especially to its commissioner.

Carol: I'd like to say something for myself, my family and other families everywhere, as a citizen. This is a fine school. It's fantastic. It achieves in areas where few others can achieve. Closing it would be a great loss to students and families. Its services are desperately needed by people everywhere.

A.G.: I'm sorry, but you're out of order.

Carol: (under her breath) Look who's talking.

Me: I must say that even this hearing is a continuation of this harassing process. Every aspect of the situation has been well known to your office and the commissioner's office for eighteen years. We've sent you all our materials, all our articles. We applied for approval when we started to operate in the summers. We've worked with thousands of kids. They and the world are all the happier for it. There is all kinds of testimony to that fact. Why, at this late date, is this matter again being brought up?

A.G.: The public is concerned.

Me: About what?

A.G.: That your school is a hazard, or illegal.

Me: Let's get down to the truth. The public is concerned because the media has made them concerned. They are conditioned to the media and their own taboos. Somehow, the public has been led to believe that we may be unethically, illegally or immorally letting boys and girls live together. Their own qualms, images, and guilt feelings have been aroused. Now, you people are trying to capitalize on that situation, for your own personal gain in stature, salary, and job responsibility.

A.G.: That is not the purpose of this hearing.

Me: I didn't finish. I want to state here and now that there is nothing unethical, illegal, immoral or misrepresentative about our school with regard to its treatment of sex, academics, and other subjects. One only has to read our literature or visit us to determine the accuracy of that statement. And I am further stating for the record that, until there is an official, valid complaint filed, this issue is closed as far as I'm concerned. I refuse to discuss this foolishness any further. You already have every fact and detail you need with regard to the education department.

Piggy: You don't understand. You are operating illegally in the eyes of the law.

Me: I refuse to discuss the matter. What's next?

A.G.: Are you going to cooperate?

Me: Not on the present issue. What else is to be discussed? If there are no other questions, I'm going to leave.

A.G.: That may not be in your own best interests nor those of the school.

Me: Everything has its limits. This is degradingly stupid for all of us. I have no need for Catch 22. I think you gentlemen are blindly following rules which don't apply here; you have been conditioned to do so and are being paid to do so. You have brought a cat named Fido into a dog show and rather than recognize it as being a cat, you insist on trying to judge it as a dog. You will be the laughing stock of everybody, an embarrassment to the state. Go ahead and do it if you have to. But I'll not waste my time further.

There are so many things, worthwhile things, positive things, helpful things that you could have done and still can do with regard to our program. It is a mockery to the sanity of our society that the best action you have come up with is to continually tell us we will be closed down or fined. My God! The young people in this country are being staggered by the inability of the educational system to meet their needs as human beings and citizens. They resort to every asocial act imaginable to signal that something is wrong. Our school responds to their pleadings and demonstrably gives constructive assistance and guidance in every conceivable area. Does the State Education Department rejoice? Not on your life. Do they offer scholarship funds? No! Do they try to integrate our findings and process into the existing system — an exciting, simple matter of encouraging expedition education emanating from the public schools? No way! Do they ask us to assist in setting up a demonstration school to see what can be done? No! Do they in any way encourage us to set up an institute which would teach others how to accomplish what we do? Not at all! Perhaps we have discovered a major antidote for many of our social diseases. Has the State Department of Education shown any interest? No! The only action in eighteen years is precisely that which is being rehashed again today by the commissioner and I am being expected to take it seriously and respect it. I ask you, who should be investigated — us or the department? If I was the commissioner, I would make the last two years of high school optional for any qualified student who desired and was qualified to enter a citizenship / environment / discovery program such as ours. The overall improvement in their state of being as well as improvement in the health of the environment would obviously be highly advantageous to everybody. I would be happy to fully cooperate with the commissioner in such a program. But I'll be hanged if I'm going to put any more energy into the foolishness of this inquiry. Now that's final. Period. cooperate with the commissioner in such a program. But I'll be hanged if I'm going to put any more energy into the foolishness of this inquiry. Now that's final. Period.

Carol: Amen!

A.G.: That is practically contemptuous. I —

T.B.: A.G., I have a few questions.

A.G.: Go right ahead, T.B.

T.B.: If I may, Mr. Bryce, I note that you are completely and properly licensed with regard to the operation and maintenance of an interstate motor vehicle. There is no question about that. But what color is your school bus?

Me: Yellow.

T.B.: The state law specifically states that only school buses for approved schools may be painted yellow. All others must be of another color. You are not an approved school.

Me: Yellow is the safest color. It protects the passengers — who are school children. That's why we paint ours that color. It's a safety factor. People are conditioned to it, they recognize us as a school. They are extra careful.

T.B.: It is illegal.

Me: Are you telling me that the law is written so that to be 'legal' we must endanger the lives of students? It would seem more sensible to change the law than change the color of the bus, don't you think?

T.B.: It does seem ludicrous, but the law is to be obeyed. That's my job.

Me: My responsibility — my job — is to safely convey students and I will continue to do so. I can't believe it! First the law refuses to give us approval because we might be unsafe. Now the law openly refuses to let us operate safely. You fellows ought to get together with Dr. Sullivan over there. He's a psychiatrist.

Dr. Sullivan: Thanks, but no thanks, Mr. Bryce. I'm here because the medical board wants to determine if you are practicing medicine without a license. It's a very serious offense.

Carol: Dr. Sullivan, you know exactly what Wally is doing. What do you think? Is he harming anyone?

Dr. Sullivan: That's not the point. One needs a license to practice medicine or counseling. If that is what Mr. Bryce is doing, then he needs a license and special training.

Me: Do I need a license to expose kids to their God-given social and natural environment?

Dr. Sullivan: That's not my department. I don't think they have a license for that — yet.

Me: That's all I'm doing. I'm helping kids see what their eyes and ears can be used for besides listening to conscious or unconscious orders. I'm taking them around so they may see their world — their environment as it really is — how others live and cope. Is that illegal?

Dr. Sullivan: The environment to which you expose them includes full 24 hour / day contact with members of the opposite sex, is that not correct?

Me: You know it is.

Dr. Sullivan: Yet you insist that illicit or illegal sexual acts or relationships are not taking place.

Me: Precisely. Have you ever heard any evidence to the contrary?

Dr. Sullivan: No, but how do you explain that these same young people, who have to be chaperoned and kept apart at home to fulfill the requirements of legal and moral laws, are able to relate sensibly and socially when they are together all the time on your school?"

Me: You've just explained it. In addition, it's been covered in books and articles about the school.

Dr. Sullivan: Oh? What is it then?

Me: The environment on the school. They are in a repeatable but different environment than at home: the contracts, the agreements, the trust, the atmosphere, the purpose, the concept, the freedom, the involvement, the respect, the friendships, the visible effects of each action and relationship, the feedback, the encounters, the outlets, the confrontations, the honesty, the openness, the self and environmental responsibility — just to name a few. The fabric of the society is different on the school. We purposely make it so.

Dr. Sullivan: But it's made up of the same kids, is it not?

Me: So what? You will admit that the environment in a family is completely different than in a school classroom or party, but it is made up of the same individuals. It is rare that young people have sexual relationships with members of their immediate family. But teenagers and adults in the same family share a house and its bedrooms. Why are you not investigating families which have teenage youngsters of both sexes? You would do well to just think of our school acting and relating like a large, close-knit, happy family unit. Then maybe you'll get it straightened out in your mind. And believe me your image will be accurate.

On the school, we face the consequences of our actions. There is no place to escape. We choose to live in the effects of our actions and relationships — those with adverse effects are curtailed until we are in an environmental setting where their effects are not harmful. At home you may have sexual desires for your sister or for someone besides your wife but you don't necessarily act them out. The effect would be hurtful. That's exactly the process we learn and practice on the expedition. Otherwise, we would not be able to exist. From this hearing alone it becomes obvious how difficult it is for us to exist even when we have nothing to hide. The fact that we hide nothing is undoubtedly a catalyst for the aroused feelings of those who are secretive.

Dan: May I say something, sir?" (Dan was immaculately dressed in a full suit with a vest, hair combed, face washed, wearing a borrowed Phi Beta Kappa key as a tie pin and an antique masonic pin in his lapel. I think he would have worn a Distinguished Service Medal if he thought it would have helped.)

Dr. Sullivan: Go right ahead.

Dan: I have a statement here signed by all the students and teachers and parents. It is to the effect that the school does not encourage nor in fact indulge in asocial activity, including illicit or illegal sexual acts. In speaking for the students, I would like to say for all of us that the testimony given here by Wally Bryce is accurate as are all the books, articles, and radio and TV statements we have heard him make. We know because we've been on the school for a year and the school he has been talking about is us. We would be happy to so testify. Thank you.

Dr. Sullivan: Thank you, Dan. I'm happy to see you and Arty here and actively involved in issues which are important to you and others. It shows 'good conditioning' and great determination on your part. (Dr. Sullivan smiled and winked at me when he said this. That's strange, I thought. What did he mean by the smile? It felt supportive! Had Sullivan already politically gained what he wanted from the hearing? Did our letter have some effect? Was the hearing now just a sham? Had he given up?)

Dan: You might be interested to know that eleven of the signatures are of professional reporters and educators who have spent extended periods of time and observation on the school.

Dr. Sullivan: For how long?

Me: Two days to three weeks.

Dr. Sullivan: (to me) Do you advertise healing or cures in any way?

Me: Yes, apathy. We cure apathy and the rest takes care of itself. We do it through travel, encounters, confrontations, and questioning.

Dr. Sullivan: Travel? That's it! That's out of my department! You're a travel agent. That's OK with me. I'm satisfied." (Obviously something had happened — he was copping out. Had Dan's testimony been overwhelming?)

A.G.: Do you have a license to be a travel agent?

Me: Well, actually, I drive the bus and I do have a license for that. Frankly, that's the only license I think I need for what I do.

A.G.: Do you have a teaching license?

Me: There is presently no training course to teach what I do. I show students how to teach themselves and each other. I help them turn the world into questions and then have them find the answers themselves. Why would I need a license of any sort to do that?

A.G.: The state requires licensing for many forms of education or business where public welfare is concerned. Even certain corporations need licenses to exist.

Me: I'd like to say something about that, if I may. Licensing corporations is a futile, ineffective stopgap measure. Rather than spend your time investigating me, you ought to do the world some good and put your energy into outlawing corporations as they presently exist.

A.G.: Mr. Bryce you're interrupting ...

Me: That would be a task worthy of your office — to make it illegal for any corporation to have the same rights and status in society as an individual. That would be an immense step in the right direction educationally and environmentally. Corporations are merely images. They are the manifestation of people's images and desires to indulge in business and economics.

A.G.: Mr. Bryce, I ...

Me: ... They are the epitomy of mankind's desire to devour the natural environment and convert it into materials and energy for the armor we create to protect ourselves from our fears of nature. To give such images the same rights and privileges as an individual human being is nothing short of obscene. Yet, we do it. That's where corporations get their power.

A.G.: Mr. Bryce! ...

Me: ... That's why the natural environment is being ruthlessly overhauled and destroyed by habitat destruction and pollution. It's an inhuman act which is being performed by nonhuman conditioned forces.

A.G.: Mr. Bryce! You are off the subject of this hearing!

Me: I think not. You are trying to determine if we are harmful or hazardous to the welfare of the public. Our school helps young people become aware of their responsibilities to themselves, to others and to the environment. Both you and present corporation laws are part of that environment. You consider us harmful because we tend to make people aware of the harm that corporations and a business-controlled government can bring. We're a threat to the status quo, and you are now trying to eradicate that threat by eliminating us. Limited corporate power would greatly enhance the ability of people to live directly in harmony with their environment and each other. No corporation should in any way, fashion or form have the ability to lobby or influence a government "of, by, and for the *people.*" Corporations are not people, — even though they are so recognized. They and you, their purchased-through-lobbying servant, don't want the people to be aware of the situation, for people might decide to change it through the power of their vote. Licensing or limiting our operation increases corporate power. That makes my statement very much in order to this hearing.

A.G.: You should go into politics if you feel so strongly about it.

Me: If I did, that would not be the first thing I'd do. The first thing I'd do was to legalize suicide, so people would at least begin to understand that they, not the government, are fully responsible for their own lives, welfare and environment ... their "pursuit of happiness". It's incredible that the government has laws that forbid a person from committing suicide. If a person isn't even free to own his own life, what does he own? Where is his real freedom?

And that's about where it ended. Permanently? I doubt it! I think Dr. Sullivan had the wind taken out of his sails. He obtained his promotion; in addition he was confronted by our letter, our observations, and my testimony at the hearing as well as Dan's. I think he could see Dan's obvious improvement. Arty's, too. I believe they both get help from him occasionally. Without Sullivan as a motivating force I suspect A.G. and the rest of the gang will have no reason to continue the investigation. There will be no complaint to work from. It's been almost a month and we've heard nothing further from the foursome.

What, you the reader of this journal say you're surprised? You thought I was in jail? Where did you get that idea? Oh, I get it, you thought that because I was writing this journal from jail, therefore I was in jail. I can understand that. I misled you, just as Dan misled me at the telephone. I purposefully exposed you to just one incomplete image. Your conditioning did the rest. You had a very reasonable supposition based on a conditioned, pre-set idea: "One who writes from a jail 'lives' there." I was in the jail singing folk songs to entertain inmates. Sorry to disappoint your images. In reality, I would quit the school before going to prison over it. Be careful when you trust incomplete images. They are misleading. They can lead to grave consequences, like the formidable fearsome foursome, environmental deterioration, "innocent" oil refineries and misadvertised products. They all take advantage of you just like I did, but they won't reveal themselves as readily.

Don't worry about the school. We'll be around. We've already made escape arrangements so that at the last possible moment, when all attempts to be sensible fail, when we've changed the education department as much as it will change, when it's do or die, we're going to do it. Yes, sir, we are thankful that a former parent has made arrangements to, if necessary, move the office and mailing address into a blessed state licensed, fully inspected, hot-shot, improved and approved, completely sterile, reinforced concrete-fashionable, first rate "A" number one, ipsy pipsy, yankee doodle, high class HOTEL!

What a travesty! What a symbolic turnabout! The school, which leading educators have described as being an innovator in the field of environmental education, is forced to end up with offices in the N.Y. Hilton. The school which the New York Times in 1976 described as being "a pioneer in the environmental education movement" — one which those who know have described as "perhaps the most valuable revolutionary educational program in the country," is forced against its desires, to offices buried in cement. A school designed to expose its participants to the elements of *both* the natural and social environment is overcome by powerful, conditioned images and elements of the social environment and compelled to place its offices in a tomb epitomizing man's distance from nature, in a fortress sealing its inhabitants from every energy of the natural elements, in a liquor licensed mausoleum of machine-made air conditioning, radio, television, walls, flooors, plumbing, heating, lighting, smells, services and scenery, in a sickening, dead atmosphere of social affluence and annihilation of nature.

Business friends have predicted that such a move will help our enrollment, the public will go for our new image. Of course they will — so will a poor fish to bait — so what? It's damned close to having the state say we must mislead the public if we are to exist. But that's conditioning for you; that's where we're at folks. Believe me, we'll fight such stupidity every inch of the way before moving into the Hilton. Everybody's got to start things rolling somewhere, right? We'll start here.

Sarah and I were born and raised in N.Y.C. Without courses it's taken us thirty years to learn there's more to life than what we learned there as kids. We'll not easily be driven back into that escape from the natural world.

I understand that now there's a move on in the statehouse to rectify our school's approval situation by changing the licensing laws. Some senators have begun to realize how unfair our present legislation is. I know we've helped create that realization by not giving in.

Recently we've been receiving requests to teach others how to operate expeditions similar to ours out of public and private schools as well as conservation societies. Two national organizations have offered to help us establish an institute for that purpose. Perhaps something positive will emerge from the hearing after all.

I envision the institute to be a permanent "ark" which will sail upon America's stormy sea of madness. It will be manned by experienced people who have a reverence for the life process. The institute will help others discover their environment, their conditioning and themselves. It will help people find real freedom: the freedom to select a sane way of life.

I recently mentioned the idea of the institute to several friends. Ben and Carol thought it was a terrific idea and promised to help in whatever way they could. So did Dr. Gitman. But, best of all, both Dan *and* Arty were equally excited about being part of it! It seems that we have all reached common ground.

XVII

I was in Woods Hole when the petroleum barge, Florida, went aground, spilling oil. I saw the shorelines littered with continuous windrows of dead fish and dying marine animals of all kinds. As the oil was liberated from the muddy bottom, others were dying. The clams were lying limp with their syphons extended or gyrating in the sand. The death list went on and on. The sands were stained yellow and the air reeked with the stench of death and oil. Clean-up crews were desperately trying to dispose of the dead animals to avoid adverse publicity. The oil is in the mud and is being picked up by the clams. Perhaps they'll never be healthy again.

From a composition by Dan Miller, age 16.

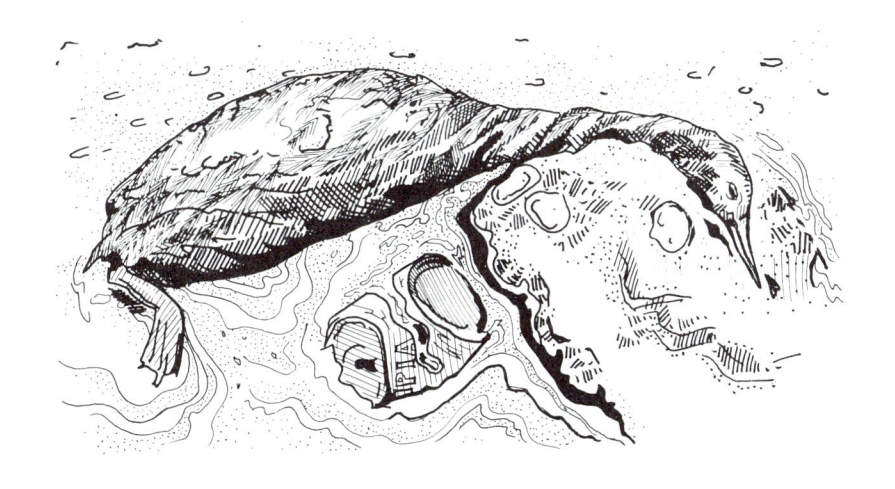

From *The Downeast Gazette,* October 11, 1975
In the international poker game of oil, all the high cards are held by the cartel giants. Oil men are very comfortable with putting on the pressure until what they want gives. The energy crisis is part of the game. It's part of the global scale muscle flexing in practice for the past fifty years.

Michael Raymond
World Business Weekly

Journal entry by Sarah: June 11, 1978. Whitehorse, Maine. Fog and rain.

Life seems to be one battle after another for us folk. Just when you have one small victory to celebrate, another enemy seems to loom up on the horizon.

That certainly has been the case for Danny Miller. Just as the trial was ending in our favor a year ago today, Danny began to be embroiled in one of the toughest battles a seventeen year old boy could ever wage. As the year unfolded, Danny would challenge the most powerful conditioning force in American society. He was to attack the guiding light of the western world, the mighty, the all-powerful ... what's that you ask? Did he take on the judiciary system? The church? The TV networks? No, Danny Miller took on the toughest enemy of all: money. The profiteering of Big Oil and the Richton Corporation.

For over seven years, Richton and its missionary-like representatives had been lobbying tirelessly to convince the people in our "impoverished and backwards" corner of eastern Maine that we were missing out on the "benefits of the twentieth century." Here on the last wild section of the eastern U.S. seaboard, Richton wanted to build an oil refinery — a refinery that would "raise our standard of living for decades and decades to come." With steadfast fortitude and perseverance, the Richton plague had slowly crept from household to household through Northpoint and the surrounding towns. Front-men had preached the Richton doctrine at every available podium, pleading with townspeople to accept Richton into their lives and to support the construction of this mighty outpost, a forerunner of oil refineries up and down the wild coast.

"We'll make you rich," they exhorted. "We'll bring the world to your doorsteps! We'll improve your schools, hospitals, and streets. We'll wipe out filth, crime, and alcoholism with a new fleet of garbage trucks, street lamps, and a community recreation center. Trust us, dear townsfolk. We have YOUR best interests in mind."

Slowly the word spread, and gradually the ranks of the opposed began to diminish. Those who spoke out against the refinery were labelled "hippy environmentalists," "wealthy folks from away," or "old-fashioned fogies." Divisiveness and slandering became common. Local politics took over from there. Richton had carefully infiltrated the town's political ranks, trickling large amounts of money and propaganda into the hands of a chosen few in high positions. Outspoken opponents began to drift back into the woodwork from whence they came.

It was the same story with the supposed "regulatory" agencies. The local, state, and federal environmental authorities consisted of people trained and skilled in economics, the essence of our culture. These government officials slowly neutralized their initial oppositions to the refinery proposal. Ultimately they too would give their consent. Cultural conditioning had made "profits" worth the risk of an environmental disaster. Even the Canadian Government whose rocky and treacherous waters would be the passageway for American-bound oil, but who would never see a drop of the finished product, fell to economics. Suddenly and mysteriously they would reverse their opposition.

All of this was too much for Dan Miller. His "bottom line" had been reached. He was no longer able to contain the torment he'd felt for so long. Richton was proposing to threaten and probably destroy the truest friend he'd ever had. No one could appreciate the intricacies of the Northpoint Bay area like Danny could. He knew every inlet on this coastline. He knew the names of every living entity in the bay. He'd spent hours, days, and weeks living and breathing the pure salty breezes, watching the whales and the seals and the tiny shellfish. He could no longer bear the image of this most treasured of worlds polluted by another human enterprise, a mockery in the name of progress.

With heartfelt furor and a clear head, he lashed out. He began to campaign openly and vigorously against seemingly overwhelming odds. Unencumbered by "normal adolescent hangups," his energy knew no bounds. At a time when most area residents, including Wally and I, had been conditioned to the inevitability of the refinery's approval, Dan was striking out and challenging the very heart of our complacency. Unconditioned, his images and energies were drawn directly from the source of life, from nature, from the will to survive.

Dan became a fireball. Lightning sparked wherever he paused. He began to attract small clusters of concerned citizens and was encouraged to pursue his goal.

He started out by writing an article for the local paper. Arty helped him with it. As they expected, the paper turned it down, claiming that it was "too controversial."

"The sons of bitches," Dan thought to himself. "They're totally controlled by the Richton machine." Undaunted, he sent the article, along with the following letter, to the regional paper in Bangor. To his and Arty's delight both were printed. The article appeared as a leading editorial:

                                                      37 Oak Street
                                                     Whitehorse, Maine
                                                      July 8, 1977

To The Editor
The Daily Star
Bangor, Maine
Dear Editor,

We understand that in Russia they charge $4,300.00 to have a tooth extracted. Dentists there have to remove teeth through a patient's ear or nose, a costly process. This is due to the fact that in Russia one is not allowed to open their mouth.

Have you recently checked the price of dental work in Northpoint?

We wrote the enclosed article, "A Russian Naval Base In Northpoint" for the local Northpoint newspaper. The editor there turned down the article. He told us that he feared the reaction to it from those who would object to its anti-oil pollution message. We went as far as to offer to buy advertising space and to place the article in it. This offer was turned down for the same reason.

It is a sad day in this country when a citizen's opinion cannot be heard because it does not please a large corporation. It is a very sad day when the free press and its advertising policy is controlled by big business interests and fear. One might rightfully say it's not a very pleasant or healthy environment in which to live; E.P.A., B.E.P., and D.E.P. take note.

Things are not running very smoothly down east because they're being lubricated by a fluid called oil. The right solution is unpolluted sea water.

                        Very truly yours,
                        Dan and Arthur Miller

Guest Editorial: A Russian Naval Base in Northpoint
by Dan and Art Miller

A little known error was discovered in the White House after President Nixon resigned. One of Mr. Nixon's tape recorders was left operating and it still is! A chambermaid friend of mine has discovered it and left it intact. She's been sending me recent tapes she thought might be of interest. The following is an alleged recent conversation between the new president and his secretary which should be of interest to citizens of Maine.

President: What's in the mail today? Did my Sears Roebuck catalogue arrive? The commissary tells me we're running low on toilet paper. Order some from Sears? No, we'll use the catalogue; just as good, you know, and you can read it too. It's either that or raise taxes.

Secretary: Mr. President, there's an incredible letter here from a member of the Northpoint City Council.

P.: Northpoint? Where's that?

S.: Maine, sir.

P.: Where's that? Oh, I remember now: Northpoint, Maine, the tidal power city that the Indians say they own. What's the councilman have to say for himself?

S.: Sir, this is absolutely unbelievable. It's a long letter in which he says — get ready for this now — he says he has arranged with Bresynev and the Russian navy to make Northpoint into a Russian naval base . . . for missile laden submarines, troop carriers, and warships.

P.: #@%$&-(*&)!¢#*&/... by golly Charlie he can't do that!! My God! Impossible! It's downright dangerous!

S.: The letter says he thought you might react that way at first but he says you shouldn't worry one little bit, it's not dangerous at all. The water is plenty deep for the ships, he says, and the Russians are going to help out a bit and dredge some in the shallow areas just to show their good intentions. Don't worry about anything going wrong, he says, they've even been careful enough to put old tires along the dock so it won't scratch the Russian ships at all. He promises it will all be safe, and so do the Russians.

P.: Doesn't that idiot know the Russians are potential enemies of this country, that they're not going to do us any good! My Lord, where's the man been all these years?

S.: His letter, sir, says exactly the opposite. It says here that in all his dealings with the Russians to date they have been friendly and even cooperative. They promise they won't do anything to hurt anybody. If they break their promise and invade or shoot rockets they say we can fine them and even make a speech to spoil their image at the United Nations. They've even offered to let the Northpoint people have their Tidal Power Dam as long as they put in locks under Russian control. That way the troop ships can get into the bay so the soldiers can go flounder fishing near the fertilizer factory dock. Some good fishing there, he says.

P.: The man is insane! The Russians will use the base to invade the United States when they please. We'll be within missile range. Businesses will be destroyed, what will happen to our balance of trade? Our bargaining power at the arms race table? Our national security? Our 200 mile fishing limit? Our mighty fishing fleet? Our . . .

S.: Mr. President, isn't it even possible that people might be injured or killed?

P.: Oh yes . . . People . . . American citizens might be injured or killed.

S.: And Canadians.

P.: That's correct, and Canadians, too. The whole idea is insane — it's madness. Why the hell are they doing this anyhow?

S.: Sir, the councilman says the area is ECONOMICALLY DEPRESSED. He says the naval base would really perk things up: pier construction, hammer and sickle sharpening, borscht made from Maine sugar beets and Maine potatoes, cannon cleaning, machine gun lube jobs, battleship tune-ups, uniform pressing and alteration, button and medal-shining, concessions, underwater parking meters for submarines, pay toilets, and souvenirs. Why, he says here it might even bring in the tourist trade. People from far and wide will want to come and gape at just how far a city will go to make money. They'll put a toll booth in just before the Indian reservation. They'll never be economically depressed with a full fledged Russian naval base in town.

P.: Madness! Don't those Maineiacs know that "economically depressed" is an advertising term which simply means that some people can't afford to buy everything that big business would like to sell them. Whew! They've fallen for the big business "economically depressed" brainwashing in a big way up there, haven't they?

S.: You mean down there, Down East, correct, sir?

P.: Up, down, anywhere around — they're still U.S. Citizens! Don't they realize they're far better off than anybody else in the world?

S.: The letter says, sir that they're sick and tired of being themselves. They want to be real Americans — like it shows on the TV or in the ads of the Boston paper. They want big money jobs like Americans are supposed to have and to hell with gardening, carpentry, logging, fishing, handcrafts and the like. They want more than to just be able to live peacefully in a beautiful place like Washington County. They want it ugly, polluted, and developed like it is from Bangor to Norfolk, Virginia! They haven't had a spectacular robbery, suicide, rape, or murder down there in years; so naturally their newspaper has nothing exciting to say. All it talks about is who visited whom, which boats came and went, when the tide will be high or low, and which local club met where and when. That's front page news down there. People have lost their sense of American pride . . . they figure they're just like a minority group . . . He says the naval base will change all that.

P.: Don't they know what uncontrolled, uncaring foreign personnel can do to a town when they're just visiting? Don't they care about how their neighbors in the area might feel about such a development, about having a prime military target being moved into their locality?

S.: Evidently sir, they're not thinking about later on. They seem to be all hot to trot and want to make money now, ignoring the long term effects. The Russians have even agreed to pay rent for the land so it's a new source of city revenue. The town council is excitedly looking forward to being bigshot politicians.

P.: The fools! They can't do it! I'll call the Pentagon. General Nuisance will take care of this situation with a bang! The federal government will protect its citizens from this kind of craziness. That's what we're here for, and by golly the army will see to it that this happy horsesh-play with the Russians will stop immediately! Now!

S.: Mr. President, hold on! Get this! The councilman says in his letter that if the federal government makes them stop, they'll put in an oil refinery instead. Most people, he says, would much rather have the Russians because they won't screw up the environment as much in the long run . . . and at least you can ask the Russians to leave if it doesn't work out. There's no getting rid of oil refineries. "As long as they make money, they stay. They're a big stationary investment. Matter of fact the letter says they are known to multiply and spread out along the coast, and get bigger once established. But, it says right here that if a Russian naval base it isn't, then an oil refinery it is!

P.: An oil refinery? They'll pollute and develop the last natural area north of the Carolinas? Does that make sense? Don't they care about themselves? Don't those misled few know a refinery means many more tankers, many more chances of oil spills and pollution? A polluted, destroyed environment pollutes and destroys the people in it. Don't they read or believe in history or the Bible? God told Noah for his own welfare to take and keep *all* the animals *on* the ark. The City Council sounds like it is planning to kick off some of them with poisonous oily water and sulphuric acid fog from a refinery! It states right in the Bible, "That which befalleth the son's of men befalleth beasts . . . as one dieth so dieth the other; yea, they have all one breath." (Ecclesiastes 3:18) Is Northpoint full of self-destructive heathens?

S.: Why doesn't the federal or state government stop it just like you can stop the Russian naval base? Protection is needed in this situation, right?

P.: It's not in our make-up or nature. It's an internal matter.

S.: Excuse me, Mr. President, sir, but what about the Environmental Protection Agency, E.P.A.?

P.: Are you kidding? The E.P.A. just makes big business gobble up the environment more slowly. I'm sure E.P.A. would never directly say "NO" to a refinery in the same way that the government and the Pentagon would say "NO" to a Russian base. The E.P.A. listens to BIG OIL money, BIG OIL public relations, BIG OIL lobbying, BIG OIL profiteering, BIG OIL spills, and BIG OIL excuses in just the same way that the public does. Just read their Environmental Impact Statements. E.P.A. is willing to risk Big Oil spills. At best E.P.A. fines Big Oil a piddling sum of money if they disobey some pollution law, but that's not protection. Now when I call out the armed forces and say "NO," that's what one might call protection!

S.: Mr. President, sir, how then does the federal or state government protect the environment and the people in it?

P.: Whoever told you that we did? You're so bewildered I can't believe it! You believe the Environmental Protection Agency is an agency for protecting the environment. I know, it's exactly the same words, but just because it sounds like it protects the environment doesn't mean that it does. E.P.A., B.E.P., D.E.P., C.R.A.P., they're all the same. Just look at the state of the American environment today and you'll know exactly who in this country *protects* it. NOBODY, that's who! The way it works is if people can't distinguish between the powerful brainwashing of the mighty businesses in their economy and their own everyday well-being — if the people don't come to their senses and protect their own environment — than nobody will.

S.: How can they be brought to their senses?

P.: We must reinstate and expand one of the old 18th Century laws of this country.

S.: Which law sir?

P.: Back then it was illegal for a witness to testify to any act he observed while looking through a window pane. His testimony was inadmissable.

S.: Why was it inadmissable, Mr. President?

P.: Because in those days the window glass was warped. It presented a strange distorted picture and view of the world. At least our forefathers recognized a window's misrepresentations and legally dealt with it. Today our culture and conditioning present an equally warped picture but we totally ignore it. Yet that's the window through which the government and big business observe this nation.

S.: What should I tell the councilman, sir?

P.: Tell him that if he wants to represent oil companies he should get a job with them. If he wants to represent the people's welfare like he's elected to do, then he should encourage them to take care of themselves by writing letters to E.P.A., taking E.P.A. to court, electing concerned councilmen, and passing resolutions over and above the council which will protect the environment in a permanent manner. If people tell him they are helpless when it comes to environmental protection what they are really saying is that they are lazy or scared. There's plenty they can do, especially if they get together. And tell the councilman to forget about investing in Russian-to-English dictionaries. When it comes to protecting the American people from foreigners, the federal government will do it pronto — you bet, because big business will let us; it profits when we fight. But big business has become too powerful. It won't let us really protect the American environment, or the people in it from their own overwhelming desire for gold and what it can buy.

S.: I'd sure like to tell the councilman what you've said, Mr. President, but I'm afraid I'd have to learn to cluck. Evidently, they have poultry serving on the council in Northpoint.

P.: Poultry?

S.: Yes, sir, the councilman who wrote the letter is a chicken — he didn't even sign his name, and the rest duck the issue. Isn't that fowl? An oil refinery? They can't pullet off without being a bunch of turkeys.

P.: Eggsactly!

As you might have imagined, the boys' letter caused quite a ruckus in town. Letters began pouring in from different parts of the state, demanding more detailed investigations of the proposed refinery. The town paper was criticized for turning down a local citizen's attempt to speak out. Public resentment began to be voiced against the local political ringleaders and the E.P.A.

But, Dan was just warming up. Next he hit the regional high school and his former schoolmates.

"We've got to stop this thing," he cried. "Richton has taken over the adult population in this community! Soon the area's going to be filled with rich oil barons. High land prices and high taxes will leave no property for us to settle on later. Most of us will have to move on and locate elsewhere." Dan's words were like electricity. His old classmates were alarmed. They'd never really thought about this refinery thing, but the "freak" was actually making sense!

"He's right, we've got to do something," they angrily conceded. "We've got to stop this thing and NOW!"

Danny and Arty began organizing battalions of kids to set up neighborhood information centers. A network was organized around the bay. Kids began to talk earnestly with their parents, many of whom were delighted.

Arty got hold of a civilian band radio transmitter and set it up on a hill overlooking the bay area. He and his friends began broadcasting news items and facts about the status of the Richton refinery proposal. They could reach most of the bay area towns. After a period of time they put together a ham radio transmitter which could broadcast throughout the county.

Adult groups began to sense the new air of excitement. Danny appealed to bingo clubs, bridge clubs, the booster club, the veteran's association, the Elks, the women's club, the charities — like a whirlwind he sped from shopkeeper to shopkeeper, begging them to fend off the enemy in their backyards.

He spoke at rallys, screaming for justice, self-reliance and civic pride, reading from (yes) the Bible and the Constitution, and the Declaration of Independence. He led groups in prayer whenever he spoke. He appealed to the independent Yankee Spirit that had heretofore seemed doomed to the history books. He brought long-buried anger and frustration to the surface. Pointing to the battlegrounds and local monuments of townspeople's ancestors, and demanded remembrance of their fights for freedom in battles past. He made each man, woman and child feel what they already unconsciously knew. Home was more than a house. Home in Northpoint was gulls, beaches, clean air, gardening, fishing and the sea. Home could be destroyed by a refinery. "We must fight for our home," he cried.

Almost singlehandedly, Danny began to bring out a new sense of pride amongst his neighbors. At churches and fairs, sporting events and flea markets, on the fishing piers before sunrise and again at dusk, Danny appealed to this pride — a pride that he knew was buried in all of us. His talks would often leave his audience choked up and determined as he would paint elaborate emotional portraits designed to snap people out of their conditioned defeatism. Conservation easements by land owners became popular. Sentiment and signatures poured forth for a State referendum against coastal development.

It was a brilliant and successful campaign. Dan had mastered the art of emotional appeal. He capitalized on deep-seated resentments, reservations and anxieties just as he had done years ago with Bob Hitch in the rose garden.

He proved himself to be an adept political tactician as well. He had studied carefully the backroom maneuverings that had characterized Richton's campaign. He appealed to the same prominent and outspoken citizens to assert their independence to refute their alliances with the Big-Oil "foreigners." To political aspirants, he pointed out strategies to higher offices. He outlined ways in which they could gain widespread favor and positive regard by being "man" or "woman" enough to publicly admit they'd been misled by Richton's promises and to call for more local discussions of the proposal.

Ever so slowly the political climate changed. It climaxed when the deputy town manager publicly tore up a Richton campaign donation of several thousand dollars. He was just one step ahead of Dan Miller who was ready to expose him to the public. The deputy had been given the money as a bribe for issuing an illegal zoning permit to Richton.

Danny had certainly matured over the last few years. He was no longer the alienating and disturbing little menace that used to turn everybody off. He'd learned to talk to people on their own levels and to capitalize on their conditioning. His experiences in our school had taught him how deep-rooted some of our resentments could lie, and how good it felt to bring them to the surface.

One of Dan's brightest moments turned out to be at the local Congregational Church, the very same church in which he'd had his unfortunate "Bible experience" two years earlier. The event was a public meeting to discuss people's grievances. Danny was given ten minutes at the podium and was he ever sharp.

"... You see friends, Richton has led us along like donkeys following carrots dangling in front of our noses. Big Oil money has infiltrated our town for seven years! They've put down everything we've ever had as being substandard. They've harped on the negative, pointing to the weaknesses in our institutions, emphasizing our crime and unemployment rate, our dirty and poorly lit streets, our dilapidated piers and patched-up fishing boats, but they don't ever acknowledge the beauty and charm and lack of tension that is particular to our little towns.

Don't you see what they've done? They've made us look at our towns in a new and faded light. Crime in Northpoint is low by any other town's standards! The reason that we've got a law enforcement force of two part-time fellows and a '67 Chevy is that the last crime here was when somebody stole the "Budweiser" sign off Penny's grill last Fourth of July. And even that turned up on the Elk's float during the parade (chuckles and applause). Our poorly-lit streets never seemed to be a problem around here until those city-slickers started making such a fuss. No wonder they all have to wear those fancy glasses (more laughter). The condition of our boats is a tribute to the Yankee ingenuity of a few fine men who have kept the vessels afloat day after day, year after year! Why, some of those hulls are as old as this town (standing applause). They've put down our favorite traditions too. When Richton gave the Memorial Committee $2,000.00 for the Fourth of July parade, they were really saying, 'Your parade stinks, here's some money to make it better.' Those parades have always been the high points of my summers, how about yours? (applause) What about when they hired chefs from Boston for our annual August lobster feed? That was a direct slap in the face to the people in this town who'd kept the feed going for twenty-five years, folks who were better lobster cooks anyways! (laughter and applause.)

"You see, Richton has made *us* feel ashamed because they've told us *we're* SUBstandard. *They've* given us that image. I bet nobody here ever thought too much was wrong around here before the Richton people came along. Sure, we could use a few more jobs, and a large dose of money would be nice for *any* town, but who's thought of what else a refinery would bring — more noise, pollution, strangers (and not just the summer visitors we've got now), bigger stores and supermarkets, traffic lights, more bars — probably even a new church. We can't fit many more in here anyhow (a few chuckles). It'd be the end of the small town spirit I've always known, that's for sure.

"The Richton proposal is the latest phase in a long chain of events that began when the first aristocrats began to get fellow humans to do their menial tasks. From that point on, people have desired to get further and further away from the vital day-to-day chores necessary to keep them alive. Fishing, farming, washing garments, cleaning one's home all became the slave or the servant's tasks; they would help protect their master from all the harsh realities of the environment. Money became the conditioning stimulus and reward; self-reliance and survival took a back-row seat. The natural world fell prey to the people's conditioned responses to money.

"Today we've got conveniences like dishwashers, central oil heaters, and supermarkets instead of servants. These helpers perform the same duties as the slaves did. They protect us from the environment. And *all* of them demand oil to keep them (and us) going. But the end result is that now *we're* all slaves to *oil!*

"Richton has used money to hypnotize us. The Richton people have offered massive transfusions of cash, like blood to an ailing person. But we don't need the transfusions. We're not ailing. We have enough fish and other foods to stay well fed. If a family has a hard year, their neighbors are always nearby to lend a hand. Our children are healthy, our older citizens are honored and cared for." (Danny was crying now, making no attempts to restrain himself). "We have a wonderful clean environment just like our parents and grandparents had. We don't need anyone to tell us what our problems are. We know we've got problems just like every other small town. But we've also got a heritage in this area. We've got a past, two centuries of people living by the sea, a god-given life that no one can ever take from us — no one, that is, but ourselves." (Danny was openly sobbing.) "I know all of you feel this way but Richton has you scared to speak out. Now I ask you, what in God's name is there to fear?"

For what seemed like minutes, the entire congregation of over three hundred people were silent except for the sounds of sobbing. Then, as if by a silent agreement, the people began to clap, and cheer, and stamp their feet. They rose to their feet, and applauded this fine young man. This eighteen year old had said it all. He'd addressed every doubt they'd ever had, and more.

The results of Danny's talk were astounding. Letters were now pouring in to the local paper by the hundreds. The local, state and even federal environmental agencies were besieged with mail begging them to halt the construction of the refinery. Pressures mounted on governmental agencies to review the decision.

Finally, on August 31st, the E.P.A. rendered its heart-stopping conclusion. They'd agreed to postpone any decisions regarding the Northpoint refinery for six months ". . . to further evaluate the letters and impact of said proposal."

It was a wonderful moment for all of us. Old people, young people, fishermen, shopkeepers, school teachers, preachers, and town officials, all felt the burst of local spirit. The air was alive with the buzzing of good cheer. A new flagpole was raised, fences were painted, and park benches were repaired. A sense of civic pride abounded. Yes, it was a wonderful moment, if only it had lasted longer, if only the refinery had been stopped.

Hold on a second! What did I mean by that? I'm afraid that, as some of you may have guessed, our victory was short lived. Six months to be exact.

Most of us had never dreamed that when the E.P.A. announced their final decision in February, the Richton proposal would be approved. This had seemed out of the question six months earlier. In fact, most of the townsfolk had put the entire conflict out of their minds.

Apparently the Richton people had pulled one over the eyes of the unsuspecting public. They had used the six month delay to their own favor. Whether it was to arrange a last-minute OK by some of the newly elected town officials (who had since reversed their positions for a second time), or put pressure on the E.P.A., it now appears that the refinery is here to stay. E.P.A. had again proven itself to basically just be a group of economically oriented Americans.

As for the refinery, there remains one final E.P.A. contingency to be met. Tomorrow, at the crack of dawn, an empty supertanker will pass through Canadian waters and into Northpoint Bay in a trial run to determine the safe passage of the vessel. Once it is conclusively demonstrated that the tanker can handle the dangerous Fundy tides, the refinery will be given the official green light. Construction at the site has actually already begun, the test is a mere formality.

Richton has spent thousands of dollars and man-hours surveying the channel floor. As required by E.P.A. they've brought in a special master commander to guide the ship into the harbor. The specially trained commander has personally inspected every tide and swirl in the channel. It's a sad, sad day in Northpoint, a sad, sad day indeed.

Finally that fateful day arrived. As the sun slowly peeked over the islands in Northpoint Bay, the gulls and shorebirds began their morning rites. Porpoises surfaced in the harbor and harbor seals perched themselves on flat rocks, awaiting the first warming rays of sunlight.

The sun crept further above the horizon and brilliant colors shone off the waters in the bay. Along the shorelines, in the little towns of Whitehorse and Northpoint, curls of smoke emerged from chimney tops. A milk truck bustled down one of Northpoint's gravel roads. Cows slowly wandered into the new day's pasture.

Out beyond the bay, on the eastern-most neck of land, several young white-tail fawns leapt about in a dandelion meadow. An osprey brought fresh salmon to her young.

And beyond on the open waters of Fundy Bay, a fin whale surfaced, kicking up a fan-like spray of foam. A bald eagle soared high above the glimmering waves, gently gliding with the rises and falls of the ocean breeze.

Nature's creatures innocently began, once again, to dance their early morning ballet. Suckling from the warm and supportive breast of Mother Nature, all these living things followed patterns that had been set down thousands of years before. Each and every creature, independent but ever so interrelated, commenced its dance to a natural rhythm that played deep within every ounce of living, breathing matter.

But something was amiss in the striking natural scene. A foreigner had arrived in the waters of Fundy Bay. There, at the mouth of the long, winding channel that ran from Northpoint to the Bay of Fundy, sat the Maru Suma, a hulking, floating mass of steel. As high tide approached, the Maru Suma lay at anchor awaiting her appointed destiny.

The Maru Suma's size alone polluted the scene. She was an awesome craft, almost three city blocks long. Her angular, unnatural lines contrasted sharply against the smooth curves of the gently undulating sea and islands.

A stranger had arrived. Unbeknownst to the wild inhabitants of the area, the forerunner of millions of gallons of oozing, sticky, polluting liquids had calmly entered their domain.

And aboard the Maru Suma, another breed of living creatures danced to a different rhythm. They too were independent, but interrelated characters in a larger scheme. Each and every creature aboard that craft served a vital role: from the engineers deep in the ballast chambers to the drum major in the special Marine Corps band that had assembled on deck for the occasion, from the piccolo player on the third tier of the fourth deck to the stern faced, heavy-set gentleman who surveyed the scene from high above on the bridge.

Master Commander Gimball Perkins peered forward from the bridge, a man of composure and fortitude. The Commander tapped his foot to the beat of the Marine Corps drummer, eyes fixed towards the rocky coast a half mile away. He stood glaring across the expanse of water at the narrow mouth of the treacherous strait. The Commander had prepared for this moment for four months. Locked away in his Merchant Marine Academy suite, he'd scrutinized every chart that had ever described this channel.

"A wonderful day for it, Commander sir," offered Roberts, the youthful First Mate.

Machine-like, the Commander gazed ahead, hands folded behind his lower back. His broad-shouldered frame remained still. His staunch, still presence commanded the awe of all those around him.

"High tide is approaching, sir," bubbled the navigator. "We're awaiting your command."

Perkins' eyes studied the scene. Before him he saw series after series of markers and reference points. Radar charts and topographical inventories flashed across his screen of vision. He remained still.

"Commander, sir? We are awaiting your instructions as to when to commence with the Canadian National Anthem," pleaded Major Fuller, the USMC band director.

. . . Azimuths, compass points, soundings, depths . . . the commander's checklist was now complete. The time was 9:33 a.m. The tide had almost reached dead high.

Suddenly the radio blared, "This is Command Headquarters of Superior Coast Guard Operations. All crafts have been directed out of the area. Commence with entrance and docking procedures at will."

Still glaring ahead, Commander Perkins proceeded to sharply recite the order of the day. "Navigator, proceed at one-quarter speed ahead," he barked, still facing to the bow.

The ship slowly glided smoothly forward, in direct line with the channel entrance. The craft was alive with activity. Crewmen moved methodically about, each carrying out a role they'd rehearsed on many occasions. And high up on the bridge, perhaps the best rehearsed of all, Master Commander Perkins carefully scrutinized the coastline ahead, eyes transfixed on the shoreline. Stealthily, the ship crept through the passageway. The Commander remained perched in place. Suddenly the radio again blared:

"This is Command Headquarters of Superior Coast Guard Operations. Simulate laden weight and attitude. We repeat, simulate laden weight and attitude."

"What the hell does that mean?" thought the First Mate.

Commander Perkins immediately demonstrated his superior knowledge and special training. He quickly ordered, "Open all water intake valves and have the ship take on water in ballast to bring it to its fully loaded level."

"This procedure is a Coast Guard and E.P.A. requirement to simulate the actual weight, maneuverability and depth at which tankers to follow will operate when fully laden," he explained to inquiring faces.

The Mate responded with lightning precision. "Take on water in ballast. Open port and starboard stopcocks fore and aft!" he radioed to the engineers below.

"Major Fuller you may proceed with ceremonies," directed Commander Perkins.

Major Fuller proudly stepped to the podium, keeping tune to the beat of distant Marine Corps drummers that forever marched through his consciousness. He pointed his baton at the Canadian shores, then at Commander Perkins, and finally at his sharply attentive musicians. With an imposing sweep of his hand, the band began a rendition of "Oh Canada" followed by "The Star Spangled Banner."

The radio cut through the silence which followed the termination of the music.

"This is Command Headquarters of Superior Coast Guard Operations. Please demonstrate safety procedures in case of emergency. Repeat: Please demonstrate safety procedures in case of emergency."

The Commander rapped out another order. "Navigator, slow vessel speed to a full stop!"

The navigator echoed, "Reverse all engines. Come to a full stop."

"Prepare to demonstrate emergency safety procedures," demanded the captain. "Prepare to abandon ship."

"Sir?"

"This is a drill, Mister," he barked, still facing forward. "Prepare to abandon ship per drill order #0185. It's Coast Guard regulatory chicken shit."

"Prepare to abandon ship," echoed the Mate, over the intercom.

The ship slowly glided to a halt in the dead high motionless channel of Northpoint Bay. The sun was now high in the sky, shining brightly on the vessel. Eighty-seven crew and band members stood poised, awaiting the Commander's orders. Minutes seemed like hours.

"What a strange time for a drill," remarked a crewman below.

"There must be a reason for it somewhere," remarked another. "Don't worry. I've been with this outfit for a long time. They've always got everything under control."

Finally, the order came. "Abandon ship!" ordered Perkins.

"Abandon ship," echoed the Mate.

Major Fuller suddenly appeared on the deck, way below the bridge. "Commander Perkins, sir?" he hollered from below. "About this drill, sir. My men were wondering; should we leave our instruments on board? We're under orders never to leave our instruments unguarded."

The Commander was already below on the main deck. The First Mate hollered back down.

"Yes, damn it, leave the bloody instruments!" ("Oh shit," he thought to himself, "I'm supposed to be in the lifeboats before the Commander. My ass is grass.")

"But Roberts, will there be a guard left on board to watch over the instruments?" shouted the Major.

"No, we're abandoning ship and that means everyone!" Seconds were flying by; Roberts was panicking.

"My orders are to never leave the instruments unguarded!"

"My orders are not to clutter the lifeboats with trombones and french horns. You are on my ship. I am in command!"

"But you are a Merchant Marine. I'm USMC. I'm a Marine."

"You're on my merchant vessel," screamed the First Mate. "Now let's go down to those boats or you're going to find a piccolo where you'd least expect it!" With that, Roberts rushed to the main deck, only to find the last boat already being lowered and Perkins angrily awaiting him.

"What the hell," he sighed, and took a flying leap overboard with Perkins immediately behind him. He landed on the lifeboat, which was already overloaded with Marines and sailors, as well as trumpets, fifes, drums and a french horn. "What the hell?" he screamed, trying to pull his foot out of the mouth of a tuba.

"Major Fuller's orders," smirked a drummer. "The major yelled, 'take the instruments,' as soon as his life boat left the ship and hit the water out of your jurisdiction."

The boats pulled away from the Maru Suma to the required three hundred yards and awaited the Commander's orders to return. Commander Perkins kept his weather eye on his watch. The boats were to stay at three hundred yards for seven and one-half minutes after the last boat arrived. At four minutes and nineteen seconds, a cry went out from one of the boats.

"She's listing to port!"

Commander Perkins looked up from his watch to observe that, indeed, the Maru Suma was on an angle to the port side. "Oh shit," he thought. "What is that all about? Screw it, we've only got two minutes to go."

At exactly seven and one-half minutes the commander's boat began its return to the tanker. The others followed. Unfortunately, a reboarding was no longer possible from the starboard side, so the boats made their way around to the port side. As they rounded the starboard, there, high above, the puzzled sailors observed that a log had accidently jammed the open bow portal. While the port side portals had swiftly been taking in thousands of gallons of water, the bow starboard ballast had remained relatively empty. Thus, the explanation for the now seriously listing vessel. Hurriedly, the Commander and crewmen scampered aboard. But it was too late. The port side stopcocks were now unreachable, well under water and the ship was beginning to go the same way.

"Oh fudge," muttered the Commander, and then suddenly he shouted, "Fuck, shit, and molasses! The bugger's going down for sure.

For Chrissake, ABANDON SHIP, THIS ONES FOR REAL SO TAKE YER GAWDAMN INSTRUMENTS!"

This time, the First Mate beat the Commander to the lifeboat by thirty-five yards. As the boats quickly pulled away from the tanker, they turned to watch in amazement as the listing ship's deck reached the water-line. With a dramatic shudder and a howling of escaping air, the Maru Suma disappeared below the surface, presenting a formidable blockade to anything other than small vessels which might still pass through the channel. Otherwise the passage was closed. Nothing else could possibly slip through.

All of this activity had been observed by the Northpoint residents, who at first had gaped at the offshore doings with utter amazement. Now however, many were cheering wildly. They realized what this all meant. Not only was the Maru Suma sunk, but so was Richton!

A lengthy Coast Guard investigation was undertaken almost immediately. Numerous witnesses were subpoenaed, records were checked, and divers scanned the sunken ship for the unusual. No signs of sabotage or wrong-doing turned up through the entire investigation. Every single order had been obeyed to complete satisfaction. Each crew member had performed his duty up to par. All had reacted with well-conditioned military precision. The log was a purely coincidental mishap. The tanker would have sunk even sooner without its interference.

The only unexplainable circumstances of the entire episode were the orders Master Commander Perkins had given. Not only were the orders, "Simulate laden weight and attitude" and "Demonstrate emergency safety procedures" completely inappropriate orders but neither were official marine terms at all! Lengthy investigation of the commands revealed that neither order had ever been uttered in the entire annals of maritime history!

Commander Perkins was subjected to psychological examinations, lie detectors, brain wave tests, and more. All seemed to arrive at the same mysterious conclusion: Perkins must have been given a post-hypnotic suggestion, perhaps by radio! But how?

Perkins himself pleaded that for over a month he had kept himself virtually locked away in his Merchant Marine quarters, studying the Northpoint area charts. With the exception of his wife, he'd hardly exchanged a word with anyone. The investigators certified that his wife was a completely innocent contact.

Commander Perkins testified he had no other extraordinary contacts in the days preceding the sinking except for a visit from a young college reporter who had interviewed him with regard to Perkins' feelings about the work he did. The only thing Commander Perkins could remember about the reporter was that he had a very penetrating, inspiring air and tone of voice.

He also remembered one other unusual thing. The reporter used the bathroom and returned with his fly unbuttoned.

EPILOGUE

THE DOWNEAST GAZETTE, Monday, November 18.

COFFIN TO BE EXHUMED

Northpoint, Maine. After 3 months of bickering and deliberation the U. S. District Court today gave the Northpoint City Council permission to remove an unidentified coffin found on the Richton Corporation site for a 7.4 million dollar nuclear power plant. The discovery of the coffin last August halted construction due to state ordinances governing the disturbance of cemetery lands.

Proponents of the power plant claim that the halting of construction was costly and unnecessary. According to them, the delay postponed the reaping of economic benefits to residents and businesses in this economically depressed, remote area.

The wooded nuclear power plant site, formerly a city park, had originally been proposed for a 250,000DWT oil refinery. Refinery plans were halted two years ago after the catastrophic sinking of a supertanker in the Northpoint channel.

THE DOWNEAST GAZETTE, Tuesday, November 19.

EXHUMED COFFIN CONTAINS NOTE

Northpoint, Maine. The controversial coffin which has stalled construction of the Richton Corporation nuclear power plant was today dug out and opened under a court order by Judge Arnold Harrison. Experts believe the coffin was buried approximately 3 years ago. The coffin did not contain a corpse. It instead contained a typewritten note whose content was made public this evening:

" TO YOU WHO HAVE DISTURBED MY RESTING GROUND

My spirit lies in this coffin as a guardian of this undeveloped, wild place. It is important to our spirits that this site remain wild.

Each remaining square inch of wilderness gives nature a better chance to survive while offering us a better chance to understand her, and thereby, to reduce our fears of her. As we understand Mother Nature so shall we fear her less, become comfortable living compatibly with her, and exploit her no more.

We were born out of wilderness. In wilderness is our preservation. We must learn to sustain and to relish the substance of wilderness.

It is imperative that the effort to preserve wild places does not fail. Our spirits must be committed to this effort."

THE DOWNEAST GAZETTE, Wednesday, November 20.

COFFIN MYSTERY DEEPENS

Northpoint, Maine. A backhoe today partially uncovered another coffin while excavating the wooded site of the Richton Nuclear power plant. It is the second coffin which has been unearthed on the former park and refinery site and raises the question of whether others remain undiscovered.

Judge Arnold Harrison issued an injunction against further excavation on the controversial site until an accurate appraisal of its legal status could be determined.